Maverick, Movies & Murder

Mary Seifert

Books by Mary Seifert

Maverick, Movies & Murder
Rescues, Rogues & Renegade
Tech, Trials & Trouble (fall, 2022)

Maverick, Movies & Murder

Katie & Maverick Cozy Mysteries, Book 1

Mary Seifert

Secret Staircase Books

Maverick, Movies & Murder
Published by Secret Staircase Books, an imprint of
Columbine Publishing Group, LLC
PO Box 416, Angel Fire, NM 87710

Book layout and design by Secret Staircase Books
Cover images © Patrick Marcel Pelz, Boyan Dimitrov, Aleksey Telnov,
W. Scott McGill, Ayutaka
First trade paperback edition: June, 2022

First e-book edition: June, 2022
* * *

Publisher's Cataloging-in-Publication Data
Seifert, Mary
Maverick, Movies & Murder / by Mary Seifert.
p. cm.
ISBN 978-1649140876 (paperback)
ISBN 978-1649140883 (e-book)

1. Katie Wilk (Fictitious character). 2. Minnesota—Fiction. 3.
Amateur sleuths—Fiction. 4. Women sleuths—Fiction.
I. Title

Katie & Maverick Cozy Mystery Series : Book 1.
Siefert, Mary, Katie & Maverick cozy mysteries.

BISAC : FICTION / Mystery & Detective.
813/.54

ACKNOWLEDGMENTS

Many hands helped make my dream a reality. I am blessed and wish to thank Stephanie Dewey and Lee Ellison for their trust and exceptional guidance in making the transformation from computer page to book page. And to those who have given valuable advice: Lois Hurley, Colleen Okland, Sam Okland, Sandra Unger, Joan Christianson, Molly Silbernich Johnson, Deb Van Buren, LeAnn Atchison, Margaret Sullivan, Tim Sullivan, Patty Gehlen, Brenna Gehlen, Tory Leitch, Deborah Peterson, Hal Neely, Ruth Neely, Kindra Szymanski, Evy Hatjistilianos, Joey Nytes, Anne Christianson, Beth Johnston, Dr. Tom Haas, Dr. Steve Bell, Cathy Szymanski, Dean Stier, Jenifer Leitch, Kelley Johnson, Kati Phillipi, Dianne Krizmanich, Jill Benson, Carol Dahlstrom, Nancy Hafner, Marla Michaels, Cheryl Hoskins, Caryl Antil, Dr. Anne Bruckner, Dr. Emily Ellingson, Joanne Haugen, Nathaniel Fremling, Dr. Danica Seifert, Kathy Voss, Joanne Haugen, Craig Holmgren, Tracy Duininck, Jason Duininck, Donald Calhoun, Luke Seifert, and any others I may have missed—you know who you are—for all the encouragement, support, assistance in answering weird questions, and taking time to read, but mostly Colleen for her indefatigable nagging.

Thank you to all who choose to read.

Writing classes at the Loft were supported in part by a grant from the Southwest Minnesota Arts Council with funds provided by The McKnight Foundation.

Life's a gift and I don't intend on wasting it.
—Leonardo DiCaprio as Jack Dawson.

CHAPTER ONE

The bullets changed everything for me. Sometimes I wished I'd taken a bullet too, because I lost the most important men in my life. My dad still fought every day to reclaim his confidence, mobility, and wit from the bullet that creased his brain. But my husband of seventeen days took our dreams with him when he died. They never caught the shooter.

"Promise me." Charles's bloody hands gripped mine. "Promise me you'll be happy."

I had to try to keep that promise, so after a year of indulging my sorrow and wading through mind-numbing platitudes, I threw away the flood of sympathy cards and letters. I needed to return to the world, to sink or swim.

And my stepmother wanted me out of there.

At her insistence, and to the surprise of my therapist, I circulated my résumé. Neither of them, however, congratulated me when I accepted a position one hundred fifty miles from home. New town. New people. A job in my area of expertise. Truth be told, I accepted the only offer I received—teaching high school math.

I'd be lying if I said I wasn't apprehensive. I missed the fairytale life I had planned—an adoring husband, challenging job, devoted family—but I packed my meager belongings and moved to Columbia, Minnesota, determined to make it my home. The gem of a town snugged into prairie grasses surrounded by rich farmland, acreage dedicated to wildlife management, and lots and lots of water.

Following a second fruitless week of apartment-hunting, I returned to the bed and breakfast with a little less spring in my step.

"He was a real gentleman today. Let me get him," said the desk clerk. He disappeared into the recesses of the office.

I heard the rhythmic clack of nails across the tile floor before I saw him and steeled myself for the onslaught of Maverick's ecstatic welcome. He rounded the desk and buried his black nose between my legs, drooling all over. His tail whumped against the desk and he pawed my thigh.

"Sit," I said. "Sit." Maverick jumped and licked my face then circled behind me, wrapping the leash around my legs before his rump hit the floor.

"He missed you. Look, he's smiling."

Maverick gazed at me with sparkling brown eyes. To me, it looked like laughing.

"Find anything today?"

I'd been searching for a place to park my belongings, anxious to live life out of a closet instead of a suitcase. The Monongalia Bed and Breakfast provided good food, clean bedding, daily vacuuming, and fresh towels every other day, but the expense was eating into my savings and my first paycheck was weeks away.

"Nothing yet. Do you have any hot prospects for me?"

Mr. Walsh had recommended a cheery coffee shop, a delightful deli, a local market, walking paths, and a hardware store that had one of just about anything but apartments.

"The film people will be finishing up soon." He tapped a notice on the front desk. The words written in cherry-red marker stood out: Servers needed. Great pay. The attached article stated that although most of the filming had been completed on a sound stage built for the movie, when the director needed a crowd, he came home for the extras and a docudrama about the *Titanic* needed plenty of extras. After months of shooting, the director planned to re-create the famed ship's final dinner and take promotional shots.

"You should do it. Half the town is in the movie. You'll see Columbia in all its red-carpet glory and know what you're getting yourself into."

Maverick stood and pulled at the leash. I sighed. The clerk said with a satisfied grin, "He can stay with me Friday night."

The promised compensation would help stretch my dwindling funds, so I signed my name on the next line: Katie Wilk.

CHAPTER TWO

Three days later at the movie soirée, outfitted in a frilly white apron tied over a simple black dress, with a starched cap perched on my head like a nest, I imagined Charles chuckling at my uninspired attempt to play the role of a member of the ship's waitstaff. My heart skipped. My first transatlantic flight had taken me to England and the Royal Holloway where I studied cryptography. I'd promised my dad I intended to study hard, earn my degree, and there'd be no foreign entanglements, but Charles wore me down. On our first date, we visited the *Titanic* Museum in Southampton, and we found it easy to imagine ourselves as first-class passengers. The memory warmed my heart.

Amid notes of "Shine on Harvest Moon," I wound through stands of spotlights and vivid green panels that surrounded the tables crowding the convention center and served deviled quail eggs with caviar to the dinner guests. I shimmied past swaggering men clad in tuxedos and glossy shoes, and women, teetering on high heels, dressed in Edwardian evening attire of delicate fabrics that shimmered with oodles of beads.

Bright lights ignited gleaming crystal goblets, cobalt blue-and-gold china, and eight-piece silver place settings. Candles flickered on the tables next to menus propped on miniature easels that guaranteed a sumptuous over-the-top meal. Cameramen circled the room catching snippets of the evening's proceedings.

A tall woman with twinkling blue eyes stepped up to the podium. The microphone crackled as she lowered it to her lips and quieted the rumbling crowd.

"Ladies and gentlemen. Welcome to this astounding re-creation of a *Titanic* dinner. As you are aware, we're filming, so smile. We'll get our first look at the movie after dinner. If you would please take your seats, we'll take you back in time."

On my way to the kitchen to exchange my empty appetizer tray for oysters, a man's size eleven stepped into my path. I caught myself before launching headfirst onto one of the tables and tugged on my collar in relief. My finger stroked my good luck charm, a smooth ring that hung on a chain around my neck, and I looked up into dark mocking eyes.

"Watch where you're going." The shoe's owner sneered.

"Excuse me," I said, and almost tripped again in my rush to get out of his way.

The string quartet played a haunting melody, and as the strains of music faded, the final words of the verse filtered into my busy mind: "For those in peril on the sea."

Or anywhere else, I thought.

The line of waitstaff bustled to serve each course. With a steel grip on my shoulder, the floor manager timed releases to avoid collisions. Choreographed as if on a runway, we marched in one swinging door and out another. The delivery and dish removal continued rapid-fire through all but the final course, which would be brought out following the film viewing.

Silverware clinked on the crystal, sounding like bells in a marina, and the enthusiastic conversation muted. A robust man in captain's garb waved his white cap and beckoned a tall fair-haired fellow to the microphone. The precisely cut, vintage Savile Row jacket hugged his slim frame. His intense eyes slowly surveyed the attendees.

"Hello, handsome," shouted a bold dinner guest, shifting her voluptuous assets, her lips pursed to blow a kiss.

"Good evening. For those who don't know me, I'm Robert Bruckner." Wolf whistles, cheers, and hearty whoops answered his greeting. He tugged at his shiny blue bow tie, which matched the color of the silk dress worn by the woman seated next to him. "Thank you for being here and celebrating our story-making. I would like to congratulate the cast and crew on your fantastic accomplishment. This is a project of my heart, bringing my family's story to life, and I can't wait to share the film with you. *Titanic: One Story* will be the cornerstone piece of *Bruckner's New Titanic Exhibit* opening Labor Day weekend at the Midwest Minnesota History Center."

Applause exploded from the tables. The striking raven-haired woman in the blue dress raised a fist and hooted, "Go, Robert!"

When the murmurs of appreciation died down, he continued. "We've charted new territory with an experimental filming technique, and I wish to present what we've accomplished. Together we've made better history the second time around."

I imagined waves of the icy Atlantic pouring over me and thought, *I would hope so.*

"I give you my deepest gratitude for a job well done." He raised a glistening champagne coupe. "To the *Titanic.*"

The crowd echoed his toast.

One by one, the lights winked out. Heavy music filled the large space. Those milling about rushed to their seats.

I peeled my eyes from the director, and the movie magic unfolded. I hesitated, momentarily mesmerized by the immensity of the ocean liner. The camera panned the open water and gradually zoomed in on a tan-and-brown Airedale prancing on the deck. My eyes stayed glued to the big screen as I drifted to the kitchen.

"They'll be in to film a bustling kitchen in ten minutes." The manager shouted over the sounds of rattling dishes. "Hop to it."

I removed a tray of éclairs from the cold storage unit and lined it up with the edge of the counter. I joined the other servers surrounding a sink splashing soapy water. After I dried my hands, I picked up a chunk of dark chocolate and a grater.

"Hey. I'm Samantha," said the pudgy woman sliding next to me. Her blond ponytail, laced with gray, bobbed in time to imaginary music. Weary eyes in a tired face darted around the kitchen.

"I'm Katie," I said. I lifted a white ceramic square from the top of the stack next to her.

"Are you new in town?"

I nodded.

"What do you do when you're not waiting tables?" she

asked, plating with efficiency.

"I teach math."

She froze and took a step back. Her right hand clutched her chest in a mock faint.

"Be still my heart. I hate math. I'm taking algebra at the community college, and it…Well, you know what it can do."

I nodded as the camera crew crashed into the kitchen, and the manager shouted, "Ignore them. Do your jobs."

"What are you studying besides algebra?"

"Mostly gen eds, but I was able to snag a preceptorship with the research and development department for this movie and earned a history credit. It's been a blast…from the past. I even stumbled onto an interesting old sea chest," she said. Catching the eye of one of the film techs pointing the camera, she giggled and winked.

"Aren't the dresses to die for?" The laugh lines at the corners of her eyes deepened and her contagious smile coaxed one from me. "I know a couple of the girls in the movie. They're so lucky." She swapped the tiniest jealous sigh with a huge grin. "And I know the dog."

"The dog?"

"The terrier parading on the ship's deck. Sundance is a hospice therapy dog." Her hazel eyes gleamed with shiny tears, and she sighed. "I wish I had a dog."

I almost wish I didn't.

The lights flickered on in the dining room to booming applause. The manager rapped her knuckles on the doorframe and relayed instructions before we delivered the final course.

"Let's get a move on, folks." The bossy manager pointed with her index finger. "Samantha, pastries, please."

Samantha pretended not to hear and headed in the

opposite direction.

One line of servers followed Samantha through the double doors, balancing trays of the signature cocktail served in first-class aboard the ship on its final night, Punch Romaine. I hung a folded tray stand over my elbow and carried a full platter of pastries.

I stepped through the swinging doors to the sound of heavy pounding. I scoured the large room, following the gazes of all eyes as they turned toward the hostile voice of a man leaning across the head table, hammering his fists. He looked ready to burst.

"Bruckner, you bastard!" he thundered, red-faced. The room went silent. "I didn't sign on for this. You owe me."

He grabbed Bruckner's dinner jacket and pulled him partway over the table.

The menacing voice lowered, but not enough. "You're a dead man," he growled.

Bruckner placed his own hands over those of his aggressor and peeled the fingers off his lapels.

"Hastings, we've got something sensational here," he said. "Wait and see."

Two enormous men in black suits appeared and stood on each side of Hastings. Earpieces, attached to spiral wires, traveled down their burly necks. One put a hand on Hastings's shoulder to restrain him, but Hastings shrugged it off. After releasing his grip on Bruckner, he rolled his shoulders, rearranged his tuxedo jacket collar, and straightened his tie. He yanked the front of his jacket, lifted his chin, and the man who'd delighted in my clumsiness stormed from the room.

Before I could catch my breath, rhythmic slaps punctuated the silence. Heads turned toward the rear of the room. A petite woman, wearing an exquisite amethyst gown, stood, clapping. Pearl combs pinned back her riot of flaxen curls. Her dark eyes twinkled and a contrived grin lit her porcelain-like face. "Great show," she bellowed. She picked up her sequined purse and sashayed out of the room, spiky heels clattering.

I centered the round tray laden with its artistic creations on my unfolded stand while the credits continued to roll on the screen. Chatter resumed. Bruckner shook hands around the room.

"Hey, Colleen." A plump brunette snorted. "What did you think?"

The woman in the blue silk spun in front of me. Her dress swirled and she tottered. I reached out to steady her. Another hand reached for her as well, and between the two of us, we guided her to an empty chair.

"Colleen?" The woman who'd welcomed the dinner guests brushed back a few strands of hair that had fallen over the young woman's face.

Colleen studied both of us, eyes wide as if trying to determine who we were. Then she jerked her arm away. Resentment replaced her lost look. She shook her short hair and said, "I'm an actor, portraying shock."

"Pretty convincing. Are you sure you don't need anything?" the woman asked.

"Thanks," Colleen said, the word dripping with disdain. She raised her chin and her eyes narrowed. She stood and stalked back to her table, fierce emotion crackling in her wake. The remaining guests at the head table squirmed in their seats, sneaking glances at one another. As she approached, Colleen's tablemates shrank back, searching for a means of escape. I couldn't blame them.

Colleen sat abruptly. She yanked the tablecloth and shattered a cocktail glass. As the shards disappeared, cleaned up by one of the servers, she settled into her chair with an imperious expression.

A throat cleared next to me. "Thanks for your help." She extended her elegant hand. "I'm Jessica Balponi."

I shook it and smiled. "Nice to meet you, Ms. Balponi. My name's Katie, but I'd better get back to work or my name'll be mud."

At the end of the evening, I changed out of my costume and tossed it onto the growing pile. "Samantha, I might know where you can get a dog."

She sighed. "I'm not ready for a pet."

I chewed on my lower lip for a moment and then asked, "How did Sundance become a therapy dog?"

"I'm not sure," she said. She balled up her apron and added it to the dry-cleaning bag. "But the head honcho in hospice at the hospital can tell you anything you want to know." She scribbled something on a paper napkin. "Here's her cell number."

I shoved the napkin into the front pocket of my jeans. "Thanks." The smile on my lips came from my heart. After a long week, I'd finally had an engaging conversation with another human being about something other than elusive housing.

By the time I retrieved my dog, I was dead tired and in need of a hot shower. But in one night, I earned a week's worth of inn charges.

I grabbed Maverick's leash and chew toy and gave Mr. Walsh the condensed version.

He shook his head. "I can't wait for everything to get back to normal."

I wondered what normal would be.

CHAPTER THREE

On Monday, I placed a call to the number Samantha had given me. The robust greeting caught me off guard. "Good morning. Marjorie Seydel here. How may I assist you?"

"Hi. I'm Katie Wilk. Samantha…" I faltered. I didn't even know her last name. "Samantha told me about your therapy dog program." My hands shook, and the phone slid from my fingers, crashing to the floor. I scooped it up. "Sorry about that."

"No problem. You're a friend of Samantha's?"

"I met her while we were serving the *Titanic* dinner."

"It's the talk of the town. What can I do for you?"

"There's a dog…" I had to find a good home for him; I didn't think I could take care of him anymore.

Marjorie broke in. "You're certain he would make a

great therapy dog? You've called the right place. Our trainer is coming to evaluate dogs for our next class. Would you like to set up a time for the assessment?"

"I think so."

"C'mon in and complete an application." Marjorie rattled off the address and instructions to get through the maze created by the hospital construction. "I can't wait to meet you," she said. Before I could reply, she hung up.

* * *

I mustered my courage and stepped inside. I took shallow breaths to avoid gagging from the imagined antiseptic smell lingering in the space. I trudged to the elevator and forced myself to push the button to the hospice offices. The box clunked to the third floor.

The director of volunteers met me as the doors swished open. "Samantha's quite a handful, but she's a hard worker. I suppose my cousin gave my mom a hard time." A wry smile crept onto my face and Marjorie read my mind. She said, "That's my Samantha. She thinks she knows everything. She's had some tough times, but she's super smart, and finally on the right track."

Marjorie rummaged around on her cluttered desk, straightening a stack of papers and tugging on a folder. "Here's a packet of information about our program. And the application." She withdrew the last two pages and spun them in front of me. "Why don't you fill in the blanks and sign up for an assessment time?"

I read through the list of requirements. "What is 'leave it'?"

"You never know what might be on the floor or in a trash can in an unfamiliar room—medication, old food, sharps…"

"And you want the pet to leave whatever is there. Good idea."

"Don't worry if your dog doesn't know everything right away. Our trainer can help you with whatever you need. Our patients love our dogs." She opened a photo journal that contained snapshots of therapy dogs and their beaming partners.

"Therapy dogs are a godsend. A registered therapy dog is evaluated by our trainer to make sure they are gentle, clean, and make great visitors. Petting a dog can lower blood pressure, help with anxiety issues, improve cardiovascular health, release endorphins, and may even reduce the amount of medication a patient needs to take." She proudly recited the list as if from a training manual.

"Who would the handler be?"

Her tone was indulgent. "You, of course."

"I thought maybe you adopted them," I said, stumbling on my words. I'd have to work something out.

Marjorie peered over my shoulder and read as I scrawled answers into the application. "Your dog is twenty-seven?" She laughed.

The next question asked for neutered status. Realizing my mistake, I erased my birthdate and hastily filled in Maverick's. Her eyes narrowed when she read my local address at the Monongalia Bed and Breakfast. After pulling a card from the Rolodex on her desk, she reached for her phone and punched in some numbers. "Do you still have that room to rent?" She winked at me and nodded. "You betcha."

She handed me a business card. "She'll be expecting you."

Before we headed toward the elevator, Marjorie gave

me a short tour and introduced me to some of the staff and volunteers, who eyed me with suspicion.

Aware of my discomfort, Marjorie said, "We appreciate all our volunteers, but a staff member must accompany everyone in and out, and the hospice office locks up tight at four every afternoon. Can't be too careful. We've had some trouble, so I apologize if we seem overly cautious."

"What kind of trouble?"

She leaned in and whispered, "We think someone might have tried to steal some drugs. Better safe than sorry."

Marjorie handed me off to an energetic social worker. "You don't mind taking the stairs, do you? I never take the elevator," the woman said. "One time I got stuck in the darn thing for more than an hour."

"What happened?"

"They'd started installing new elevators and had turned off the alarm bells. The old beast stopped between floors, and the construction workers were making such a racket no one heard me yelling. Hey, did you find someplace to live?" she asked.

"For the time being, I'm at the Monongalia Bed and Breakfast, but I have some new properties to check out." I squeezed the life out of the business card. Indeed, I now had one possibility I was pinning my hopes on.

CHAPTER FOUR

Armed with the address on the card clasped in my hand, I glanced through the wrought iron fence to verify the house number. I parked my car on the street under a majestic oak tree that filtered morning sunshine onto a dappled carpet of green. A covered porch wrapped around the front of an imposing two-and-a-half-story Queen Anne-style home. White gingerbread dripped from the eaves, and cream-colored siding set off the black shutters. The curtain in one of the multi-paned windows of the hexagonal corner drifted to one side.

I turned off the ignition but let the auxiliary power continue to cool the interior. I popped out of the car and, turning to my eager passenger, pleaded, "Stay!"

I closed my eyes and inhaled the soft scent of roses, fortifying me for the ascent. After the gate screeched open,

I mounted the steps and raised the handle of a shiny brass doorknocker. In answer to my rap, a quintessential female of indeterminate age wrestled the door open and a hint of Ivory soap wafted out the entry. The stout woman wore a flowing black maxi skirt and a bright-green peasant blouse tucked into a wide purple suede belt. She had wild, curly red hair held in place by a multicolored silk scarf. Huge hoop earrings dangled from her earlobes and a tangle of chains encircled her neck. A mischievous light shone in her green eyes as she raised an eyebrow.

"May I help you?" a wary voice with a curious accent asked.

"Marjorie Seydel sent me to look at a rental unit? Katherine Jean Wilk, but everyone calls me Katie." I wiped my sweaty hand on my jeans and offered it in greeting. She gave it a quick decisive shake.

"Mrs. Ida Clemashevski. Come in." She beckoned with both hands. "First, a tour."

The heavy door closed with a whoosh, and the room fell silent. Glossy wooden floors creaked as she led me through a golden-hued living room crowded with plush forest green furniture and curio cabinets jam-packed with knickknacks. Prisms dangled from lamps adorning the tabletops polished to a high sheen.

"This way, please." Mrs. Clemashevski glided around the furniture. I followed closely because every surface held a figurine or two, and I didn't want to knock anything over. I desperately needed this interview to be a success.

As we left the living room, my guide nonchalantly brightened the hushed space with a rich glissando from strings of an opened grand piano couched in the corner beneath an imposing staircase. Closing my eyes, I let the waves of sound lift my spirits and slow my racing heart.

We entered an immaculate kitchen. Copper pots and cast-iron pans hung from a ceiling rack under a hood over an industrial stove. I'd never seen so many cooking utensils and had no idea what they might be used for. Salivating over something that smelled like chocolate baking in the oven, I inhaled deeply. "You must be a great cook."

"Looks can be deceiving."

I felt heat rise beneath her gaze and sweat beaded down my back, certain I stuck my foot in my mouth. Much more at ease with numbers, I sometimes fumbled for the right words and wished I could retrieve my awkward attempts at humor.

Then Mrs. Clemashevski sighed and remarked, "I do love to cook."

She rattled a key in the lock and we stepped through a connecting door. She proudly announced, "Your kitchen."

I felt I'd almost blown my best chance at finding a place to live, so when I stepped in, I tried, again, to be witty. "A dishwasher is all I need." When Mrs. Clemashevski knitted her eyebrows, my heart thudded against my chest and I coughed to cloak a nervous giggle, vowing to keep all further comments to myself.

An oversized enamel stove and refrigerator took up much of the small kitchen. On our way through, I straightened one of the mismatched chairs at the Formica table.

I preferred simple lines and predictable patterns and adjusted the tap on the stainless-steel sink to a position perpendicular to the backsplash. Mrs. Clemashevski cleared her throat and my ears felt hot. She waved to a small pantry. "Basement access through there. Laundry downstairs." She opened a door and announced, "Guest bath."

In the sparsely furnished living room, peeling birch logs piled on a thick metal grate in a brick fireplace, waiting for fall. A wood-paneled library looked out over the back yard. She tugged on a drawer handle and revealed a twin Murphy bed.

"One garage stall out back."

We mounted a staircase and I lightly ran my hand over a smooth rail. My feet slid into slight depressions on the worn steps. At the top of the stairs, she announced, "Full bath, two bedrooms."

"Can I have a roommate?" I stammered. She glanced at the ceiling, pursed her lips, and nodded.

I sighed when we entered the white and seafoam-green bathroom. The claw-footed tub would be perfect for a relaxing soak, my favorite place at the end of a long day.

In one room, white eyelet lace hung from an exquisite canopy bed. An intricate cut-glass mister sat atop a century-old vanity, and the matching carved armoire would give me plenty of storage space.

The second bedroom was furnished with a daybed. When I added my laptop to the desk standing in the corner and stacked my books on the built-in bookcases, everything would fit nicely. Nothing reminded me of where I'd been for the last year. "This is wonderful. How much is the rent?"

"Let us go down to your kitchen. You can fill out a renter's agreement," she purred. The self-assured woman added in a perfunctory manner, "It's merely a formality, but I'll also need you to submit references for a background check."

"Certainly."

The apartment was not far from the school where I'd be working, and close to the hiking trails listed on the city map where Maverick and I could walk. It was private and far enough away from my past.

Mrs. Clemashevski explained how she had determined such a reasonable rate. "Some days, I might allow you to help with the yard." She waited for a beat and glanced out the window, nodding at the garden and the fruit trees surrounding it. "Or I might need a better set of eyes to read the fine print of the phone directory. I have a fabulous head for numbers." She tapped her forehead. "But there are new ones I cannot read. And I might need a hand changing a light bulb." She'd been so straightforward I hadn't realized that without her heels she probably stood less than five feet tall, yet she had the personality of a giant.

"So, what brings you to the county seat of Monongalia, this great city of Columbia, on the windswept prairie in west-central Minnesota, the edge of the cultural Siberia of the Midwest?" Mrs. Clemashevski set her hands on her hips and finally grinned.

"I was hired as a math teacher at Columbia High School." I concentrated, filling in the blanks on the application.

She relaxed, leaning back, folding her hands in front of her. "And I am a retired art teacher. Did they talk you into anything else?"

"I have to admit, when the principal said, 'Would you be willing to…' I said yes." Her eyebrows prompted more. I really wanted a job, that first paycheck, and with it, experience to land other jobs. "I agreed to advise the science club and mock trial team."

Mrs. Clemashevski snorted.

"I'll already be teaching my favorite subject. And acting as an advisor to a club will give me the opportunity to meet more students and their families. Mock trial sounds like fun—sort of acting out a strategy game. That won't begin until the end of the first quarter, so I have a little time to get acclimated."

"And the science club?"

I shrugged. "I'm not sure. The entire adventure will be an experiment, pun intended. I guess I might want to keep busy, because the first few weeks in a new place can be…" I trailed off, reluctant to share so easily with this stranger.

"Lonely," Mrs. Clemashevski said, affirming my reticence. "Katherine Jean Wilk, I think we will work out just fine. Would you like to move in now?"

What an unexpected bonus! "That'd be great. But…" I scribbled faster and handed her the completed form.

She impishly arched an eyebrow.

"Maverick's in the car."

Both eyebrows arched.

CHAPTER FIVE

I clipped the leash on my sixty-five-pound black Labrador retriever, sitting amid ribbons of what might once have been a map. With his huge brown eyes, sloppy smile, floppy ears, and noble bearing, people who met him thought he was a fine specimen of a dog. Tongue hanging out and tail wagging, he yanked me along as he dashed up the stoop to where Mrs. Clemashevski waited.

I cued, "Sit, Maverick." I paused. "Sit." I counted to ten and lowered my voice. "Sit."

"Sit," said Mrs. Clemashevski. His rear hit the deck. I fumbled for the treats I kept in my pocket. "He'll only be here until I can find someone to take him," I said hesitantly. I never planned on owning a dog, and this one came with responsibilities I hadn't bargained for. Hedging a bit, I added, "He's well trained."

"Does he do tricks?"

"Maybe," I said. I gave Maverick my most serious look, hoping he understood his performance could make or break this deal. "Say hi, Maverick."

He tilted his head, kryptonite to dog-loving humans, and offered a paw to Mrs. Clemashevski. She shook it and said, "Velcome home." I was so flabbergasted, I forgot to give him a treat. He'd never shaken my hand.

* * *

After leaving a thank you note for Mr. Walsh and checking out of the inn, I transferred everything into the apartment and garage, except two cartons marked "school supplies."

"Can I get WIFI here?" I asked.

"It is accessible to you."

I opened the wizard to enable the connection. My fingers poised above the keys, and Mrs. Clemashevski disclosed the password. "CQDMGY."

With my fingers hovering, I grinned back at her. "The distress call from the *Titanic*?"

"Of course. I am an ardent aficionado of all things *Titanic*, along with most everyone else in town. And you?" She inclined her head toward the bookcase. *College Kids Cook*, *Magic for Dummies*, and a few dog-training titles were crammed between bookends in the shape of a bisected four-funneled ocean liner. I shrugged.

I hadn't yet thought about food, so I relished Mrs. Clemashevski's invitation to lunch.

"What do you do for fun?" she asked as she scurried about her kitchen. She handed me plates and silverware and pointed to a stack of napkins.

"Maverick and I walk. And we're always working on

a cue. It's what the pet manuals say to do." Even if we weren't too successful yet.

I reached down to scratch behind his ears. His eyes closed and he leaned into my hand. I pulled away, not wanting to get too accustomed to his presence. I couldn't keep him. "What about you?" I asked, as I rotated an unfinished crossword puzzle on the table.

She closed her eyes and sighed. "I love to dance."

I penciled in three answers before I caught Mrs. Clemashevski's checking over my shoulder. I dropped the pencil as though it burned my fingers.

"You like puzzles," she announced.

I nodded sheepishly.

As we devoured Irish stew and nibbled warm pumpernickel bread, Maverick remained calm, easygoing, and a perfect gentleman. "He's very smart," I said. "He'll make someone a great pet."

"How did you get a dog you did not vant?"

Her comment stung a little, but I'd practiced a hundred times and the line slid off my tongue. "He was a gift I'm unable to return." My tone cut off any further discussion.

Mrs. Clemashevski placed a warm chocolate lava cake in front of me for a sweet finish. Vanilla ice cream melted on the side, and hot fudge oozed from the center.

"Maverick would make a great therapy dog." Mrs. Clemashevski looked thoughtful. "You should take him for a walk now."

* * *

I stumbled behind Maverick as he pulled me into the wildlife refuge where we could walk and I could try geocaching, an activity I'd researched for science club.

No one was around, so I unclipped Maverick's leash, allowing him to investigate unrestrained. He sensed prey or past visitors in the area and raised his hind leg every five yards to mark his territory.

The trail crunched beneath my feet and Maverick inspected every square inch of turf, sprinting between the maple and black walnut trees. I inhaled the refreshing scent of Frasier firs as I crushed fallen needles under my heels.

Happy clouds skittered across the sky. The canopy of trees cast cooling shadows that appeared to move with us as we wended our way through the wetlands. Through a channel in the trees, I caught glimpses of the mirrored surface of a small body of water peeking through the tall grass surrounding it.

I perched on one of the wooden benches built to catch the not-so-hale and hearty, opened the geocaching app, and waited for it to zero in on my location. We were two-tenths of a mile away from an easy find. When we closed in on the cache, I signaled Maverick to "sit." I fed him a tiny morsel, hoping he'd stay, then headed the last few feet toward the coordinates to begin my search. I sighed when Maverick joined my exploration, snuffling through the underbrush. He left his mark on a metal sign post, and I gingerly searched the base. A magnetic box clung to the back of the sign.

"Maverick. Cache," I said. I held the container near enough for him to sniff. "Cache," I repeated, hoping he might someday associate the word with the action and help locate them. It could be a great selling point. I needed all the help I could get.

Maverick loved playing hide-and-seek and it was the one cue I could bank on him understanding. I covered my eyes, and Maverick knew it was game on. When he found me, he lavished me with sloppy kisses and I didn't need to use treats as an incentive for the game anymore.

I put my hand over my eyes. He sat and I walked ahead until I found a comfortable spot at the base of an enormous gnarled tree. "Find me," I called.

I heard Maverick bounding down the trail, panting with anticipation. Then he veered off on one of the narrow paths, crashing through the brush toward the water. The dense vegetation hid him from view. He swam well and I didn't think he would drown, but I'd never been to the water's edge, and I didn't know what other trouble he might find.

"Maverick," I called. When he failed to return, I trudged through thigh-high weeds, thinking of ticks, spiders, a sprained ankle, or a ring-necked pheasant Maverick might chase to who knew where. Keeping him safe was sometimes overwhelming.

I found him balanced, as if on point, one black paw raised. I didn't see any wild friends, people, other dogs, or, heaven forbid, squirrels. Maverick studied the reflection on the water. He snuck a sidelong glance at me as I stepped into the narrow clearing, then returned to his watch-and-wait stance.

"Come, Maverick. Maverick, come."

He looked my way, tongue hanging out, muscles rippling, and then he closed his lips and turned again to stare at the water.

"Stay." I approached with care and knelt next to him. I wrapped an arm around him, scratched his neck, and followed his gaze. "What do you see, big guy?"

Something shiny and blue floated on the surface of the

water about forty feet from shore. An almost imperceptible line cracked the surface next to it.

"Wonder what that is?"

The wind direction changed and an unpleasant odor permeated the air around us. Maverick turned his face to me, cocked his head, and his big brown eyes seemed to ask, *do you see it now?* He wriggled free of my embrace and plunged into the slough.

"Maverick, here," I shouted, but he paddled away on a mission. When he reached the bobbing object, he took it in his mouth. "Maverick, here," I howled. He struggled with his retrieve. Gentler, I called, "Here, boy." He dropped the bobbing whatever and paddled with difficulty, progressing nowhere. He wasn't panicking yet, but I felt the first tingling of alarm. "I'm coming."

I threw down the contents of my pockets—my phone, ID, and an emergency twenty-dollar bill. I considered removing my well-worn shoes, then had a vision of the things that might be lurking in the fetid water: bottle caps, glass, rocks, wet wigglies, crawly bugs, and mush. "Now I'll need new shoes, Maverick," I grumbled.

I raised my feet as high as I could, trying to avoid things I couldn't see. The pond inched its way higher with each step, soaking me to my chest. Slimy blue-green scum clung to my arms. I brushed aside the oily effluvium that snaked across the top of the water. It took forever for me to wade close enough to reach Maverick. His collar was tangled in a piece of sturdy wire below the surface. I unhooked him.

I didn't want him to get hooked again so I grabbed the flimsy fabric and tugged, but it held tight. Maverick paddled in the water next to me, captured the material, and turned inland. A figure rose out of the water and pivoted.

Milky eyes lolled in the sockets. Shredding skin fell in sheets from a pale, macerated face. Bloated hands reached for me. I sprang back and lumbered through the murky water, which felt as thick as syrup. The muck sucked my right shoe from my foot.

"Maverick!" I screamed as I struggled to shore.

He paddled efficiently, dragging the tuxedoed body behind him. When he reached the edge of the slough, he released his quarry. Water splashed from his coat, and panting, he bounded over to me with a pleased, expectant look.

"Oh, Maverick. Now look what you've gotten me into!" I cried. I slogged up the incline, grabbed my phone, and with green gunk sliding off my fingers, I punched 911. I tripped and my last vision was a crackle of fireworks.

CHAPTER SIX

Warm blood pulsed through my fingers and it wouldn't stop. A distant siren screamed, and I croaked, "Here we are. Help us!"

The gossamer threads of memories parted like a curtain as I swam to the surface, away from the nightmare that never failed to drag me into the abyss. Something warm and rough swabbed my face, and I heard a whimper. My eyes flashed wide, and I moved Maverick to one side.

A police car and an ambulance stormed the service road and parked near the end of the wetlands path.

I sat up with a start. A pain roared in my head and a wave of nausea knocked me back down. Tears filled my eyes.

"Ma'am?" called an EMT as he stepped toward me.

"Stay, Maverick," I mumbled. Maverick sidled next

to me, and he gently shook tiny droplets of water. The metal dog tags around his neck rattled, comforting me. I pointed to the shore where Maverick had dropped his find. "There's a body."

Maverick nestled close enough for me to put my arms around him, gathering support to sit upright, and keep him out of the way of the emergency assistance.

The uniformed man draped a metallic thermal blanket over my shoulders. "Roger that," he reported into the walkie-talkie clipped to his collar.

"We can't do him any good, but…you're bleeding," he said. He tore open a small package and reached down to wipe my head. I cringed from the sting and the antiseptic smell.

The EMT glanced at the body and said, "I've seen worse." He flexed his muscles so they strained against his crisp white shirtsleeves. His muscles strained against everything, accentuating his compactness. His lips hinted at a smile. Confident round eyes reflected various shades of a startling blue and green in a narrow face framed by wavy carrot-red hair. A generous sprinkling of freckles dotted his nose. "You've had quite a shock."

As the EMT continued to watch me, I reached behind my calf and, shuddering, pulled off a slimy leech and tossed it as far as possible.

A short distance away, a member of the emergency team yanked equipment she might need from the rear of the ambulance and a gurney clattered.

As the EMT looked toward the wetlands entrance, I followed his gaze. A dark Ford Explorer, with blue and white lights blazing, barreled into view. "That's the chief," the EMT said. "I'll be over there if you need anything." He tilted his head.

"Oh, Maverick," I moaned. "What have we done now?"

A tall, slender man, with a thick shock of wavy white hair and a luxurious mustache draped like a horseshoe, ambled toward us. Dressed in navy pants and matching shirt pressed into razor-sharp creases, the chief of police skirted the yellow caution tape being wrapped around the trees to cordon off the area. He turned his head from side to side, surveying the sights and sounds around him. Sunlight glinted from his badge and collar pins. He stopped in front of me. "And who are you?" his deep voice asked officiously. Hat in hand, he pushed his sunglasses onto his head.

I shook my head to clear the silken threads threatening to pull me back to the nightmare that took Charles. I didn't like having to look up at the chief, so I arranged my legs under me and stood. I staggered. The chief reached out to grab my arm, but I waved him off.

"Katie Wilk," I answered, and even to me I sounded defensive. I nodded to my side and said more amicably, "And this is Maverick."

"Lance Erickson, Chief of Police." He extended his hand and I took it. "What were you doing out here?"

I swallowed hard. "We came out here for exercise."

"Do you live around here?"

"I just moved to 3141 North Maple."

"Ida's tenant. You're the new teacher?"

"Yes." News traveled fast in this small town.

"Ida's already submitted the paperwork for your background check. What brought you down to the water, off the beaten path? It's out of the way and kind of hard to get to."

"Maverick and I were playing hide-and-seek and," I added hastily, "geocaching."

"I'd like to see that." He chuckled, wrinkles deepening in his weathered face. "You do that a lot?"

"This was my first time. I hoped it would take me someplace I hadn't intended to go." I gasped at the startling truth to my words.

"Preaching to the choir." He waited.

"Maverick took a detour to the water's edge. He found…" I spluttered. "I had to go get him."

"Is he a hunting dog?" He assessed Maverick.

"Maybe." I tried to find a hunter in his stance, but I didn't know what I was looking for.

"The body you found isn't in very good shape. Sorry you had to see that."

I was sorry I had to see that too. The dreadful memory would take a while to fade. "Is it Mr. Bruckner?"

Chief Erickson lowered his sunglasses, shielding his eyes, replaced his hat, and adjusted it to lie securely on his head.

I looked down and shuffled my feet. "I thought that maybe Hastings made good on his threat."

I looked up. The chief pursed his lips and studied me. "Don't go jumping to conclusions." He pulled out a notebook and pen and jotted a few lines.

I shifted from one foot to the other, and turned toward the entrance as a tow truck rolled in. My gaze followed the men from the truck, wearing waders, as they led a heavy-duty chain into the water. The winch on the tow truck screeched under the weight of a black car ratcheted from the water.

The sirens and strobing lights collected gawkers, so the officers erected a barrier of gray plastic tarp to discourage prying eyes and prevent cell-phone cameras from recording. An eager runner in bubble-gum pink gear jogged in place, divining possible routes around the sea of emergency personnel.

"You're bleeding," Chief Erickson said.

I put my hand to my forehead. My fingertips came away sticky and red. I glanced around to see where I might have gashed my head. Maverick stood close by and growled his opinion. "It's okay, Maverick."

"Looks like you hit your head on the NO SWIMMING ALLOWED sign." The chief paused for effect, eyeing the towering rusty metal signpost near us indicating our civil disobedience. Like I wanted to traipse around in that muck. I rubbed Maverick's velvety ears to distract me, then caught myself and stopped; I didn't want to become any more dependent on him. I concentrated on the questions the chief asked and tried to keep from breaking into a heap of tears until interrupted by the water gushing from the driver's side when the door was opened.

"The ambulance will take you to the ER. Get your head examined." One corner of the chief's mouth turned up. "I'll give Ida a call. I know where to find you in case I need to speak with you again. Got somebody to take that dog?"

I didn't expect the panicky feeling. "Can't he come with me?"

The EMT, who stood within earshot, stepped closer. "I'm afraid it's against policy." He pressed an ice-cold pack into my hands and directed it toward my head.

"Then I don't need to go." I took a step back.

As I toppled, Chief Erickson charged behind me and cradled my elbows, lowering me to the ground. "I've got you."

A pleasant voice from the crowd called out, "Chief, can I help?" The pink runner limboed under the crime-scene tape, scooted around an officer, and trotted over to us. She knelt on one knee and put out her hand to Maverick. He sniffed and bowed his head for her to scratch.

"Jane," Chief Erickson said resignedly, and tipped his head. "Katie Wilk," he said, gesturing to me.

"Pleased to make your acquaintance," Jane said with a hint of Southern drawl. "You're staying with Ida, right?" She lowered her eyes. Crimson crept up her neck. She should be embarrassed. I'd been Mrs. Clemashevski's tenant for less than half of a day and already everyone knew my business.

She looked familiar.

"Have we met?"

She searched my face. "I don't think so." Maverick changed position to get the full effect of her heavy-duty scratches. "He looks very smart. Do you think your dog will go with me if you tell him it's okay?" I begrudgingly thought he might. She wriggled her fingers into a pocket of her running shorts and dug out a business card. "Contact information, in case of emergency," she said, a light twang coloring her words. I glanced at the name under an attractive close-up of her face. It read, JANE K. MACKEY.

My head throbbed and I swiped more blood off my brow. I needed to trust someone. The chief nodded his approval.

"Maverick, go with Jane," I cued.

Before I could say any more, the chief ordered, "Jane, bring Maverick to the ER. I'll send Ida to retrieve Ms. Wilk."

"We'll be there ASAP," said Jane.

Maverick licked my cheek and nudged me toward the ambulance. I wiped my face with my shirtsleeve and he licked it again. I handed Jane the leash and she clipped it onto Maverick's collar. They jogged toward the path.

"Jane?" I called. She turned. "Thanks."

She nodded and Maverick followed her with a jaunty step and not a glance backward.

I gathered my belongings, and the EMT guided me to the ambulance. "He a good dog?" The name tag read, S O'Hara.

"Yes, Mr. O'Hara, he's a very good dog—might even become a therapy dog..." The thought evaporated, as stunned, I realized Maverick might have greater success as a cadaver dog.

CHAPTER SEVEN

Fidgeting on a paper-lined exam table, I turned to see a figure in a flapping white lab coat sail into the emergency room. The baritone voice snapped, "You can leave now."

Maverick sat between Jane and me. I presumed we weren't welcome and edged off the table. Instead, the white coat bellowed at our redheaded EMT. "O'Hara, you've made your delivery. Get out."

The young man craned his neck around the white coat and said to us, "If you need anything else, just ask, okay?" He raised his chin defiantly and stepped out of the room.

"Why did you do that?" I asked with restraint, not knowing if we'd be asked to leave next. "He was just being nice."

"And what the hell is a *dog* doing in here?" the white

coat snarled.

"Excuse me," said Jane, coolly. "I checked at the front desk. Hospital policy allows an owner's dog to visit. If you have any complaints, raise them with your policymakers."

"Sorry. It's been a helluva day," the doctor said, hands raised in surrender.

Jane handed me Maverick's leash, then inclined her head and mouthed, "Call me."

The doctor's eyes followed Jane as she marched out the door, then he turned back to us. His hands probed my forehead.

"Ouch."

"Sorry," he said. "You need stitches and suturing may leave a scar." His scrutinizing hands halted.

I felt his gaze zero in on my face. I looked up. Long black lashes framed intense dark-chocolate eyes locked on mine. When my face began to sizzle, I looked back down and mumbled, "Fine." Eyes were my nemesis, always had been. My heart raced. My spine melted. Was it guilt I felt or something else? *Relax*, I told myself.

The doctor tugged the admission papers out of my hand and read them. "It says your cut may have come from a rusty sign. Your tetanus needs to be current."

I tried to avoid those eyes. Mussed black hair curled gently around his collar, a scruffy five o'clock shadow bristled on a chiseled chin and framed brilliant white teeth. I speculated I should concentrate on the lips rather than the eyes and found, to my chagrin, my heart thumped even faster. His lips were full and sensuous and terribly dangerous. Fortunately, my thoughts were interrupted by an attention-getting cough.

"I'd recommend another," he said. "Another inoculation," he repeated. "A little prick from a local," he said. *Yup, maybe he was.* He reached for a syringe, "And we'll wait for the anesthetic to take effect."

Maverick rested his head in my lap, his big brown eyes blinking.

"Trying to get on my good side?" I asked.

"What was that?" said the doctor.

"Nothing."

The nurse wrapped the blood pressure cuff around my arm, and I repeated my calming mantra: *The past has no power over the present.* I closed my eyes and willed my galloping heart to slow to the pace of Maverick's measured breathing. In with the good air, out with the bad.

"Nice dog," the doctor said.

I opened my eyes. "Say hi, Maverick."

Maverick sat straighter, and I heard the snap of nitrile gloves being removed. The doctor put out his hand for Maverick to sniff. "Hi, Maverick." Sniffing done, Maverick offered a paw to shake and leaned in. He was a discerning dog, but hey, a petting hand also can reach a perpetual itch. I almost heard Maverick sigh when the doctor reached under his collar with an earnest scratch. "Good boy."

"Dr. Pete Erickson." He extended his hand.

"Katie Wilk," I replied. I wiped my grubby fingers on an equally grubby T-shirt and reached out.

"Pleased to meet you, Mrs. Wilk," he said.

"Just Katie."

He released the hand he held an extra moment. "Just Katie then," he said with a satisfied grin.

The nurse tapped a pen against a clip board. Auburn hair framed a youthful face. She wrinkled her nose. I sniffed. Something smelled awful. Me? My baggy walking clothes were wet and dirty and a whiff of Maverick clinched it.

The nurse grabbed my wrist and chewed her lower lip as she watched the seconds tick by on the clock.

"Are you in the market for a dog?" Maverick's head volleyed back and forth.

Doctor Erickson let out a little laugh. "Susie." The nurse handed him a penlight.

"May I?" Dr. Erickson asked. I nodded, and he flashed the beam in my eyes.

"Are you new in town?" Dr. Erickson asked.

"Yes." I should have said more, but I couldn't find any words.

"Okay?" He reached up to touch my forehead.

I nodded. I wasn't sure the local had taken total effect, but it was more uncomfortable to sit and be flustered by my inability to communicate coherently. I didn't understand my reaction. Until now, I thought I'd banished all those primal urges and they were locked somewhere in stasis.

"Looks like seven stitches." I heard, rather than felt, each and every one.

After the stitches, with a slightly sadistic glint in her eyes, Nurse Susie administered the tetanus booster.

Dr. Erickson scribbled on a pad and handed me a square. "Take this antibiotic twice a day for five days, and in seven days see your general practitioner to check the stitches and examine the wound."

"Um," I faltered. "Can you recommend one? A general practitioner?"

"You could come back here," Dr. Erickson offered.

"Thank you," I mumbled. I really didn't want to return to this ER. "When would it be convenient for you?"

"Tuesday…"

The entry doors crashed open, and Mrs. Clemashevski

bustled into the ER. "Katie, what happened?"

I faltered. "I'm fine."

"Good evening, Ida," Dr. Erickson said. Glittering lights of familiarity winked on in his dark eyes. "I'm confident I can release her into your most competent care. If you notice any symptoms of nausea or trouble walking or talking, bring her back immediately. Other than the initial dizziness and headache, I haven't seen any other signs of a concussion."

Concussion?

"Of course, Dr. Erickson," Mrs. Clemashevski gushed. She took hold of Maverick's leash and led us out the glass doors to an ancient purple muscle car. Aside from the garish color, I thought my dad would have approved of the immaculate 1970s Plymouth Barracuda.

We pulled into a drugstore drive-through to fill my prescription, and my eyes slammed shut. I woke up when Mrs. Clemashevski backed into an empty garage stall next to a Buick.

She ushered Maverick and me into her kitchen. While she fussed, I assured her we were fine, but then the dam burst, and she handed me a box of tissues. When I finished dabbing at my eyes and wiping my nose, she said, "No more of that." She sent me out to sit at a battered picnic table.

From behind her screen door Mrs. Clemashevski asked in her thickest accent, "So, smarty-pants, when will you learn to open the door?" I wondered whether she was speaking to Maverick or me. "Pull" would be the next cue for us to work on. I slid the door to the side, and she exited, balancing a tray with two glasses, cookies, and a pitcher of ice-cold lemonade.

"Maverick is such a good boy. May I walk him when you are not around?" she said.

Hearing his favorite word, Maverick wriggled. "I don't think he's going to wait for my permission. I'll hang that leash in the porch and you can walk him whenever you'd like."

"Good. That will get me outside." She paused, then added, "Katie, which is heavier, a pound of gold or a pound of feathers?" It tickled me that she remembered I enjoyed puzzles. As I started to answer, her landline trilled. "Would you get that for me, please?"

Eager to please, I sprang into action, nearly vaulting inside, but was brought up short by a stabbing pain behind my right eye. I slowed and picked up the receiver. "Hello. Clemashevski residence."

A tentative female voice asked, "Am I speaking with Ida?"

"No. Hold on. I'll get her. May I tell her who's calling?"

"Elaine Cartwright," she barked.

I pulled the receiver back from my ear and stared at it. "Mrs. Clemashevski. It's for you. Elaine Cartwright?"

A stone like mask fell over her features. She drew herself up to her full four feet and some inches, bracing herself before taking the few steps inside, and put out her hand for the receiver.

"This is Ida." She listened, nodding her silent responses. She rolled her eyes and pointed to the pitcher, indicating, I hoped, I should begin pouring. I was happy to oblige. A few moments later she joined Maverick and me on the deck.

I handed her a glass. Her forehead scrunched with worry lines. Without trying to seem too nosy, I asked, "Is everything all right?"

"Miss Cartwright is not a very happy person right now." Mrs. Clemashevski took a dainty sip.

I dug for more. "Why is she unhappy?"

"She was asked to resign from a job she loved."

I waited.

"I know many people in town, and she had the impression I could help her." Mrs. Clemashevski took another sip.

"*Can* you help her?"

"I do not think so. There were some photos of improper behavior with a student."

"Who asked her to resign?" I held a cookie too close to Maverick's tongue and it disappeared.

"The school board chairman," Mrs. Clemashevski said.

"That's too bad. What did she do for the school?"

She leveled her eyes at me and said thickly, "Yourrr job!"

CHAPTER EIGHT

I finally understood the phrase "the silence in the room was deafening."

A sigh slipped from Mrs. Clemashevski's lips. "Last year, the chairman of the board called Elaine before the school's attorney. She denied any wrongdoing, and the attorney admitted the photos they received could have been doctored, but rather than drag the student in question through an inquiry, Elaine resigned. No charges were filed. She will not, however, sit idly by. She vowed to find out who did this to her and why. Sadly, she now seems to be the subject of many police investigations."

Mrs. Clemashevski took a long drink of lemonade then rattled the ice in her glass. "Elaine played in my yard. She grew up in my house. I never doubted that she loved teaching. I think she would do anything to protect her students."

"You said she held my job?"

"Her degrees are in video production and mathematics. But her sullied reputation preceded her. She couldn't get a job with the movie crew either."

We finished our dinner in grim silence.

After we cleared the dishes, Mrs. Clemashevski steered me to my kitchen table and sat me down. "You have medication to take." She retrieved the pill bottle from the counter and handed me a full glass of water. She stayed rooted until I re-secured the cover on the bottle and downed the entire glass of water.

I thanked her and said goodnight. As I waited for the sandman, I tugged out my journal.

Busy day: Maverick found a dead body. Met Jane Mackey and Dr. Pete Erickson. Nice to know I can still appreciate a good-looking man. To top it off, it seems the last person to have held my job was asked to resign.

* * *

The next morning, Mrs. Clemashevski shared her daily newspaper and, fortified with hot black coffee and a warm cinnamon roll dripping with sugary frosting, I perused the front page of the *Columbia Sentinel*. A photo of the water-fowl protection area and tall headlines trumpeted our gruesome discovery. The article didn't mention my name; it described a new resident out for a stroll with her dog and the horrific welcome they'd encountered.

The victim was Arthur Condive—entrepreneur, school board chair, local businessman, and owner and operator of Ye Olde Auld. A fifty-eight-year-old widower with four grown children, he traveled the tri-state area searching for odd treasures. He specialized in collecting antiques, archaic office supplies, old paper, ink, furniture, and ancient business records. The article gave an account of his valuable service to the community and a list of those who would miss him.

"This man signed my employment contract," I said. "Did you know him?"

"Katie." Through Mrs. Clemashevski's sadness, pinpoints of light twinkled in her captivating eyes and she puffed up a bit. "I have lived in Columbia longer than you've been alive. I know almost everyone."

Filing that thought away for future reference, I continued scanning the article. "It says he might have died under suspicious circumstances. I should say so. It wouldn't have been difficult for him to drive into the slough, but it would have been almost impossible for him to have floated out of the car with the doors closed."

Mrs. Clemashevski's eyes grew huge.

"Did Mr. Condive request Elaine's resignation?"

"He did."

Maybe not everyone would miss him.

* * *

My school was minutes away by car. Over the tops of the boxes I hauled in, I heard chuckling and peeked around to find the clerk of the Monongalia Bed and Breakfast. "How's that pup doing?" Mr. Walsh asked. He grabbed the top box.

"You work here too?" I asked, flabbergasted.

"I loved my engineering career, but I couldn't find enough to keep me occupied at home after I retired and the missus passed away, so here I am. I love the energy and as a custodian I have no home work." He winked and delivered me to the math department. "I'll leave you to it."

I tore through my boxes for items to cheer up my classroom and adorn the sterile khaki walls. I tacked up a few posters, and organized what I considered to be a prime selection of books and puzzles. I planned to show my students how math is used in a variety of disciplines. Maybe one of the posters or books would inspire a student to pursue a career, and they'd see how math connected to the world around them.

Or not!

The stack of teacher's manuals teetered on my desk. When I opened the new advanced math book, the spine made a crackling noise. The pages smelled fresh and inky. I took a deep breath, then set to work writing out lesson plans, supplementing daily instruction with card tricks or new vocabulary words with numerical meanings, such as *sesquicentennial*: a 150-year celebration. I matched biographies of mathematicians to the topics I would teach. If my students seemed bored with a lecture, I could change it up with an outlandish number story or brainteaser.

When I returned to my apartment, Mrs. Clemashevski said, "Elaine called again. The police brought her in for questioning. She believes she is a suspect in the death of Mr. Condive."

"Have they determined how he died?" I asked.

"She did not say, but their questions alarmed her. They asked for an alibi she does not have. She is one unlucky girl."

"Could she have done it?"

Mrs. Clemashevski sighed and shook her head.

"What can you do?"

"Prove she is innocent."

* * *

Mrs. Clemashevski had two automated doggy doors installed, elevating Maverick to king of the yard. His new collar activated an electronic keyed entrance to the porch and my kitchen. He enjoyed lying outside in the warm sun and occasionally cooling himself in the shade. However, his favorite place when I was in the apartment was underfoot.

Mrs. Clemashevski and I lounged in lawn chairs and sipped iced tea. Maverick leaned into her scratches and beamed in satisfaction. If he were a cat, he'd be purring.

"Boyfriend?"

I forced a smile. "Not right now."

"We'll work on that. Favorite music?"

"I like music from the 1940s best."

"Me too. Color choice?"

"It changes, but today, purple."

"Mine is rrred," she said. "Favorite food?"

"Anything I don't have to make myself. You?"

"Anything I make myself." She laughed. "By the way, a dear friend of mine gave me a few bottles of Zinfandel. I do not drink red wine. If you do, please consider it part of your housewarming gift." She nodded at a carton on the deck.

"Thank you. I'd love it." I carefully crafted my next question. "If they determine foul play in the death of Mr. Condive, and you believe Elaine is innocent, who do you think might be guilty?"

She stopped scratching Maverick.

* * *

Each day, the formidable Mrs. Clemashevski relaxed her attentiveness a bit more. I took Maverick for walks, although we avoided the wetlands for more populous territory. Walking on leash tethered his joyful sense of adventure, but our yard was the only acceptable location to be free. I feared what he might find if I allowed him to roam. He repaid me by chewing the strap off a sandal he found by the back door, gnawing a perfectly good McIntosh apple, and shredding a day-old newspaper.

After the week passed, I welcomed and dreaded the return trip to have my stitches removed and come face-to-face with Dr. Erickson again. No one was at the desk, however, when I entered the ER. I felt relieved for a bit then peeved. My stitches were begging to be scratched.

Sitting in a red Naugahyde chair, I watched the ticking hands of the clock hanging behind the desk. I could have sworn it took two hundred forty seconds for the minute hand to complete one revolution. I didn't wear a watch, and the sign at the entry had asked us to turn off our cell phones so I had no way of knowing how long I sat there.

By the time Nurse Susie bustled in, I had lined up the chairs, straightened the tables, and paced off the dimensions of the room. She uttered a displeased, "Oh," then began the strange business of organizing the desk in front of her.

Sweaty skin stuck slightly, making an embarrassing sucking noise as I stood and walked red-faced to the admission desk. I did the traditional throat clearing and asked to see Dr. Erickson.

"He's not available," she replied brusquely. "Come back tomorrow."

What else could I do?

When I returned, Mrs. Clemashevski eyed my stitches, perplexed.

"No Dr. Erickson," I volunteered with more acidity than planned.

She handed me a key. "For the garage. After our walk, I closed the door and left Maverick in the yard. I watched him stand on his hind legs, pull the handle down on the service door, and push it open." She frowned but her eyes laughed.

I made my way to my room and penned another note in my journal.

Maverick! What a dog! And no one was available to remove the stitches or examine my head. Strike one, Dr. Erickson.

CHAPTER NINE

When my persistent questions about Columbia drove Mrs. Clemashevski crazy, she shooed us outside.

In the evening, she implored, for the eleventh time, "Come with me and meet some people. Vivian Green said, 'Life is not about waiting for the storm to pass. It is about learning how to dance in the rain.' I dance. That is how I keep my svelte figure." Her hands smoothed the sides of her solid hourglass shape and she did a little shimmy.

I acquiesced and accompanied her to what she said would be the easiest class, ballroom dancing.

Mrs. Clemashevski wore a flowing paisley skirt and a silky violet blouse. Her hair swirled in a French roll; she applied her makeup with an artist's eye; jewelry glinted from her earlobes, fingers, and neck. I dressed for comfort and donned my well-worn burnt orange yoga pants, Tommies T-shirt, and lime-green sneakers. I pulled my light brown hair into a ponytail, closeted the rest of my shoes, and said goodbye to Maverick.

I hadn't anticipated a dress code.

We arrived at the dance studio with fifteen minutes to spare and found a dozen dancers divided into small groups. Mrs. Clemashevski led me to a welcoming threesome. The tailored teal dress on the tall dark-haired woman swayed gently as she turned to greet me. "Ms. Balponi?"

"Call me Jess, dear." She smiled warmly and gave me a knowing look. I wondered what she knew.

The tall man, capped with poorly dyed dark brown hair, sported an incongruous graying goatee, and his rheumy, greenish eyes made him look as though he'd pored over pages and pages of text during the course of his career. His name was Edward Scott. "Not Eddie, nor Ed," he insisted.

The clean-shaven shorter man had a round face, full pink cheeks, a bulbous red nose, and the most intense sapphire blue eyes in the room, which distracted me from staring at his tonsured head. The fabric of his well-worn plaid suit strained across his plump midsection, and if it had been December, I could have seen Cash Schultz playing the role of Santa in the local mall.

"Can you guess our occupations?" Mr. Schultz asked. His eyes blazed with mischief.

I guessed Jessica to be a costume designer. Mr. Scott looked like a professor, and Mr. Schultz, maybe a trucker. Wrong on all counts.

Mr. Schultz's eyes twinkled and he offered a soft, dry hand. "Professor emeritus, history."

Putting her arm around my shoulder, Jessica laughed. "I'm retired tech support for my family's software company. I supervised research for our *Titanic* movie. And Edward drove a snowplow for thirty-five years."

Mr. Scott raised his chin. "I retired from MnDOT last year and moved here from Bloomington. In the spring I'll assist with the high school baseball team."

"I'm teaching at the high school. Maybe I'll see you there," I said.

"Katie," Mr. Schultz said, "take me out and scratch my head. I'm now black, but once was red. What am I?"

"My secret's out. I'll have to think about that one." Mrs. Clemashevski ignored my evil eye and dragged me over to a younger threesome. The pert, smiling blonde had two handsome hunks lingering on her every word. Jane Mackey wore a fluorescent pink salsa dress, short in front, longer in back, flowing to mid-calf, exposing narrow ankles and glitzy four-inch stilettos. She'd pulled back her curly blond hair and pinned it up with an easy elegance. Her too white smile accented a flawless complexion. Vertically challenged, however, she needed the heels to see over the hulking shoulders she attended to on both sides. All right, so my thoughts were just a tiny bit catty, and I owed her big time. But I never felt so under-dressed and regretted the comfort my clothes afforded.

"This is my new renter, Katie Wilk. Katie, meet Matthew and Stephen. And you have already met Jane." She paused for effect and whispered conspiratorially, "Did Jane tell you she is the new high school history teacher?"

"Hi there," Jane said with a more pronounced drawl. "I'm so happy we can share these nice gentlemen." She rested one hand on each man's forearm. "They plumb tucker me out every time I come here. They take turns and I have to dance every single dance." She took my hands in both of hers and with genuine sincerity said, "I sure am glad you came." Then she added quietly, "When do you get those stitches out?"

A thickness welled up in my throat as she drew me in with her sunny smile. Maybe I'd find a friend behind those sparkling eyes. I smiled back. "The doctor wasn't in."

Stephen and Matthew offered their hands and took turns pumping mine like the jack handle on a monster truck.

Carrying a clipboard with him, the instructor wrote down the information I supplied. I paid a nominal fee for a trial month of classes, which would give me time to decide whether I enjoyed the dancing enough to continue after earning my first paycheck.

We waltzed the entire hour, working on form, space, and rhythm. "Relax, head up, straight back, and count. Step, rise, close. Gentle pressure from the lead, opposing movement and a box step," the teacher recited, guiding us through the dance. Jane and I took turns dancing with Stephen and Matthew.

I noticed something familiar about the way Jane floated across the floor. Just before the last dance, the answer hit me like a hammer. "You're her," I said.

"I am *a* her," she said with a giggle.

"You walked out of the *Titanic* screening. I've been racking my brain trying to figure out where I'd seen you before."

"Pleased to meet you, Katie, under much more pleasant circumstances." She smiled and shook my hand. "Someday I'll tell you about it."

When the class ended and we funneled toward the door, Jane said, "I don't know about you, but I'm always on the lookout for things to do. This is sort of a quiet town, don't you think?" I refrained from commenting. "I'm sort of an exercise geek. Do you run? Or bicycle?"

"I don't run," I answered, "but I walk Maverick every

day. I do have a bike, but it's been a while since I last rode."
My palms began to sweat.

"Let's bike." My forefinger traced the scar on the inside
of my left arm and a wave of panic washed over me. "Did
something happen?" she asked and reached out to touch
my arm. "You know what they say. If you fall off a horse,
the best way to conquer your fear is to climb back up on
it."

In with the good air, out with the bad. In my mind I
heard the words *Move forward*. "I need to walk Maverick
early, ahead of the heat. Then I'm going to try again to get
my stitches removed, but the rest of tomorrow is open."

"I live down the street from Ida. How about I swing by
at ten and we'll give it a go?"

"Sounds good," I said, then turned to Mr. Schultz.
"Does 'match' answer your riddle?"

He glowed.

* * *

Before Mrs. Clemashevski and I parted on the porch, I
gave her a quick hug. "Thank you for taking me."

She nodded toward my front door. "Time to call it a
night."

I released her and dragged my tired body upstairs. I
luxuriated in my fabulous tub, filling it with warm water
and soaking the day's cares away, smiling at the pleasant
turn of events as wisps of steam circulated a lavender
scent.

CHAPTER TEN

I didn't really want to go to the ER, and once I arrived, a curt triage nurse directed me to the urgent care clinic where an on-call physician would remove the stitches for a reasonable fee. "The ER is for e-mer-gen-cies," she said impatiently.

I sauntered past numerous computer-generated flyers displaying the words "Pardon Our Mess. We Aim to Impress," to the opposite end of the hospital, down an elevator, through creepy quiet corridors, cluttered with tools and tarps. I pushed through a set of double doors and down a ramp into a brilliant white hallway toward a blood-red phone with a sign above it that read, FOR EMERGENCY USE ONLY. The exit doors became visible only after I walked halfway through the long passageway that connected the clinic and the hospital, which must have crossed beneath the street. I heard the rhythmic thrum of traffic above, punctuated by my echoing footsteps, which gave me the unnerving feeling of being followed.

I followed paper arrows to the clinic, both relieved and a little saddened that I might not meet Dr. Erickson again. While waiting, I picked up the *Sentinel*. I scanned the headlines and turned to the page of cartoons and games. I retrieved an old receipt and pencil from my bag, copied the cryptoquip, and scribbled until I worked out SJPFMLVFPI NISJVN MPL to ARITHMETIC SCARES HIM. I'd heard that before.

When I returned to North Maple Street, I found Jane engaged in a conversation with Mrs. Clemashevski, both smiling, but arguing about what each considered to be part of a healthy diet. Food high in fiber and protein, low in calories and fat—Jane spoke well of her diet, vitamins, minerals, and home-grown herbal supplements. Mrs. Clemashevski argued with equal adamancy, defending homemade foods full of real butter, sugar, cream, and, of course, the most important ingredient, love. Neither was going to give an inch.

When Jane saw me, she said mid-argument, "Hi, Katie."

"Look at you."

"My favorite color." She struck a pose in her hot pink padded biker shorts and pink-and-white jersey. She modeled black wraparound sunglasses with pink piping along the top, spotless white cycling shoes, and an eye-catching pink-and-white helmet to literally top it off. At her side was a white custom Colnago M-10; she was no amateur cyclist.

"I'll just be a minute," I said, and scurried to change. My generic black biking shorts used to fit better; now they sagged in all the wrong places. The two pockets in my polyester shirt carried only the necessities. My unfetching metallic green helmet and my sunglasses were department store specials, but I prepared to ride.

Taking one step at a time, I marched into the garage stall and approached my red aluminum Trek bike with trepidation. I curled my fingers around the handlebars and pulled it away from the wall, fingering some of its battle scars; it was well broken in. I shook my head and wheeled my bike to the service door, where I stood watching Mrs. Clemashevski and Jane laughing.

As I rolled my bicycle toward them, the textured handlebar tape evoked painful memories—the thwack of metal as it struck its mark, the scrape of plastic against pavement, and the sound of a gunshot. Waves of nausea rolled over me, and a riptide of sorrow threatened to pull me under. Maybe biking wasn't a good idea. My vision narrowed. Coursing blood pounded in my ears.

Jane asked, as if from a great distance, "What happened, girlfriend? We don't have to ride today if you don't want to."

I gulped fresh air and fought to recover. "Must be the removal of my stitches." After a few tipsy starts, I swallowed hard. It was only a bike. You didn't forget how to ride; sometimes you just didn't want to remember.

Gathering my courage, I followed Jane to the bike path for a smooth trail with little traffic. We rode for about six miles at a relaxed pace, taking in the trees, the birds, the wildflowers, and the gorgeous blue sky. My gauge told me the speed, time, and distance. My shoulders relaxed. I worked hard and felt invigorated. Now that I was back in the saddle, the sense of being in control gave me strength.

"I suppose I acted a bit immature at the movie screening," Jane said. My response was labored breathing. "I met Robert Bruckner on a flight to Minneapolis, coming for my job interview, and he told me all about Columbia. After I accepted the position, we met a few times for coffee, and, until a week before the screening, I thought I was Robert's date. Then his assistant called and told me he couldn't take me. Fortunately, I still had an invitation in hand. The film *is* remarkable, and Robert did a terrific job. But when Damon made such a show, I felt a childish satisfaction letting Robert know I was there. And that's all there was to that.

"This is great. If I have someone to bike with, I'll keep at it. You can be my conscience and I can be yours."

"Accountability." Sweat rolled down my back and I huffed. She didn't.

As we rode, Jane puffed up when she recited her crazy health rituals. She took vitamins K and D, a daily multivitamin, calcium, and iron. It sounded like a gigantic cup of capsules to down every morning.

"I'll text you the list and you can see if anything interests you. Each component of this regimen has its own special health-giving property. I eat quite a bit of seafood and some poultry."

Her words moved like molasses and were easy to listen to. "I seldom touch red meat." She continued, "but I love fruits and veggies. Only sweets in some form of chocolate ever cross my lips, but what's one vice? And I drink red wine for my heart. Do you think you want to try anything?"

I waited a beat. "The wine and chocolate sound fabulous." We both groaned.

"You know, everyone should take calcium, vitamin D, and fish oil."

"I'll think about it," I said.

Because school workshops wouldn't begin for four more days, we made plans to ride again. I assumed Jane was entering the event on her calendar when my phone pinged with a text message. I glanced at the screen, opened the text, and found her menu of healthy habits.

"Thanks," I said.

While we were stopped, she pulled a small plastic pill bottle out of her pocket. She rattled the contents into her palm and tossed something into her mouth. I cocked my head.

"It's an antacid. A little indigestion," she said. "Can you do another five miles?"

I struggled to catch my breath and begged off. "I can't. I have to let Maverick out."

She rocked on her toes and said, "Stephen and Matthew want to show me the sights and evening lights of Columbia at Take Your Best Shot on Friday. Why don't you join us?" When I hesitated, she begged, "Please?"

I wondered what Take Your Best Shot might be. "I'm sure they only wanted to invite *you*."

"Even if that were true," she said, "I couldn't keep both of them happy. Take Your Best Shot is supposed to be the best club in town." She took a breath, and a smile crinkled her eyes. "Actually, it's the *only* club in town.

"Let's go together. Then we don't have to walk into unfamiliar territory not knowing anyone. There is a dress code of sorts—no T-shirts, no torn jeans, no flip-flops. And I always, *always* have an escape plan." She giggled. "We need a code in case we need to get away from there."

I needed only a second to come up with an idea because I'd used it on occasion before. "We need to let Maverick out."

"I knew it." She chortled. "Eight o'clock, Friday."

Mrs. Clemashevski greeted me from the porch and patted the seat beside her.

"I'm sweaty and I reek," I warned.

"Sit!" she ordered, so I sat.

She opened the *Columbia Sentinel* and pointed to an article I'd missed. The story detailed a drug bust the day before and the overdoses of four recent Columbia High School graduates found at the scene. An anonymous caller had alerted the trauma team, and it appeared none of the students would have any residual ill effects from the combination of drugs found in their systems. Names were withheld pending an investigation. The article continued on page five, but I didn't finish reading it.

"That's awful," I said. "Did you know any of the victims?"

"Not all the children, but I know their parents," she said. "Keep reading."

I turned to page five. What first caught my eye was an article about the discovery of letters being researched and authenticated before being sold to Bruckner's *Titanic* exhibit. Mrs. Clemashevski tapped the article, which continued from page one, and I read aloud, "Hometown son Dr. Pete Erickson…" I glanced at Mrs. Clemashevski then back at the paper. "…returned to Columbia six months ago after completing his medical training and residency at Chicago's Cook County Hospital. After a long night reviving four recent Columbia High School graduates, Dr. Pete pleaded with the community to assist the police in putting a stop to the drug pipeline. 'Lock up your prescription drugs. If your kids mention a Skittles party, they're not talking about the fruit-flavored candy. They're talking about throwing together whatever drugs they can find: Ritalin, Tylenol, Xanax, Vicodin, Adderall and then taking turns grabbing and swallowing whatever they select. Talk to your kids. It's suicide.'"

Before calling it a night, I amended my journal.

Maybe strike one wasn't entirely his fault.

Dr. Pete, hmm. I let the name slide off my tongue.

CHAPTER ELEVEN

To commence my evening of fun, Mrs. Clemashevski served an iced tea with a touch of Limoncello, and asked, "Katie, what begins with 't,' ends with 't,' and is filled with tea?"

"A teapot." I answered with ease, but I had a feeling her riddles were going to get more difficult.

Before she set off to her next dance class, I had her survey my attire. Although I couldn't compete with Jane, I didn't want to embarrass her either.

Wearing white jeans for the last time this season, I had cinched the waist with a safety pin, then added a draping salmon-colored sleeveless top and matching flats. I used a flat iron and turned the ends under, so my hair curled softly against my shoulders. I brushed on dark-blue mascara to complement my light-blue eyes and applied a shiny lip-gloss.

"Not bad, but…" Mrs. Clemashevski hesitated then walked out of the room. She returned with a delicate turquoise pendant on a flat silver chain. "Around and down," she ordered. I turned, bent my knees, and pulled my hair out of the way. "A pop of colourrr!" she said, the "r" purring as she encircled my neck and clasped the necklace from behind. She tapped on my shoulder, and I stood for a final inspection. She took her time and had me worried. "You vill do," she said at last. Then she picked up her elegant black evening bag and headed out the door.

It had been too long, so I punched in a phone number I knew by heart.

A female voice answered with its characteristic sharpness. "Katie? I told you to wait until the doctor approved. He's doing as well as expected. Give it a rest." She hung up. I didn't appreciate my stepmother's reminder and stared at the phone in my hand. I'd monitored my dad's measured recovery for eleven months and she'd welcomed my initial involvement, but at the last care conference, she strongly suggested I back away for a while; this exile was excruciating.

Seventy-six minutes later, a knock sounded at the door.

"Coming," I called.

I opened the door. Jane didn't bat an eye. "I came for Katie."

I pouted. "Jane. It's me."

Her eyes popped open wide. "You look so different, girlfriend. What happened?" Then her big brown eyes winked.

"And I thought I did a fine job."

"You did. I was just teasing. And what a beautiful necklace!"

"It's Mrs. Clemashevski's."

Fingering the delicate pendant, she said, "I love lockets." It opened under her gentle ministrations. She rotated the jewelry, and I peered at the enclosed photographs: grinning faces in sepia tones of yesteryear. "Nice." Jane gently secured the clasp then snapped her fingers. "Now let's blow this joint. I'll drive."

Maverick whined. "I need me time, my friend," I said.

She sat high up in the driver's seat of her forest-green Ford Edge, talking nonstop. "This car has plenty of room to cart a bike or two." She hunched her shoulders and let out a sigh, as she ran her hands around the steering wheel. "And don't you just love the smooth ride?"

As she careened around each corner, I inspected my seat belt. "A stop sign!" I cried.

"Merely a suggestion," Jane said. I latched on to the strap as we squealed through the intersection, taking the corner on two wheels. I didn't breathe until we stopped.

When we entered the bar, Jane surveyed the establishment, bobbing her head in time to the music, playing air drums.

Most of the crowd were twenty- and thirty- somethings dressed in skirts and jackets, shirts and ties. Panning the room, I spotted S O'Hara. He inclined his head and tipped his brown bottle my way. I nodded and smiled in return.

We located Stephen and Matthew, seated to the right of the dance floor at a high-top table surrounded by stools, most of them filled. Jane cocked an eyebrow, and I shrugged my shoulders, deciding to dive in.

"Heya, chickies," Stephen called with a broad smile, slurring his words. "What's cracking?"

"Hi, Stephen," Jane said, and gave him a peck on the cheek. She leaned over and greeted Matthew similarly, then beckoned me into the circle with a kind incline of her head.

"Heya, Katie," Stephen said thickly.

"Hi, Katie," Matthew chimed in.

It appeared our group had begun socializing earlier in the evening.

Tables and chairs were pulled together, and we were introduced, shaking hands all around. I desperately hoped I wouldn't have to repeat any names because the music boomed loud enough to keep me from hearing the important parts of the introductions. The guys ordered another pitcher of beer and two more glasses. Popcorn and peanuts in the shell magically appeared and just as quickly disappeared.

I left the table for a minute and when I returned, some dark-haired guy had taken my chair. His broad back to me, he wore a crisp blue shirt with sleeves rolled up on his biceps. As I neared the table, I heard Jane describe exaggerated cycling escapades I didn't recall. Her riveting storytelling had them glued to their seats.

"You should have seen her legs go. She was Ms. Speedy Gonzalez. I could barely keep up. She bikes every day *after* walking her dog for miles." She saw me, grinned, and continued. "She's on this health-food craze and…" She was describing herself to a tee except she was using me as the subject. I didn't know if I should be annoyed or giddy. Jane got up and grabbed another chair and thrust it next to the guy who'd hijacked my seat. "Katie," she said. "I was telling everyone about our riding schedule."

I stepped on the bottom rung and began to haul myself into the seat, ignoring the guy next to me.

"It's my Saturday off, and tomorrow's weather is supposed to be perfect. Mind if I join you?" the guy asked, and my sharp intake of breath had me close to hyperventilating. My heart had figured out way before my head that the guy sitting in my chair was Dr. Pete. Way to let me down, head!

Jane said, "Sure thing, Doc. But put your cycling special together 'cause you're in for one heck of a ride."

"Good evening, Just Katie." Dr. Pete held my chair as I finished sliding onto the seat.

At that moment, a huge brown tote jangling Michael Kors tags slammed down on the table between Dr. Pete and me, and an auburn-haired woman grabbed his shoulder. "Hi, Pete." She kissed him on the cheek then wiped off some of the red lipstick left by said kiss. She wore a short, frilly, orange skate dress with an open back, leaving little to the imagination. She'd applied her makeup with finesse, and her heart-shaped face and turned-up nose were the cutest things. Ugh!

"Susie. You remember Katie?" Dr. Pete nodded over her shoulder to me.

"Hello." She wrinkled her nose.

"Let me introduce you all around."

"I know everybody, Pete," she said, pouting.

Jane piped up. "I don't think I've had the pleasure. Jane Mackey." She offered her hand.

Susie balked at first, looking at Jane's hand as if a coiled snake were poised to strike, then took it cautiously and said, "Hello." Evidently, she knew all the men at our table, who were now drooling, and she had no time for the women.

"How do you know Doc?" Jane asked.

"I'm his nurse."

"I must have missed you the other day."

Susie rolled her eyes and turned her attention back to

Dr. Pete. "Could you go with me to the Mall of America tomorrow to shop for my fall wardrobe? I really need a male opinion."

"Actually, no." The "no" lingered on his lips. "As it turns out, I'm biking tomorrow."

"I can bike," she said, changing her plans with the flip of her tresses.

"For exercise," he continued with a patronizing smile.

"I *do* hate to sweat." She turned to us and said confidentially, "It isn't very ladylike."

"With Jane and Katie," he finished.

"Oh," she said sourly. "Well, gotta run." She wiggled her fingers, grabbed her unwieldy bag, and disappeared into the crowd.

"Is she your girlfriend?" Jane asked, taking a sip of her beer.

"Not anymore," he said. "She's too young and way too high-maintenance." Dr. Pete laughed. "But she's great at her job."

Jane's mischievous brown eyes blazed over the top of her glass. "She likes you well enough."

He sputtered, "I'm like a brother to her."

Jane added in a singsong voice, "Just sayin'."

Turning red, Pete glanced around the room. He frowned, and when I followed his gaze, I found S O'Hara at the receiving end.

"I *do not* like that jackass," he took a long pull from his beer. His eyes never left Mr. O'Hara.

"How can you say that?"

"I just open my mouth and the words fall out." I tried to keep my disappointment from showing. He added carefully, "Sorry. It's just that he's always hanging around, and he rubs me the wrong way. He has this macabre habit of sitting here watching, sitting in the ER watching, sitting just about anywhere watching. I also think he sometimes tests the limits of his position." He sighed. "I'll try to think better thoughts. I know he helped you the day of your"— he paused, thinking— "accident." He took another long swig from his bottle. Changing the subject, he asked, "What do you do for fun?"

"I walk my dog. I play with my dog. I train my dog. Did I tell you I have a big dog?"

He nodded. "We've met. Tell me something about you I don't know."

"Once upon a time, in my checkered past, I was called upon to use my acute powers of observation and—"

Dr. Pete interrupted. "I observe cuteness."

Heat radiated to the tips of my ears. I took a deep breath and continued. "I've always enjoyed following clues or decoding patterns. The NSA broadcasted a tweet that looked like it had come from a drunken sailor, but the intriguing nonwords formed a coded recruiting pitch. I ended up attending school in London, studying encryption. I wrote my master's thesis about the use of cyphers and codifying machines like the ENIGMA from World War II. I thought I wanted to be the next Elizebeth Friedman, an expert cryptanalyst." *But I found true love.*

"And, Doctor—"

"It's Pete, please." I liked that.

"Math is a process of decoding. It seemed like a logical progression." *And I needed a new path.*

He nodded.

"I read about the kids."

Pete spoke more seriously. "During my residency at

Cook County, I thought I'd seen it all." He breathed slowly, checking his emotions, and continued. "It's happening here as well, and I thought I knew my town so well. Drugs are pervasive."

"I can't understand why so many kids would want to take a mix of unidentified drugs to get high."

"Drugs have a strange effect on people. And so does peer pressure." He shook his head. "One of my Chicago ER patients came in with a severed forefinger and thumb on his right hand. He'd been high and tried to loosen some debris on his lawn mower while it was still running. We fixed him up as best we could. A week later, he returned with an identical wound on his left hand. When I asked him what had happened, he said he was trying to show his buddies how the first injury occurred." He shook his head. "Some of the drugs the kids get a hold of are animal grade prescriptions."

On one of our spins on the dance floor, Dr. Pete shouted, "Sorry I wasn't there to take out your stitches."

"No problem…"

"Long week. I had a body come to the coroner's office right after you left the ER. I turned it over to law enforcement and they are investigating."

I hoped I didn't give away my surprise, but his week was much rougher than I originally thought—students overdosing and Arthur Condive's death. "You're the coroner?"

He bowed.

"How did Mr. Condive die?"

He gave me a sly look.

"I found the body. I'm curious."

"Arthur enjoyed getting a rise out of people and his

death is suspicious so I sent samples off to the lab."

"Any suspects?"

"Why do you ask?"

"The doors and windows on his car were closed so he must have floated out of the trunk…"

Pete stared at me.

Jane plopped down on the chair next to him and fanned herself. "We'll never be able to ride tomorrow if we stay much longer. Don't you need to let Maverick out?"

* * *

I tiptoed into my quiet apartment; Maverick's eyes followed me from his personal kingdom, his cushioned doggy bed, without a tail wag. The bag of treats I remembered hiding in the cupboard sat on the floor next to him, the top torn open.

"Message received, my friend. I was, however, talking about you. That has to count for something." His brooding eyes followed me up the stairs.

I sat at my desk and wrote an entry in my journal.

Lacking finesse in the art of social graces, I've often found it difficult to make friends. I'm almost afraid to write these words and jinx my good fortune, but I believe I can count Jane as one of them.

CHAPTER TWELVE

Walking at four miles per hour, Maverick and I set out to cover new ground. After thirty minutes, we turned around and headed back before the cooler temperature evaporated in the sunlight. At the twenty-five-minute mark we entered the Lake Monongalia neighborhood filled with elegant homes. Spectacularly tiered landscaping covered the gentle slopes with colorful blossoms. I caught a hint of acrid smoke; perhaps an early riser couldn't wait for the warmth from the sun and had lit a fireplace.

We headed around the water in the cool stillness just before dawn. According to Mrs. Clemashevski, most of the homes on this side of the lake belonged to summer-only folks. I spotted long gated drives, huge stone pillars, and a few lights aglow. The great old trees had been carefully trimmed, retaining enough foliage to provide as much shade and privacy as possible.

I wanted to remember this location for a return trip, so I snapped a photo of the street signs at the intersection of Lake Street and Ivy Avenue. The flash from my phone camera reflected off the grille of the car parked in front of me—a shiny black classic Bailey Electric Light Car. The Bailey Electrics were ecologically minded vehicles built more than a hundred years ago. While researching "being green" for my science club students, I'd come across a surprising number of electric cars dating back to the early 1900s.

As the sky brightened, yard lights flickered off. The outline of a vintage Chevy materialized behind the Bailey. Its creamy off-white paint gleamed, and the polished chrome reflected daybreak. The black ragtop shone like new. The blue-and-white license plate read MYCHEVY2. I wondered what MYCHEVY1 looked like.

Sunlight reflected haloes in the treetops as the temperature rose. Maverick dragged me toward a park that appeared through the haze of dawn. It was unusual for him to pull me off the pavement into a yard, but our walk in the wetlands had demonstrated nothing was impossible. Frustrated, I pulled back. My training guides nearly outlawed the used of the word "no," so I spun on my heels and redirected Maverick toward home.

Home. I wondered when I'd begun to think of it that way.

* * *

After securing everything Maverick could get his teeth into, I loaded my bike, shoes, helmet, sunglasses, and water bottle, and cruised through the sleepy Saturday streets on a serene and glorious clear-blue-sky day to the bike trail.

While keeping an eye out for Jane and Pete, I took a swig from an ice-cold water bottle before sliding it into the holder. I felt, rather than saw, the good doctor and turned to greet him. An all-black racing machine pedaled into the parking lot, and once again I felt slightly underdressed.

He unclipped one biking shoe, and glided to a stop in front of me. "You look ready and raring to go."

"Good morning, Pete please."

"Got me," he snorted.

Payback, I thought, massaging the ache in my thigh from biking with Jane the past few days. Still, I was tingling, anxious for more torture.

"This trek is seventy-miles round trip, so how much are you interested in doing?" My eyes popped, and my face registered panic. He laughed. "There's a coffee shop at the eight-mile mark. We could stop there and reevaluate."

I looked at his eager face and said with all the enthusiasm I could muster, "Sixteen is good." The coffee shop would be a nice place to catch my breath. My cell phone buzzed in my back pocket. I contorted, removed the phone, and read "JM" on the lighted display.

I turned away from Pete. "Where are you?" I whispered.

"And good morning to you too," Jane replied softly.

"Sorry. Good morning. Where are you?"

"Listen hon, I'm not feeling well. I won't be able to ride. With workshops coming up and school starting, I simply can't get sick. I have allergies, and I think the pollen count is up as high as it can get." She said all this with the feeble voice of someone who sounded miserable.

"Sorry you don't feel well."

"Have a good ride." She ended the call.

With clammy palms, I turned to Pete. "Jane isn't feeling well. I guess we should postpone our ride until she feels better."

"Are you all right?" he said with doctorly concern.

"Sure."

"Then we might as well ride. We're already here."

"You know," I hesitated. "That wasn't me Jane was describing last night. *She's* the big biker."

"I know."

I suspected I didn't look much like an avid biker, but still … "How did you know?"

"You have a nice bike, but she described a carbon-fiber Colnago. She knew way too many particulars. I wonder why she let it seem like it was your bike."

"Yeah, I wonder too."

Pete chuckled. "She's a trip, isn't she?"

"A trip." I bounced back and forth between feeling sorry for her and feeling sorry for me.

"Coffee shop?"

"Okay," I said.

He clipped his shoe into the pedal. I snapped on my helmet, and we rode out of the parking lot onto a newly paved time-worn train bed with curves and bends through open farmland and an occasional copse of trees. The air whooshed, and the wind whisked by my face. Birdsong hung on a breeze that prevented our overheating.

Biking eight miles took thirty-seven minutes, traveling at an average speed of thirteen miles per hour. My riding with Jane had paid off. I wasn't gasping for breath. At least not as much.

I secured my bike in the rack of CAFÉ LOT and stashed my sunglasses in my helmet. I reached into my back pocket for my "in case" cash. Pete remained balanced on the tips of his bicycle shoes. Perhaps he hadn't brought any money with him.

"Since you worked out this great plan, how about I spring for coffee?" I closed the gap between us. "Or tea or water?" He looked as though he wanted to continue his ride. "Why don't you go farther down the trail? It's a beautiful day. I'll have tea and a rest, and I'll start back in about forty minutes. That'll give you a few more miles, and I can travel at my snail's pace. You'll catch me on the return."

He brightened considerably. "Only if you're okay with it." Then he flashed a smile. I couldn't resist reaching up and pinching his cheek, just to the right of a deep and splendid dimple. The simple contact was pleasantly electric, and I pulled back my hand.

"Yup. And if you take too long, I might be home letting Maverick out." I chuckled, trying to recover from the scintillating touch.

"I'll catch up." Pete pushed off the curb and rapidly disappeared down the trail.

A cup of tea, a completed crossword puzzle, and forty relaxing minutes later, I decided I wanted to see how fast I could ride. No black-clad biker appeared on the horizon, so I popped on my bike, turned off the ringer and started the stopwatch on my phone. With my head down, I pedaled furiously, pumping a familiar rhythm.

Although the distant landscape didn't alter much, the pavement beneath my feet blurred. I traveled fifteen or sixteen miles an hour with no obstacles in my path and no pleasant company to distract me. The wind roared in my ears as it caught the baffles of my helmet. Grainy fragments—sand, tree leavings, or maybe bugs—pelted my face in an effort to slow me down, but my wraparound sunglasses protected my eyes, and I kept my mouth closed to flying protein. The miles melted away.

I slowed when I neared the parking lot at the trailhead. I pulled up next to my car, dismounted, and unsnapped the front wheel to put into my car. Before removing my helmet and gloves, I glanced back, and caught a black flash rocketing my way. My face flushed with embarrassment. What if Pete had seen me and thought I'd been racing away from him. He didn't look angry. I took a deep breath and waited for him to close the gap. I floundered for my next smart remark, grinning as he neared, but instead of slowing, he bobbed his head and continued on his speedy way.

I saw red. What a jerk! What did I do?

I opened the driver's door, threw my helmet and gloves onto the passenger seat, sat down, and slammed the door. Both hands grasped the steering wheel. I lowered my head and sobbed.

CHAPTER THIRTEEN

After a few miserable moments, it occurred to me I'd done nothing wrong. Sadness and anger assailed me—saddened that the beautiful day, which had begun so well, had changed in an instant, and angered that I let some bicycle nerd make me feel… What did I feel? Initially I hoped he'd enjoy my company and we might become friends. I leaned forward, pulled a tissue from the glove compartment, blew my nose, and wiped my tear-streaked face. First his absence from the ER when I needed my stitches removed and then flying by on his bike. "Definitely strike two, Doctor Erickson," I muttered.

I retrieved my cell phone. There were seven missed calls. I listened to the three voicemails.

Having made a miraculous recovery, Jane sang, "Sorry I left you high and dry, hon. You didn't need a third wheel, and I thought you might want a little one-on-one time. He's not *my* type, but Doc seems like a good guy." I firmly pressed "delete."

In the second, Jane spoke hurriedly. "If Pete's still with you, he needs to call the ER immediately. Susie called *me* looking for him."

I listened to the last voicemail. Mrs. Clemashevski's voice was shaky. "Katie, please pick up."

I returned calls to both Jane and Mrs. Clemashevski. Neither answered.

I arrived at North Maple Street, parked my car, and ran up steps to the porch where Mrs. Clemashevski sat, her mascara smeared by the tears streaming down her face. Wild hairs stuck out around her scarf. Maverick leaned into her, nudging.

"Don't let Maverick bother you," I said, and flopped into the seat next to her. "Maybe I should ask Samantha McCoy if she's ready. She really wants a dog."

Mrs. Clemashevski turned her face to mine. "There's an APB out on Samantha. They think she started cooking meth again. I thought she was doing so well. Now, it seems she's on the run." When she moaned, Maverick nudged her. "Oh, Maverick!" She rubbed his ears. She bent forward and touched foreheads.

I put an arm around her shoulders. Mrs. Clemashevski leaned against me, her head nestled under my chin. Her shoulders heaved as her breath caught between sobs. Then it dawned on me that she no longer had any accent. I gently held her away from me. "Mrs. Clemashevski?"

"I'm sorry, Katie. I'm just a silly old wannabe actress, hoping to be a star someday. I like putting on a show, but I simply can't now. I'm sorry." Her face crumpled.

"It's all right," I replied and hugged her again.

I asked her what had happened. Though tears still pooled in her eyes, a smile tugged at the corners of her mouth as she pulled her memories together.

Mrs. Clemashevski ran her hand lightly over an elaborately embossed leather album and opened it on her lap. Her fingers traced the matte that secured an array of photos set against the frayed black paper. "She was helping me organize my family history. She loves research. What am I going to do?" She hiccupped. "The meth lab exploded. That's why I called to speak to Pete."

"Pete?"

"Dr. Erickson has the most experience dealing with drug interactions, and one of the first responders is in critical condition."

I regretted the selfish thoughts I'd had as he'd whizzed by on the bike path.

She turned the album pages, and a life blossomed before me, snippets of childhood, adolescence, and young adulthood. Mrs. Clemashevski stopped on a page and ran her finger around the edge of a wedding photo, lightly brushing the face of the smiling groom. She sighed, then said, "Casimer."

"Mr. Clemashevski? He was a handsome man. May I?" I lifted the tome from her lap and made a mad grab for the loose papers, photos, and a manila envelope that slid from under the back cover. In one photo, I recognized the familiar twinkle of mischief in the eyes of the groom on a sepia-toned wedding photo, the bride trying unsuccessfully to suppress a smile as she blocked his hand from tugging at her necklace.

"One of my scandalous ancestors with her first

husband. He was supposed to follow her to America aboard the *Titanic*. He was listed among the rescued, but she never found him. She had their baby in June and ended up marrying her sponsor, her husband's best friend. She truly believed her first husband perished that April."

"She's lovely. It must have been from the same sitting as the photo in the locket."

Mrs. Clemashevski cocked her head. "What locket?"

"The turquoise pendant you let me wear. Jane opened it. I think the photos inside are of the same couple."

Hefting her weary body from the chair, she retrieved the necklace. I took it from her hand and gently pried open the clasp. Her eyes grew wide.

"Sinead and Padraig," she breathed.

We continued to match the loose pages—copies of birth, baptismal, marriage, and death certificates—detailing a family history that had begun with the marriage of Padraig and Sinead on April 7, 1911. Fascinated, I lifted each document by the corners, read the data, and handed it to her. Sinead was seventeen and Padraig was twenty-eight. *Funny, I don't even know where my marriage license is.*

Mrs. Clemashevski emptied the envelope that contained love letters from Casimer and a sketch—a faithfully rendered architectural pencil drawing of the *Titanic* with numbers denoting measurements. It was signed "Bobby."

"One of my former students drew this for me." When we closed the scrapbook, she added, "I can't believe I could've been so wrong about Samantha. She had trouble with Arthur too."

"Does the chief know?" She shrugged.

CHAPTER FOURTEEN

Chief Erickson sat in our back yard with a cup of tea in hand and a cookie on a napkin. "Well, Ida?"

Mrs. Clemashevski furrowed her brow and looked askance. "Samantha McCoy had a disagreement with Arthur. He thought he should take possession of an old trunk she found, but she wouldn't give it to him."

Chief Erickson inhaled. "That man has made my job very difficult. He angered Samantha and fired Elaine."

"Do you think one of them killed him?"

"We aren't sure how he died. Ida, would you excuse us?" Mrs. C disappeared inside.

"I gave Ida the results of your background check. No arrests, no warrants, no record."

I wriggled a feeble smile. "That's good, isn't it?"

"Your reference, John Trainor, said I could rely on you."

I looked at my shoes. "John is a psychologist and a dear friend."

The chief paused, gathering his thoughts. "I read the report about your husband's death. I'm sorry for your loss."

Dishes clattered from Mrs. C's kitchen.

"While I assisted in my dad's recovery, I took advantage of John's medical expertise. He gave me tools to cope." *And a safe place to be.* "I was terrified after the shooting. But with John's help, I started rebuilding my life, piece by piece, and I came here."

"You seem to be doing well now."

I nodded. "I'm much better."

"Ida can help if you let her."

I cast a glance through the window to a woman I was going to trust with my deepest sorrows.

He closed his notebook and stood. "I know you and your husband did some investigative work but murder may be out of your league."

"It's murder then?"

"Trust me to do my job."

After Chief Erickson left, I sat down at Mrs. C's kitchen table. When the teakettle whistled, she brewed two cups of herbal tea and lined a plate with a dainty paper doily to show off her delicious powered-sugar-dusted lemon shortbread.

I began my story with a weak smile. "I considered myself a fairly serious student and never planned for a relationship. But best laid plans and all of that." Chuckling, I related Charles's incessant teasing, his erudite riddles, and his ceaseless pursuit of what he called "that damn Yankee." I hadn't thought about that in a long time.

"I never met anyone like him." I closed my eyes,

bringing to mind his brilliant smile and bright eyes, his curly light-brown hair, his broad back, his strong arms. "He could make me blush from across a room. Our cryptography team interned at the New Scotland Yard in security, solving some of the assigned code work and creating our own—the basis for my thesis. I had nearly succumbed to his relentless pursuit when I found out who he really was."

My cool teacup was replaced with a warm one. Mrs. C patted my hand.

"Charles and I were assigned the task of unraveling some mysterious text messages. The woman receiving the texts had no idea who was sending them and considered it harassment. When we deciphered the code, which pinpointed a meeting place and time, the rest of the message fell into place. There was no guile in the sender. Poor Adelbert. It turned out the messages were meant for his fiancée; his dyslexia contributed to an endless transposition of numbers. His fiancée gave us all kinds of examples of his mishaps, and they both apologized profusely.

"To celebrate the positive conclusion, Lady Victoria Colton invited us to a picnic-on-the-grounds at her home, an exquisite seventeenth-century manse. The incredible meal filled three serving tables."

"No yoga pants?" Mrs. C teased kindly. I shook my head.

"Lady Victoria invited us to ride," I continued. "I'd never ridden a horse, but Charles convinced me to try. I was outfitted with breeches, boots, gloves, and a jacket. When Charles finished dressing, he saddled a majestic horse. Then he gave me a boost and handed me the reins, laughing at my horse's name—Abacus. He pulled himself into his own saddle on Magic and gave me a few pointers while lazily following our guide along a curving path out of the yard, toward a grove of trees. As we passed the back side of the stables, a young boy, all knees and elbows, twisting and turning a cap in his hands, intercepted us and asked if we'd seen Bonnie—Lady Colton's field trial champion with a multigenerational pedigree. She'd escaped from her kennel the night before and couldn't be found.

"We joined the search on horseback, meandering through the thicket, calling her name. Abacus followed his own path and I wobbled on his back, straining to stay upright. His intuition paid off though. We found Bonnie. She'd been struggling to escape from the teeth of a trap, and her bloodied paw was shredded. I slid off Abacus's back and screamed that I'd found her. I don't know how, but I pried open the steel jaws as Charles rushed through the trees. He scooped her into his arms and laid her across his saddle, then mounted Magic and carried her back to the outbuilding, murmuring gentle words of encouragement.

"The stables weren't what I expected. Polished wood gleamed, and the floor was immaculate. A brooding man, wearing a starched white coat over creased blue jeans, met us. The brim on his hat shaded his face, but I'll always remember the precise words the on-site veterinarian spoke."

I took a sip of tepid tea. "'Give her to me, sir.' He gave me a look I couldn't identify. 'Just hope she didn't get into any trouble with the mongrel next door. Welcome home, your lordship.'

"I was standing behind Charles. His back stiffened. I pictured Lady Victoria and him side by side, their familiarity, the way he fit in, their matching merry gray-blue eyes. They were siblings. I felt betrayed. I headed for the car and a quick escape. Charles raced after me and grabbed my hand. I tried to pull away, but he hung on tight. He never said a word. He drove me back to London, and the next week I flew home to Minnesota."

I searched her face for encouragement and found understanding.

"On the flight back across the pond, I must have looked awful because, over a steaming cup of Earl Gray tea, the attendant asked if I was still in love or if I'd forgotten." One corner of my mouth turned up. "But he followed me home anyway. And we married shortly after." Then I choked back a sob.

"Apparently, Bonnie had an assignation with a neighborhood dog and, five months later, that snooty vet showed up on my doorstep with Maverick and his 'less-than-stellar' ancestry."

She looked disappointed. "You don't want Maverick because he's not a purebred?" she asked.

Tears sprang to my eyes. "No, no," I cried. "Every time I look at Maverick, I'm reminded that if it hadn't been for me, Charles might still be alive."

CHAPTER FIFTEEN

"Tell me about Samantha," I asked Mrs. C.

"She spent her first stint in rehab at the age of fourteen. The last time, she resolved to make a change. She enrolled in online classes and continued her coursework when she was released. After she graduated from the halfway house, she lived on and maintained a property near the lake bequeathed to the city by one of its founding residents. Early this morning, the caretaker's unit exploded, and they found evidence of methamphetamine. The gases are toxic, and one of the firefighters succumbed to the fumes. And with Samantha's history of substance abuse…"

"Maverick and I were there this morning," I moaned. "I thought he was just being obstinate. Maybe, if I'd followed him, we could've helped."

"Katie, cleaning up an explosion like that requires a

special team. You'd have only been in the way."

I wasn't so sure. Maverick had been almost as determined to go his way as I was to go mine. He must have sensed something; he never ceased to amaze me.

* * *

I tried to refuse, since I'd already sent up so many unanswered prayers, but Mrs. C insisted I attend Sunday Mass with her. At the end of the service, the priest announced the afternoon's visitation for Arthur Condive. Mrs. C whispered in my ear, "Come with me?" Though visions of his dead body nearly brought me to tears, I promised to join her.

Rifling through the week's newspapers, another article about the *Titanic* letters caught my eye. A violin confirmed to belong to Wallace Hartley, the ship's bandleader, sold at an auction for six figures. The letters written by a survivor had been offered to *Bruckner's New Titanic Exhibit,* and, if they proved authentic, they'd be worth a bundle too.

Mrs. C entered the kitchen, dressed somberly in a navy-blue two-piece suit, black kitten heels, and a matching pillbox hat. When we arrived at the visitation, the line already spilled out the funeral-home doors and snaked around the corner. A rumble of conversation followed us to the entrance and abruptly converted to a tense hum once we were inside.

"What a crowd! He must have been well thought of," I whispered.

Mrs. C didn't answer; we shuffled forward in the slow-moving line.

As we neared the family and the photo display, Mrs. C's resolve softened. "Look at their lovely wedding photos. Her dress was so beautiful, and wasn't he a handsome groom?"

A memorial collage contained snippets of a happy family. Mrs. C pointed out the children. "That's David and Fiona, Brigid and Finn."

Over time, the subjects in the photos changed; the woman became thin, pale, and frail, then wheelchair bound. "She died too young," Mrs. C murmured. "Cancer. And Arthur was never the same after she passed."

We followed the line to a table covered with eight-by-ten frames, a conspicuous array of memberships, honorariums, awards, and handshaking photos taken with people I assumed were local celebrities. An ego was on display. A professional painting of an older man with a head of unnaturally dark brown hair and skin too taut and tanned hung prominently above an ornate urn set on the dais. Bored hazel eyes belied a wide, forced smile that framed perfect teeth. I grimaced back. "Not a very kind likeness," I offered.

"Actually, a pretty fair rendering," she said. "He could be a difficult man."

Mrs. C introduced me to Fiona, and we gave her our sincerest condolences. She was thirtyish, fine featured, with the same unblemished skin and intense hazel gaze as her father. She shook my hand perfunctorily, and then, as if a light switch flipped on, she grabbed my hand with both of hers, pumped up and down, and said, "You found Dad?"

"Y-y-es." Caught off guard, I stuttered, then repeated, "I'm sorry for your loss."

"Thank you." She called to a young man. "David, this is Katie Wilk. She found Dad."

He shook my hand as well. "Thanks. We might never have known what happened to the old bastard," he said. Fiona gasped, blushed beet-red, and tears filled her eyes.

"It's true, Fiona, and you know it. A lot of people wanted him gone." David turned and stalked away.

I looked questioningly at Mrs. C, but she watched David.

"Have the police told you what happened?" I asked Fiona.

"My dad didn't drive into that horrid water." Bright red splotches flushed Fiona's cheeks. "I just know Kelly did it."

I paused as I carefully chose my words. "Do you know why Kelly would want your father dead?"

"No." Deflated, Fiona said, "He was despondent after Uncle Ray died. But then out on one of his jaunts, he said he'd found someone he truly enjoyed spending quality time with." The word "quality" dripped with sarcasm. "My dad was good at keeping his own confidence. We never knew where he found his unusual pieces, his treasures. He didn't want his competitors to tap his sources. He promised to introduce us to Kelly when he got back from his latest buying trip. I informed the police, but they don't believe there ever was a Kelly." She shrugged and marshaled her emotions. Raising her head, she took a deep breath, smiled sadly, and said, "But thanks again."

Over the drone of the crowd, David's voice rang clear. "What more do you want, Elaine? He's dead. He's gone. Isn't that enough?"

Mrs. C stiffened. I turned and caught a glimpse of a long black dress and short spiky black hair sweeping out the double doors, the visitors parting like waters of the Red Sea.

Mrs. C sighed. "Oh, Elaine."

As we made our way home, I worked up the courage to ask, "Who do you believe murdered Mr. Condive?"

"He could rub people the wrong way." Mrs. C shrugged. "There were times I could have throttled him myself. He wanted to cut art from the curriculum."

Maverick and I found Mr. Condive. If he had died at the hands of another, maybe I could help bring the perpetrator to justice. They never found the person who killed Charles. It shattered me when I couldn't do anything about it and my heart hung heavy with guilt.

Maybe I could help someone else.

If I excluded Elaine, Condive had a secret friend named Kelly, angered Samantha, and even got a rise out of Mrs. C.

Frantic barking pulled us from our reverie as I steered into the driveway. Maverick raced from one side of the yard to the other, looking for who knows what. He appeared to be tracking some unknown prey, but no quarry appeared.

Mrs. C and I searched the rooms one by one, and only found the tattered remains of a stuffed animal. I put Maverick's running around in the "overly active column" since he'd been cooped up alone for too long.

"Are you ready for tomorrow?" Mrs. C asked. I started to answer, but as she opened her door, her ring tone jangled. She waved and closed the door behind her.

I will be. My heart knocked against my chest.

CHAPTER SIXTEEN

I waded through the lemony scent in the hallways of the central office building, finally able to launch my teaching career. Jane joined me in the office, and we met the new communications teacher, Andrew Kidd. We fulfilled our orientation obligations: completing paperwork, touring areas we would frequent, and meeting various school personnel.

Drew, his preferred moniker, let it be known he'd graduated summa cum laude from Duke with a double major in communications and philosophy and minors in human relations and psychology. In my opinion, he should've worked harder on the human relations. He stood just over six feet, carried himself ramrod straight, and white-blond hair hugged his scalp. Coke-bottle lenses set in horn-rimmed frames magnified his deep-blue eyes, and if that wasn't bad enough, he wore a skinny pink-and-purple necktie.

"Which is it? Girls? Women? Ladies?" he said. "I like to be politically correct. Where are you from and how do you occupy your time? Where did you attend school? Any family nearby?" Drew's unending questions intensified, and he didn't wait long for answers.

"I hail from Atlanta," Jane said. Her restful weekend must have done her a world of good; she bubbled. "My history degree is from Emory," she said, as if she had another degree from some other place.

"What brought you to this end of the universe?"

"I followed a dream here." Jane sighed. The sparkle in her eyes brightened, and she continued. "I'm happily single and a bit of a neat freak. I keep fairly active—running and biking." My ears picked up a few more interesting tidbits. "My record mudding time is three hours and thirty-seven minutes."

"What's m-mudding?" I asked Jane, but Drew put in his two cents first.

"A challenge course from Hades. My personal best is two hours and fifty-eight minutes on a twelve-mile course. What was your distance?"

"Mine was a twelve-mile course too. What was your toughest obstacle?"

"The ice cube pond. While I was thawing during the remaining run, pins and needles jabbed at my feet every step of the way. How about yours?"

"The wall. I couldn't quite reach as high as I would have liked." She grinned.

Feeling left out, I asked, "What else do you do, Drew?" *Sotto voce,* I muttered, "What don't you do?"

He rewarded me with his rapier wit. "I absolutely love to read—mostly non-fiction; can't waste time on novels. I use a new word every week. This week it's 'persiflage.'" Eyeing me skeptically, he added, "It means 'banter.' I'm also a graduate of the Institute for Culinary Education summer program. I'm an oenophile—a connoisseur of fine wines. My current favorite is a JCB red blend called Knockout." He stopped to take a quick breath. "And I'm an avid ballroom dancer, presently without a partner." Jane's eyes flashed at me. I could only imagine what she was thinking.

Drew talked nonstop. As I tuned out his dissertations about wine and bicycles, the toughest Tough Mudder, his expectations of the first day of school, and cooking, Jane's eyes glittered. My mind wandered far afield—to a walk with Maverick. Jane nodded appropriately, and her one-syllable rejoinders kept him talking through every break in our workshop.

I checked out supplies and snagged an interactive white board that connected to a classroom computer for projection. On the teachers' lounge bulletin board, I posted a photo of Maverick under the heading "Great dog looking for a good home." My phone number was written on tabs clipped across the bottom of the page. I had to admit, he took adorable pictures.

We were given an hour for lunch so Drew followed Jane and me to a deli and coffee emporium just off Main Street, sandwiched between Carlson's Hardware and Bella's Boutique.

Drew ordered first. Jane and I each ordered a Cobb salad, a seven-layer bar and iced tea. He took the tray laden with his goodies to a table, and the cheapskate left the bill for Jane and me to split.

We were sitting at a sundrenched table near the door, dust motes dancing in the beams that pierced the window, when a shadow cut through the light and Damon Hastings materialized next to Drew. My fork clattered to the floor when his fist slammed onto the table. He leaned forward, fingers splayed, his face invading my space. "So, you're the little bitch who turned me over to be grilled by the constabulary. You'll get yours," he growled. Satisfied he'd adequately thrown his weight around, he stomped away. I finally took a breath and swallowed.

"You do realize Hastings doesn't have a single original thought in his empty head," Jane said, chuckling. "He may have a pretty face, but those lines are straight out of a movie script. He's full of hot air and little else."

It sounded like Drew had been holding his breath as well. "I heard the police hauled him in for questioning about the body found in the waterfowl protection area. He sold the guy a box of valuable family heirlooms and claimed he'd been cheated."

My eyebrow rose all by itself. Hastings, Kelly, Samantha, and Elaine?

After a moment of strained silence, Jane asked, "Where are you from, Drew?"

He heaved a contented sigh after the first bite of a humongous red-and-white cake. "I began my career in Chicago. Schools there need someone with my particular attributes."

I almost asked what those attributes could possibly be, but Jane jumped in. "And do you have a significant other? What secrets haven't you told us about yourself?"

He blanched and coughed. Then he glanced at his

wrist. "Look at the time." He stood and bolted for the door, leaving half his dessert untouched. Jane's shoulders shook behind her silent chortle. Unsurprisingly, he left his dishes for us to bus.

"He's kinda cute. Do you think he can dance?" Jane smiled dreamily.

I rolled my eyes.

* * *

The next day, after the opening ceremony kick-off, I met two of five members of the mathematics faculty.

In a plaid sport coat and skinny black tie, Jerry White possessed an aloof, authoritative air. He earned it. He chaired the math department, and he coached the girls' basketball team to five straight sectional titles. He was a man of few words. "You better not screw up," he said. His icy-blue eyes peered down at me from some six and a half feet overhead. "We're watching you."

"Don't let him scare you." Tall and graying with a tuft of stiff hair above his upper lip, Tom Murphy was the boys' baseball coach. He sported a blue-and-gold argyle sweater vest, and he was one of the veteran eleventh-hour hospice volunteers I met when picking up information about the therapy dog program. "How's it going?"

"Well, thanks."

"Everything? I heard you found Arthur."

I paused. "Not the easiest introduction, I'll admit. But I'm getting there."

"Arthur ticked off a lot of people," he said. "As school board chair, he signed off on all the hiring and firing of teachers. He even got one of our own tossed out on her ear last year." Tom's eyes circled the math office, and Jerry

White's comments took on a greater significance referring to Elaine.

"You know Columbia hasn't had a murder in forever."

My ears perked up.

Tom shrugged. "Condive had a successful antique business. He found some great deals, but word was he sometimes shortchanged the seller. One guy came to a school board meeting loaded for bear—I mean, he was mad as a hornet. When he wasn't given any chance to speak, he ambushed Condive outside. He threatened him. Name was…" He brushed at his mustache, thinking. "Hastings."

Tom continued. "Condive lost it when his wife died, and, since then, thrived on inciting trouble. He even pitted his children against one another. Before the reading of an uncle's will, he told the uncle's namesake, David Ray, he'd been disinherited. It wasn't true, of course, but Condive sure screwed with his kid's head. Only the kid's sister helped him get through the reading. I doubt he'll ever easily trust again."

"Why would he do that?

"Just to stir the pot," Tom snickered. "He and his son never did get back together." He glanced at the wall clock. "Gotta run. If you need anything…" The sentence trailed off as he walked away.

I put the desks in order, and carefully laid out the seating charts. My SMART Board had been delivered and I set to work enabling the communications connection with my computer.

I hung my favorite poster, a print of Sir John Tenniel's drawing from *Alice in Wonderland*. It looked like gibberish but I couldn't wait to share the literary passage of mathematical magic with my students. Then I remembered that the last time I'd stood in front of a classroom full of kids was five years earlier when I did my student teaching. I quelled the butterflies flitting in my chest repeating the motto Charles had shared with me: fake it 'til you make it.

In one corner of the white board, I wrote an obscure Vigenère cipher and its key. I glanced around the room with approval. "Yes," I hissed, and pumped my clenched fist.

CHAPTER SEVENTEEN

It wasn't that I didn't trust Drew, but I did look up "oenophile" and "persiflage" and determined he was a sesquipedalian—someone who used long words.

I dressed with more care. No yoga pants anyway. I even applied a little mascara, a dab of lip-gloss, and brushed my unruly hair. Mrs. C gave me the once over and grimaced. "Could be worse."

I met Jane at the studio. Stephen and Matthew appeared, looking sheepish, each escorting a girl from Take Your Best Shot.

The music played softly as the instructor skirted the perimeter of the room, taking the names of new students and collecting fees, when a tall tuxedoed man appeared in the doorway. His shiny black shoes glided onto the floor and straight up to Jane. He bowed, grabbed her right hand in his left, and swept her onto the dance floor. Everyone backed away as the couple floated artfully across the room, tilting, spinning, turning, Jane's fuchsia gown swaying in time to the music. They were light on their toes, perfectly matched. The horn-rimmed glasses were gone. A smile softened Drew's features.

When the song ended, applause erupted. A huge smile radiated from Jane and she placed each of her hands along Drew's jawline and pulled him down, way down, into a lip lock. His ears flushed red, but he, too, beamed when he came up for air. "You dreamboat, Drew." Jane sighed. "Wherever did you learn to dance like that?"

Straightening a lime-green bow tie, he said, "Gramma figured every young man should learn to dance, so after Sunday dinner, we practiced in the foyer."

They crossed the dance floor through a stream of awestruck accolades. Drew looked content and flushed. Jane was simply effervescent.

"Evening, Fred," I said. I knew Mr. Astaire would have been pleased with Drew's performance.

Drew took Jane's small hands into his and brought them to his lips. "I brought a friend. I hope that's all right." Jane looked around, momentarily nonplussed, thinking, perhaps, he'd brought a friend of the female persuasion. However, a lone male figure stood in the shadow of the doorway. Drew crooked his forefinger and motioned to his friend. My heart skipped when Pete stepped nervously onto the dance floor.

"Pete, this is my friend Jane and—"

Pete interrupted him. "Hi, Jane. Hi, Just Katie. We meet again." He bowed deeply. Damp hair curled at the collar of the black sport coat he wore over a black T-shirt and jeans. He appeared self-conscious about his polished shoes, sliding one in front of the other across the parquet. Thank heavens I left my yoga pants at home!

The instructor clapped his hands, calling the class to order. He gave a few directions then turned up the music.

"Shall we?" Pete took my hand. After a moment he whispered, "I owe you an apology."

"It's all right. Really." My left hand settled on his shoulder.

We were up close and personal, and he looked and smelled delectable. We weren't as graceful as Jane and Drew, but we worked diligently, followed instructions, and with a few snickers here and there and an occasional faux pas, we succeeded in doing a bit of a waltz. It took concerted effort to dance smoothly when we both wanted to lead. I think my face turned crimson when he said, with a smile, "You stand on the top and I'll stand on the bottom." Oh, what a night!

I couldn't wait to write the words tumbling around in my head in my journal: *I could have danced all night.*

The words evaporated when I returned home to find Chief Erickson on the porch with Mrs. C. He leaned against one of the columns.

"Good evening, Chief."

"Evenin', Ms. Wilk."

"Katie, please."

I sat on the porch swing next to Mrs. C and nestled into the fat floral cushions, the caning tickling the backs of my knees. Chief Erickson folded his lanky body onto the Adirondack chair next to the swing.

"What can I do for you, Chief?" I wondered if he needed my help in spite of his earlier comment.

"I have a job for you."

I knew it.

"As a young new teacher, you're apt to be more in tune with the kids. I'd like you to let me know if students ever meet surreptitiously. Maybe they stop speaking when you come into a room." He looked at me uncertainly.

"Hold on. I have to shift gears. What are you talking about, Chief? I assumed you needed more information about our finding Mr. Condive's—"

"Never assume, Ms. Wilk." One eyebrow rose. "I suppose you read the article in the *Sentinel* about the teenagers—kids really—who overdosed on a hodgepodge of drugs." He shook his head. "They had quite a mix on board from a cancer drug to an animal grade pain-killer." I was bewildered. "I'm asking you to keep an eye on your students and let me know if anything gets your guard up."

"You mean spy on them?"

"In a manner of speaking, yes."

"Why me?"

Chief Erickson cleared his throat. "You impressed your past supervisors. It seems you have been successful connecting somewhat disparate dots." It surprised me to be the subject of a police inquiry. "The students don't know you yet and I hoped we might enlist your aid."

"It's been a while, you know."

"We certainly could use your help."

"I suppose I could watch out for strange student behavior. But I also wouldn't want to get anyone into unwarranted trouble."

An owl hooted.

"The drug use is wreaking havoc on our kids. It's happening all over our area. And now a meth lab near Lake Monongalia blew up. One of the guys is fighting for his life."

My stomach churned. "If I'd have followed Maverick

Saturday morning, we might've been able to help." I gasped, nervously bobbing my right knee.

The chief reached out to calm my frenetic knee jerks. "There was nothing you could've done." He paused and sat back. "I'm asking you to let us know if you notice any out-of-the-ordinary behavior."

My good old Catholic guilt reared its ugly head. "Of course."

"I also wondered if you'd keep an eye on Ashley Johannes. She hung out with Samantha McCoy. Ashley's been a good student, so a change in her attitude may indicate she needs to talk to someone. She's living with her grandmother, finishing school here, while her parents are on an archeological dig in Montana."

Sadness deepened in his eyes as a sigh hummed in my throat.

"Please?" he said, eyes imploring, then handed me his business card.

"I can do that." I just added another description to my job.

CHAPTER EIGHTEEN

After a hearty breakfast, I noticed a note from Mrs. C. "PYZYB NY CDBCEV HW HBU QWXYHAEPF PYS. BYXYXNYB, CXCHYGBQ NGEKH HAY CBO. TBWDYQQEWPCKQ NGEKH HAY HEHCPEJ. Have a great day." This was going to take some sit-down-with-a-pencil time.

I selected my first day attire for its austerity. A teaching-methods instructor once told me it would be easier to maintain inflexible order initially and later lighten up with students in a classroom than it would be to be lenient at the onset and then try to clamp down to create order from chaos. I wore tan pants, a silky white blouse, a tan cardigan sweater, and glasses I didn't much need. I pulled my hair back in a tight chignon and prepared to take on the world as a draconian schoolmarm.

* * *

I stepped through the pine haze rising from the spotless floors. Staff herded excited students down the pristine halls on their first day. They might not have been as ready for classroom studies as they were for the social interaction with friends they hadn't seen in a while, but the bustle and commotion filled the air with positive energy.

The math classrooms surrounded a common area crammed with tables where students congregated and shared schedules. The teachers' office buzzed with students, freshly coifed and newly attired. Some of the students eyed me suspiciously, so I slipped into my classroom. I aligned the desks, recounted books, and organized erasers, paper, pens, markers, and mechanical pencils.

My desk occupied a space in the back corner near the door, closer to meet and greet my students. Since I was the rookie, my room had no windows, so technically, there'd be fewer distractions, but also no sun to warm the disposition of my space from the outside. In the absence of doors, well-placed acoustic wall dividers muffled the sounds between rooms but the murmur of youthful voices floated on the air, and nervous tension crawled up my spine. Tendrils of excitement wrapped around my new beginning.

When the students converged on my classroom, small clusters of curious scholars halted in the entryway, craning their necks, unsure, awaiting instructions. I nodded for them to enter and sit while I observed long-time friendships, quiet conversations, and not-so-quiet conversations.

When the second bell rang, signaling the beginning of class, three desks remained unoccupied.

Muted conversations continued, so I pressed a button on my computer, and *Symphonie Fantastique* drifted into the corners of the room. I reached for a length of rope. Although I practiced the trick dozens of times, my palms were sweaty. I looked each student in the eye. I stretched the rope taut, snapped it, folded it, knotted it, held it in a circle, and supposedly cut it in half. When I pulled the knot loose, the rope was whole, minus the inch I'd palmed. I heard a few gasps.

The elements essential for my second bit of magic included a small cake tin and cover with a secret compartment. The ingredients lined the table in the front of the room. I exaggerated pouring in a heaping tablespoon of sugar, another of flour, and a dash of salt. I cracked an egg, always a crowd pleaser, and separated the yolk from the white, then splashed in the yolk, the white, and brandished the shell until it too was added. Then I smothered the ingredients with the lid, waved my hand over it, pronounced the magic word, "Numbers," and revealed a beautifully decorated cupcake. All eyes were glued to me.

"Welcome to Advanced Math. Expect the unexpected," I said brightly. "We'll begin with an exam. Read the instructions carefully."

Groans filled the air, and I chuckled. At the head of each row, I delivered copies of the first math test of the year. Then I sat down, picked up a pencil, and attempted to decode Mrs. C's cryptoquip, ignoring every raised hand. The explicit instructions provided the clues necessary to complete the exam correctly: "Remember, 'read the directions and directly you will be directed in the right direction' (*Alice in Wonderland*). Please read the entire exam carefully before answering any questions. Use ink. If you need a pen, there's one on my desk." A few students rose tentatively and rummaged through the cup of writing utensils.

Each question was a riddle of sorts, a way for me to break through some barriers. I observed many students in a rush to be the first to finish the exam, diligently writing out answers as they read each question rather than waiting until they read through the entire page. There were multiple-choice answers to questions such as, "If there were three apples and you took two, how many apples do you have? a) 0 b) 1 c) 2 d) 3." Another read, "How many animals of each sex did Moses take aboard the ark with him? a) 0 b) 1 c) 2 d) 4." Moses didn't build the ark so the answer was "a."

The final instruction read, "For an A, please print your name at the top of the page in the right-hand corner and hand in your test with no other markings." Any other markings besides the name on the exam would invalidate it. I attempted to make certain that, in the future, directions would be followed after students paid careful attention to detail.

Usually the more assertive students hurried to be the first to hand in their papers. When one gangly, bespectacled six-foot-three-inch bean pole rose from his desk, shoved his glasses back on his nose, and shuffled to the front of the room amid a few moans, I could only wonder if he was the most competitive kid in class.

He smirked, nodded, and placed his test paper, facedown, on the corner of my desk, then returned to his seat, miming whistling.

I found his name, Irwin Albright, right where it should be. I gave him a thumbs-up as he slumped back into his chair. A prominent Adam's apple punctuated his long neck, bobbing up and down as he swallowed. His brown-rimmed spectacles constantly slid down his nose, and his mousy hair could use a good stylist, but who was I to say. To top it off, he sported a pen protector in his right breast pocket, occupied by three writing utensils and a mathematical compass. As he waited, he absentmindedly spun a silver ring on his right hand.

One by one, my students finished plugging in their answers and finally arrived at number twenty. I heard sighs and a few pained guffaws. I hoped this would make a good start to the year. The students brought their exams to the front. Most smiled then returned to their seats. One sandy-haired young lady, however, clearly didn't enjoy a good joke, mathematical or otherwise. Glancing at her exam, I read her name: Lorelei Calder.

When all the papers were turned in, I said, "Please keep the contents of the exam to yourselves. We'll begin by—"

Lorelei interrupted, saying crisply, "We've already begun." Her smug smile beckoned confrontation. Uncomfortable silence gave me only one thing to say.

"Lesson learned. We'll begin again. It's important to read through an entire set of instructions and to follow directions carefully. The language of mathematics is universal and precise. Missing the word 'not' undoubtedly will get you a wrong answer."

We spent the rest of the class period repeating some of what I expected had concluded last year's math class so we could move on toward a calculus curriculum. Near the end of the hour, I asked, "Any questions?"

Irwin raised his hand. "What does that mean?" he said, pointing to the large letters printed on the white board.

"It's a coded message. The word 'math' plays an important role in the solution. Feel free to share your answer when you decrypt it."

Lorelei raised her hand. "You found the dead body,

right?" I could've heard the proverbial pin drop.

With a sigh of relief at the claxon of the bell ringing in the nick of time, I dismissed my students.

I had no doubt the format of the first period exam would be shared as the day progressed, so I'd prepared six separate exams, each with a different trick question that essentially would terminate the test.

I also prepared an answer to Lorelei's question should someone ask it again. "As it is an ongoing investigation, I'm not at liberty to discuss it." I practiced it under my breath, but no one else dared to ask.

Tom Murphy popped into my room at the end of the day. "Don't you have Ashley Johannes in Advanced Math? I seem to remember she'd be one of your students but I don't suppose she was in class today. She's pretty shaken up by the events surrounding her neighbor. I think they got on well." He walked around the classroom, examining my posters, and stopped in front of me. "Samantha McCoy is nothing but bad news."

I looked over the day's attendance record and discovered my only absentees were in first period.

"Do you know anything about these other two?" I asked him.

Tom glanced at my attendance list. "Those three girls are inseparable. Best friends, always hanging out together. In fact, recently they were all cast as extras in some flick about the *Titanic*." He feigned ennui.

"That sounds great to me." I tried to keep my spirited emotions in check.

He said a little overenthusiastically, "Pray tell, what exists out there besides Cameron's fiction?"

I ignored his sarcasm and listed DVD and video

titles, ticking them off on my fingers. "There's the classic *A Night to Remember,* the 1943 banned German *Titanic, Raise the Titanic* with Alec Guinness, *Titanic* with Barbara Stanwyck—"

He interrupted, both hands up in surrender. "Okay. You should've been here when they filmed the crowd scenes. The movie will be shown when the exhibit opens. And those three girls made the cut, I think. Best friends." He shook his head.

"Then, hopefully, Ashley will have a built-in support group," I said. I began straightening chairs and desks.

Ignoring me, Tom stared at my *Alice in Wonderland* poster. Mumbling, he read what Alice said. "... and four times seven is—oh dear! I shall never get to twenty at that rate." He smirked. "What's that all about?"

I put on my best teacher voice. "I wanted to give an example of math in literature."

"And...?" He waited.

I made it as short and sweet as was possible. "In base eighteen, twelve means one eighteen and two ones or twenty, which is four times five. Right?" He nodded. "In base twenty-one, thirteen means one twenty-one and three ones or twenty-four, which is four times six." Tom's eyes glazed over in utter boredom. I'd never get to the pièce de résistance that indeed Alice would never get to twenty. "I hoped if I used some unusual mathematics found in popular literature we could have some fun."

He nodded absently, but clearly wasn't amused. I had failed—and with someone who should've understood the math. So much for *Alice in Wonderland!* When he left the room, I sagged into my chair. The cryptoquip called to me from the desktop, a diversion. I worked a bit longer and it appeared, apropos: NEVER BE AFRAID TO TRY SOMETHING NEW. REMEMBER, AMATEURS BUILT THE ARK. PROFESSIONALS BUILT THE *TITANIC.*

CHAPTER NINETEEN

The school parking lot was nearly empty, except for the consummate Goth girl fuming next to my car. I switched my briefcase from one hand to another and bounded toward my roadworthy pride and joy, a steel-gray used Jetta I purchased when I returned from England. It'd gone through all sorts of journeys with me, long and short, good and bad, sane and crazy, joyful and bereaved. As I approached my car, she took a step closer to me, clumping on the pavement.

"May I help you?" I asked.

"Watch out," she replied. Purple spikes stood straight up in her short black hair. Metal studs curled around her ears and glinted from her nose.

"Excuse me?" I countered, uncertain I heard her correctly.

The jagged slices in her black leather jacket revealed black lace covering a lilac T-shirt. She wore torn black fishnet stockings under a short inky denim skirt. Clunky, scuffed combat boots completed the ensemble.

"May I help you with something?" I asked again.

The girl stood erect, chin up, fingers wrapped in the decorative chains at her waist, looking beyond me. "The drugs are connected to the film but no one believes me," she said through clenched teeth.

"Who are you?"

Her kohl-rimmed eyes settled on me. She shook her mangled mane and took another step toward me, her hands balled into fists. "Be careful."

My heart raced. Did she have something in those fists? Could I use any of my self-defense training? Could I remember any of my self-defense training? Could I get in my car and lock the doors before she could get around and assault me? She took yet another step in my direction and looked at the front passenger side tire. I followed her gaze.

"You need to fix that." Her voice had leveled into a robotic monotone. "This is how it begins."

Anger replaced panic, and I moved to the driver's side, unlocked the doors, and bounced my briefcase onto the front seat. I hated flat tires. I hated fixing flat tires. I couldn't remember the last time I changed a flat tire. Then I remembered my dad had insisted I purchase roadside service as part of my insurance coverage, which included changing flat tires. Hallelujah! Then, thunderstruck, I noticed the front driver's tire was flat too. "Well, that's just dandy." I complained, looking up, but the girl had disappeared.

The school door burst open behind me and I cringed.

Dreamboat Drew, wearing a skinny orange tie, whirled out of the building with an imaginary partner. He whistled a happy tune. Despite my situation, I had to laugh. I caught his eye and waved, then frowned, remembering why I was still in the parking lot.

Smiling, he nearly skipped over to me. "Hey."

"Hey, yourself," I said. He radiated happiness. His budding friendship with Jane might have merited this good cheer.

"What's shakin'?"

"Besides you?" He laughed.

"I have two flat tires!"

He stopped laughing. "What did you run over?"

"Nothing that I know of."

Drew set his briefcase on the asphalt and rolled up his shirtsleeves.

"My auto insurance covers changing a tire." I retrieved the card from the glove box, and Drew volunteered to call roadside service.

"You don't have to do that," I said, but inwardly I was pleased not to have to make the call myself.

"What are friends for? Any idea what you might've done to deserve this?"

"Not a clue." I wasn't comfortable sharing my suspicion that someone to whom I hadn't yet officially been introduced might have flattened them for me.

Drew was growing on me. Now much more engaging than the pompous know-it-all we first met, helpful Drew waited with me until the tow truck arrived.

"Thanks. I'll be fine now," I said.

"Good luck, Katie."

The tow-truck driver set to work. "Looks like this was

deliberate," he said. "In order for you to make a claim and have insurance pay for all of this, you'll have to file a police report. This wasn't an accident." He pointed out the narrow incisions on the sidewalls of both tires. "Then I'll fix you up with some new tires. Shouldn't take but an hour."

A short while later, Chief Erickson appeared. "You sure no one's carrying a grudge? Have any of your students been belligerent? Aggressive?"

I shrugged. "I still don't think I've been here long enough." However, it was as good a time as any. "Chief, I'm not sure it's connected, but there was a young woman near my car when I exited the building. She didn't stick around. And before you ask, no, I don't know who she is, and I can't say she did anything."

"What did she look like?" I gave what I hoped might be an adequate description and told him what I remembered her saying. But other than feeling uncomfortable, I couldn't offer any proof she'd done this.

"A fax should take care of the insurance requirement for reimbursement." The chief closed his notebook.

He touched the brim of his hat. "Tread carefully, Ms. Wilk."

I climbed into the truck cab. The Village People wailed "YMCA" on the radio and intensified the bumpy ride.

CHAPTER TWENTY

Each letter in the encryption is replaced with a letter a fixed number of places down the alphabet. Can you decode this message by sliding the two horizontal alphabets to match the letters?" I wrote "esp ntaspc th plhi" on the SMART Board.

Lorelei raised her hand.

"Question, Lorelei?" I asked carefully.

"No. The cipher is easy," she said, and her classmates grumbled.

"Very good," I said. "Can you tell us how you came up with your solution?" I lined up "e" and "p."

"I matched the letter used most in the cipher with the letter used most often in our alphabet and the rest fell into place."

"Excellent. An important concept for solving math

problems through logical reasoning is using some of the same skills as solving cryptic puzzles."

Near the end of each hour, I posted reminders and announcements on my SMART Board and listed assignment pages and numbers. On the calendar, I noted the extracurricular activities and mentioned the first meeting of the clubs active in the fall, including science club. Animated words flashed in neon colors—"fun," "stimulating," "wild," "magical," and "curious"— marketing strategy for my extracurricular activity. However, by day's end, my palms were sweaty and my heart pounded; the new experience had my nerves in a tizzy.

Having returned to school, Ashley, Brenna, and Allie sat quietly in my first-period class, so I was surprised to see them turn up at our first science club meeting, joining Irwin and a boy named Brock. For teenagers, they were unusually quiet.

"Can anyone tell me why you're here?" Not one expression altered. No student volunteered an answer. They even avoided looking at one another. "I suppose it could be my sterling character or my bubbly personality." That got a round of tiny snickers. "Do you know each other?" When their attention drifted around the room, I pulled a roll of toilet paper from my supply box and passed it to Irwin.

Brock commented, "Don't have this toilet paper around at homecoming. You might get in trouble." He hooted and glanced knowingly at the girls.

Irwin said in a stage whisper, "High school students can't even buy toilet paper the week of homecoming. TP-ing is considered vandalism."

"Then I'll just have to make sure this roll doesn't leave

my sight. What I would like you to do—" I began as Jane knocked on the entryway. "Ms. Mackey, welcome to our first science club meeting. Care to join us?"

"I'd love to. Thanks," she beamed.

"Ms. Mackey, please tear off what you might need from this roll of toilet paper." Jane knew how to get a laugh and tore off a hefty chunk. I continued, "This is to help us get to know one another."

Brock said, "You mean like an iceberg?"

"Icebreaker," Irwin corrected.

"What I'd like you to do is tell us something about yourself for each piece of perforated toilet paper you pulled from the roll."

Jane's face was momentarily disconcerted, and then she laughed and said, "I guess I'd better start, but I'll probably need to take a few breaks so I can use all this charming Charmin. I'm Ms. Mackey. I teach history. I love chocolate." That comment earned oohs and ahs as she slid her hand down to the next perforation. "Could someone else please take a turn?"

Each of the students told us about themselves, nothing profound, but unique facts about their siblings, their hobbies, their dreams, their eye color, hair color, and where they lived. Because of all her extra pieces, Jane described her day in detail, including how much she looked forward to helping me with science club.

I'd chosen two sections of toilet paper and declared, "I like teaching, so far, and…" I mimed a drum roll on the desktop. "I have a minor fascination with the *Titanic*." With that, everyone spoke at once. Engaged by the topic, the boys wondered how Ballard found the ill-fated ship, and its value both then and now. Jane tossed in relevant names and dates, and the girls volunteered information about being cast as extras in *Titanic: One Story*. The topic literally broke the ice, and we formed a club of seven.

As the energy of the conversation subsided, I said, "Our course is wide open. Does anyone have a pet project or a burning desire to study something in particular?"

Jane recorded their comments on the SMART Board.

"How about being green?" Ashley volunteered.

Brock said, "Like economy."

"Ecology," Irwin said and shook his head. I wasn't sure Brock was as clueless as he pretended. Money is green.

Brenna added, "Can we determine our blood types?"

"I like physics and chemistry-based experiments," said Irwin.

When the flow of ideas abated, I brought out the school's set of GPS units and demonstrated how to operate them. "We're going to try geocaching."

"What's geocaching?" Allie asked.

"It's like an electronic scavenger hunt."

"And why would we want to find whatever we're looking for?" snickered Brock.

"There'll be a prize." Bribery usually worked. "Anyone know what 'GPS' stands for?"

Irwin raised his hand for the second time. "Go ahead, Irwin. And you don't have to raise your hand here."

A small smile played on his lips. "Global positioning system. It's a space-based satellite navigation system that provides locations and times around the Earth."

"Have you used a GPS before?" I asked.

"Yeah. They're cool. Some have an electronic map with icons for gas stations and eating places, and a compass, and can tell you your speed and altitude."

"Is that what they used to find the *Titanic*?" Brock asked.

"I think they used hard work to find the *Titanic* the first time," I said, "but to find it again they might have. According to the reports, they found it at 41° 43' north latitude, 49° 56' west longitude."

"Which is latitude and which is longitude?" asked Allie.

"Latitude is made up of the circles that go around the earth parallel to the equator," I replied.

Jane brought the globe from the front of my room. "Latitude is the distance from the equator." She followed the rings around the earth with her finger. "St. Paul is on the forty-fifth parallel, a latitude of forty-five degrees north." She traced the ring until it met a perpendicular line at fifty degrees west. "Longitude runs from pole to pole. The *Titanic* was found near here. We can use the coordinates to pinpoint any location on a globe."

I projected the geocaching.com website on the SMART Board and navigated through the drop-down menus.

"Our nearest cache is a one-star search—one being easy, five being difficult." From my supply box, I pulled out samples of containers ranging in size from a small magnetic black nub with the dimensions of a pencil eraser to a two-gallon popcorn tin.

I translated the description. "'BYOP' means bring your own pencil or pen to sign the log. We might also be able to exchange swag if you'd like."

"What kind of swag?" Brock asked.

"Not much usually. Maybe we'll find something comparable to a prize from a Cracker Jack box. At my first geocache, I traded a quarter for a dime and lost fifteen cents."

"Turn on your devices and examine their faces," I said. "What do you think of the bars at the bottom?"

Brock pointed and said, "These measure battery life, and the other ones tell you the strength of your signal, like a smartphone."

"Correct. Enter the coordinates for the cache called 'Hunter,' then press the 'enter' key followed by the 'navigate' button. On the screen, we're the little green dot, and the gold box is our destination."

We exited the school building through the parking lot out into a beautiful day, sun shining, not a cloud in the sky, no wind, and I took time to notice, no flat tires. The GPS device indicated the cache might be found at a distance of .4 mile.

The students chattered about the first days of school. I asked Jane, "How's Drew?"

"He's great." Her eyes sparkled. My eyebrows rose in question. "Well, we went out after dance class." My eyebrows arched even more. "Just for one glass of wine. And we ran together this morning." If my eyebrows could have arched more, they would have merged with my hairline. "And tonight, I'm cooking dinner for him." She sighed blissfully.

Closing in on our goal, we paid attention to the ever-lessening distance blipping on the GPS units. We came to a city park filled with plastic orange and yellow playground equipment but no muggles, the term used to identify non-geocachers. A sign that read DEER PARK marked the end of our journey.

"I get it," said Brock. "Deer Park—Hunter! Now what do we do?"

"We look for a container about the size of a baseball." Jane and I planted ourselves on a bench and observed our five charges crawling around, brushing aside branches of plants in the landscaping.

Ashley held a camouflaged Tupperware aloft. "I found it," she said. "Didn't I?" A shy smile lit her face. She opened the container and found a small notebook and loot—a deck of Pokémon cards held together with a rubber band and a troll with scraggly orange and purple hair.

"Wish I had something to exchange," said Irwin. "I'd like to check out the cards and see if they're worth anything. I…er…we could make some real money on an original Holo deck."

Brock recited, "A penny saved is a penny earned—old Ben Franklin."

"I doubt anyone would leave something too valuable," Jane said, "but you can exchange them for the deck of playing cards I always carry, just in case." She rooted around in her huge bag and pulled out the cards.

Irwin's face lit up as he took the offer and pocketed the Pokémon cards. "I'll let you know if they're worth anything."

Brock chuckled. "Yeah, right."

"This is fun," said Brenna. "Are we going to do this every meeting?"

"We can do whatever you'd like, but I hope every time we meet we have something new on the agenda too," I said. I gave each student a sweet prize for his and her effort in finding our first geocache. Even Jane put out her hand. I asked if I could take a photo for our journal, and everyone lined up brandishing a caramel apple sucker.

"Can we meet every day?" Irwin asked, sounding a bit surprised himself.

"You know," Brock said, "I just wanted to add my science club membership to my résumé. I didn't honestly think I'd have any fun after the way I heard you were in your classes." No one moved a muscle. "Oops."

I was momentarily taken aback but not entirely displeased. Mission accomplished!

The students looked at me expectantly. "We won't meet every day, but let's meet tomorrow. Bring your calendars and we can plan future dates. Anyone have any other ideas about what they want to do during our time together?"

Ashley said softly, "Could we go on a field trip?"

Brock said, "The *Titanic* exhibit opens at the Midwest Minnesota History Center this weekend. That's sort of science, right?

"Well…" I began.

"We could tackle the experimental exhibits and record our findings," Irwin said. "They have a wall of ice that simulates the temperature of the water. Another exhibit monitors the weight of the water in the *Titanic* at any given time as it rushed in and broke the ship in half. You can alter the parameters of metal composition, thickness, rivet alloys, and a bunch of other variables to see if your own construction specifications would've saved the ship."

"I don't know if we have money to attend an exhibit," I said.

Ashley said hesitantly, "My grandma has a bunch of complimentary tickets. My friend and I had planned to attend the opening, but that isn't going to happen now." Tears threatened to spill past her blue eyes. The students looked at her with concern and back to me for a remedy. "I'd really like to go, but I don't want to go by myself. Could we go together?" When Brenna placed a hand on Ashley's shoulder, Brock nodded.

"I'll have answers tomorrow."

CHAPTER TWENTY-ONE

There were only two people I trusted with my total lack of knowledge of proper school procedures and who treated every question as if it deserved an answer. Mr. Walsh took care of the math department and could locate anything and everyone at any given time. And the administrative secretary knew what I needed to take the students on a field trip.

"Jane Mackey and I have five students who want to attend the *Titanic* exhibit for a science club field trip. What do I do?'

"Would you be comfortable driving a school SUV that carries nine?"

"Sure," I said. How difficult could it be?

"How much are the tickets?"

"They're being donated."

Handing me a stack of printed material, she said, "Fill in the blanks on the release forms and have a parent or guardian sign it. And FYI, there's a little petty cash stash for future educational extracurricular expenses." She pursed her lips and peered at me over the tops of her tortoise-shell glasses, adding weight to the words to follow. "Have fun."

"Thank you, Mrs. McEntee." Information in hand, I felt prepared.

* * *

After school, much to my dismay, Lorelei Calder showed up at our meeting.

"Hello, Lorelei." She acknowledged my greeting with a curt nod of her head. The SUV could seat a total of nine, but I wondered if Lorelei would find the close quarters to her liking.

I distributed the documents. "This form gives permission for Ms. Mackey and me to accompany you to the *Titanic* exhibit. You need to have a parent or guardian sign and date it. Would you like to attend a week from Saturday or Sunday?"

"Can't we get out of school?" Brock's complaint was met with blank stares, and he added, sulkily, "Just kidding."

Ashley said, "I work on Sunday." The others shrugged, the universal teenage noncommittal signal.

"If there are no objections, then Saturday it will be. Fill in the date. The exhibit hours are ten to eight. We'll leave at—"

"Nine fifteen," Brenna volunteered.

"Bring money for souvenirs. And there's a great drive-in restaurant we'll pass on our way home," Brock added.

"Mrs. McEntee told me if we're frugal, we might be able to afford a few more field trips. Let's make this one a success."

"What does 'frugal' mean?" Brock asked.

"To save," Irwin chided.

We created a list of future topics to cover. Lorelei declared ecology an essential theme, so I put her in charge of the next activity and asked that she share her idea with me over the weekend so I could find supportive materials. She acquiesced begrudgingly.

"Do you think we could meet Monday? It's Labor Day but I think we'll all be around," Brenna said, seeking confirmation from the other students.

With all eyes on me, I said, "Why not? Let's meet at four in the school parking lot."

Meeting adjourned.

I thanked Jane for her offer of assistance. I was also grateful Drew had plans during the day of our field trip so she could attend. With a dreamy quality to her voice, Jane said, "Drew called me his Terpsichore."

Even though my opinion of Drew had changed for the better, I had to drum up enthusiasm for his incessant vocabulary building. "And what does this new word mean?"

"I'm his dancing muse." She sighed. "Do you want to have supper tonight with Drew and Pete and me?" My face must have taken on a peculiar look because she added, "You're not the third or fourth wheel. I am. Drew and Pete were going to attend the opening Columbia Cougar football game then stop at the golf club to have a bite to eat. I said that you and I would join them."

I laughed. "I have to eat anyway. Can you tell me what time I'm going to the game?"

I met Jane at the entrance to the football field, and we plopped ourselves on the bleachers next to Drew and Pete. I recognized a few players' names on the program and students from my classes sitting in the stands. Some of them blatantly ignored Jane and Drew and me, and some acknowledged us with a polite nod, but almost all of them greeted Pete warmly, as did their parents. "Do you know *everybody*?" I asked incredulously.

"Not quite," he answered. "But I grew up here. I played sports here." He sat on the end of the bleachers in full view of everyone.

"Quarterback?"

"Yup."

"Basketball and baseball?"

"Basketball, yes. Baseball, no. Track. Two-miler."

I turned to look at him directly. "Two-miler? Fast?"

He looked back at me, dimples making a shy appearance. "Maybe. Nine minutes and forty-seven seconds."

He had been a supreme high school athlete, probably a top-notch student, possibly homecoming royalty material, definitely a heartthrob. No wonder he had so many admirers. Everyone in this small town had watched him grow up and likely had read about him in the *Sentinel*.

"Jock," I laughed. I nudged him with my elbow, and he flashed his luscious brown eyes. Maybe we *could* become good friends.

The final score was Cougars 21, Cardinals 17. My voice croaked from all the yelling. As we rose to leave, Pete's features hardened and I followed his gaze to a smirking S O'Hara on the field at the opponent's sideline. A ready smile softened Pete's gaze, however, as yet another parent shook his hand, breaking his grim concentration.

The golf club was famous for its late-night snacks of cheesy hamburger sliders, and delicately seasoned fries. Jane had a glass of red wine and the three of us shared a pitcher of a local craft beer. Volume control was nonexistent with the glut of satisfied Cougar boosters. Most of the tables catered to oversized ex-jocks going to seed, reminiscing about their own past gridiron successes, and they sang the fight song more than once.

"Anything new on Condive?" I asked Pete.

"No lab results yet. How's school?" Pete asked.

I could have written a dissertation on the topic but answered, "Great." Jane smiled. Drew nodded, tugging on his blue-and-gold Cougar tie. Always on the lookout for new information, I pulled up the photo of the Bailey's Electric Car on my phone. "You wouldn't happen to know who this belongs to, would you?"

Pete shook his head. "Sorry. Why?"

"It's an electric car from the early twentieth century. I thought maybe I could ask the owner if the kids could see it. I'm looking for ideas to support the earth-friendly topic the science club members want to study." Both Drew and Pete pretended to put on their thinking caps.

Jane and I begged off any later-night activities.

With little illumination from a crescent moon, I dashed to my car. It was too early for many of the Cougar supporters and golf club patrons to abandon their celebration, but I felt a presence behind me. I laced my car keys between my fingers, positioning the pointy edges like brass knuckles, and wheeled around.

"Whoa! Only me," Pete said quickly, putting his hands up. "Okay if Drew and I join you two biking sometime?"

"Sure, but remember I'm still not Speedy Gonzalez."

"See you," he said. I heard him chuckle as he strode out of sight.

* * *

The first pale amber streaks of dawn stretched across the early morning sky. Maverick and I speed-walked and practiced a few cues. By seven forty-five, we joined Mrs. C on her porch, basking in the warmth of the sun. I opened her photo album again and admired the wealth of information she had accumulated, straightening the documents as I read the life stories. A gentle wind whispered in the treetops, and the streets were silent. Maverick lay between us, eyes furtive, watching for the occasional misstep of a squirrel or bird, or any other miscreant.

She read a phone message and her shoulders sagged. "They've arrested Elaine."

CHAPTER TWENTY-TWO

Lorelei called me Monday morning with her fait accompli. "The reusable bags have an endorsement for the company inked on the side. That won't be a problem, will it?" Lorelei said with a challenge.

She wasn't going to make this easy, but it was a great idea. I emailed the principal for permission to use the bags, and he replied immediately, happy and certain we'd make nearby schools green with envy while reaping the benefits of an ecological project that was completely underwritten.

A few minutes after four, a white delivery van pulled into the lot, and Lorelei waved it over to the entry. I unlocked the school door, and we hauled the cartons into the commons area outside the main office and set up for an easy distribution the next morning.

We tiptoed through the darkened hallways to the

mathematics area where we turned on every light. Our meeting continued inside.

Lorelei led the discussion. "Plastic bags can last for generations and destroy wildlife through strangulation and entanglement. Eighty-six percent of ocean debris is plastic, killing over a million sea birds and marine mammals each year. Paper bag production requires thousands of gallons of water, and costs are high, in addition to the loss of timber around the world. We can't replace the trees fast enough, and we can't speed up tree growth."

"We shouldn't use paper and we can't use plastic. What do you suggest?" Brenna asked.

"Our refrain should be 'Reduce, reuse, recycle, refuse!'" Lorelei said. "An alternative to disposables is reusable bags. We want to make sure all bags are reused, and often. We can give these out before school tomorrow." She unboxed a foldable, frosty gray tote with the company logo printed in navy blue. "These are made from recycled soda bottles."

"Great idea!" Brock said. For the first time, I witnessed the twitch of delight at the corners of Lorelei's mouth. "I'll definitely be able to use this."

"The next item on the agenda is our visit to the *Titanic* exhibit."

"I won't be going," Lorelei said, packing up her belongings. "We can start handing out bags early tomorrow morning." Our field trip was back to seven.

I watched her leave with a degree of sadness. I'd hoped to build some bridges.

"Do you all have your signed release forms?"

Jane collected them in exchange for an information sheet containing the plan, times, place, and personnel, including contact information. They were excited and all shared something they had learned about the events of April 14 and 15, 1912. We found a website that provided a topological map of any point on earth from its latitude and longitude. Zooming in on the coordinates of the sinking, we were able to differentiate the ocean depths with disturbing clarity.

Eyes glued to the screen, Ashley said, "It looks so real, I can almost see the fish in the ocean."

Brock, who was beginning to act as comic relief, said, "They'd have to be giant fish."

After our meeting, I ventured to the parking lot and inspected my tires. They appeared to be in working order, so I checked under the car, although I had no idea what I was looking for.

* * *

I left for school half an hour earlier than usual to help distribute the reusable bags, but by the time I arrived, Jane and my students already were hard at work. They set up four tables, one on each wall of the commons area, and students flocked to see what was happening.

Lorelei's posters criticized the use of disposable plastic and paper bags. The students tolerated her complaints and happily accepted the freebie. Even some teachers came to the table to see what my students had to say. No one walked away empty-handed.

"Congratulations, Lorelei. This was a fantastic idea," I said.

The first bell rang and she harrumphed, stowed the remaining bags, and disappeared. Jane and I cleaned up the remnants of the morning activity.

* * *

After dance, I joined Jane, Drew, and Pete for a cup of herbal tea, per Jane's instructions.

"It'll help you sleep. I promise," she said.

Sipping chamomile tea in the cozy surroundings of the downtown tea shop, amid comfortable persiflage, I felt as if we were lifelong friends rather than new acquaintances.

"Are you going to the football game on Friday?" Pete asked.

"Yes, but I have to make it a short evening," I said, bubbling with eagerness. "I'm driving our science club to the Midwest Minnesota Historical Center on Saturday."

"I have to make it a short night too. I'm on second call Friday," said Pete. "How about if I drive you to the game?" Tiny bells chimed, and I nodded.

Drew asked, "Carpool, Jane?"

"Sounds like an earth-friendly plan." As we gathered our belongings, Jane said, "I'll give you a ride home, Katie."

"O-kay," I spoke the word in slow, subdivided syllables. I had hoped for an invitation from Pete.

The gentlemen walked us to Jane's car. She got a peck on the cheek from Drew, and Pete followed me around to my side of the car.

"Tell Ida I'm sorry about Elaine. Her hearing is scheduled for tomorrow," he said. "I know you're busy Saturday, but I was wondering if you might like to go out for pizza or something when you get back," he said.

Thinking about the rave reviews for Dairy D-light, and our supper plans on the way home, I answered, "Or something. Sure. When and where, Dr. Erickson?"

"Give me a call when you get back."

I slid into the passenger seat and closed the door. When I looked up, he still stood where I'd left him. I checked my watch, wiggled my fingers in farewell, and sighed as Jane backed out of the parking lot.

"You gotta keep 'em guessing!" Jane offered in explanation and we laughed.

"You really like Drew?" I asked.

"What's not to like? What about you? Do you like Doc?"

"Pete's nice." I ignored her cross-eyed look. When we pulled in front of Ida's I said, "Wait here." I ran inside and returned with a beribboned bottle of my housewarming gift.

"What's this for?" she said.

"Celebrating our friendship."

"Thank you. I'll save it for a special occasion." She hugged the bottle of wine.

I beamed as I wrote my latest journal entry.

I'm still dancing. I choose life.

CHAPTER TWENTY-THREE

For whatever reason, maybe a full moon, maybe a change in the weather, maybe too much sugar or caffeine, I couldn't rein in the vibrancy of my students, so I offered a short biography of a brilliant but jinxed political activist and mathematician. Taunted into fighting a duel and, knowing he would die, Évariste Galois spent his last evening feverishly recording numerous mathematical discoveries—some not entirely understood to this day. I also shared information about mathematician and author Lewis Carroll. After a discussion about Humpty-Dumpty's un-birthday gift of a cravat received from the White King and Queen, I had no doubt some of my students would approach their parents for their own three hundred sixty-four un-birthday gifts.

Following YouTube instructions, my science club kids

drew fairly accurate conclusions from our experiment that demonstrated the characteristics of polymers in plastic. Despite Lorelei's disapproval, we poked holes through water-filled Ziploc bags with ultra-sharp pencils, and the bags never leaked a drop.

After my car passed its cursory daily inspection, I breezed through the school parking lot and out into the afternoon. With my windows down and wind whipping my hair, I turned on the radio and sang at the top of my lungs to ABBA's "Dancing Queen." I glanced in my rearview mirror and caught sight of a small red car. I sped up a bit, pretending to lose my tail, but the car followed. I waited until the last moment to turn onto my street, attempting to misdirect the pursuer, but the car kept pace. Then I rocketed down Maple Street. The car was still there. Fear rarely took a foothold in daylight, but my mouth dried up, I stopped singing, and my heart pounded in my chest.

I sailed past the wrought iron fence covered with violet clematis and white climbing roses on the long driveway from Maple Street to the triple garage. Lurching from my car without turning off the engine, I shoved my stall door up and out of the way. The handle of the service door slid down. The door swung open and Maverick hurtled into the garage. I stepped into the cool shade and complained about him getting underfoot to the whump of his tail-wagging greeting.

A car door slammed. Maverick's tail stopped wagging. My words caught in my throat.

"Ms. Wilk," a voice called. Maverick growled.

"Maverick," I reprimanded, and although he stopped growling, his hackles were raised and he stood at attention, clearly waiting to make his own decision.

"Y-yes?" I answered. With my hand securely latched

onto Maverick's collar I peeked out of the garage. S O'Hara stood next to a gleaming red sports car. I let out a sigh. "Hello, Mr. O'Hara."

"You remember me?" he said. "And it's Sean."

Maverick rumbled. I signed for him to "sit" and "stay." "You remember Sean, Maverick." I put out my hand. "How could I forget you, Sean? You're one of the first people I met in Columbia. Call me Katie." He took the hand.

"How are you getting along, Katie?" He held tight to my hand, which made me a bit uncomfortable.

"Great."

A door banged and I heard her call, "Katie?"

"Out in the garage, Mrs. C," I replied, withdrawing my hand from his.

"Your math kids okay?" he asked.

I nodded, wondering how he knew I was a math teacher, but then again, why not? We lived in a small town.

He smiled and reached up next to my ear. I flinched. His eyes widened, and he backed away. In his hand he held a Kennedy half dollar, and he chuckled as my expression morphed to one of amazement. "You're good! I love magic. Could you teach me to do that?"

"I was wondering." He ignored my question and puffed out his chest. "I work with the athletic trainer at the football games, but if you're going to the game tomorrow, I'd love to show you Columbia afterward."

"Sorry, Sean, but I have an early evening planned. I'm taking my students to the *Titanic* exhibit Saturday morning, and I want to be fresh for the drive."

"Figured." He frowned. "What about Sunday-morning coffee?"

"I can't." His eyes flashed darkly. I added rashly, "Maybe another time?"

He brightened a bit as he stepped away. "Maybe another time. Have a good night." He flipped the coin in his hand, caught it, pocketed it, then slid into his little car.

Mrs. C stood in the doorway of the garage, scowling. "What did he want?" She sounded like Pete.

I worked it over in my mind. "I think he wanted a date."

She spun on her heels and stomped back into the house.

* * *

I scheduled a quiz for each of my Friday classes, and although my students weren't particularly happy, they were surprisingly well prepared. After the quiz, they could expect a homework-free weekend, so I sent home a puzzle for fun. "In this cipher algorithm, replace the letters with numbers." I wrote on the SMART Board, "THREE + THREE + FIVE = ELEVEN." My own weekend homework included collecting the keys to the school van.

* * *

Pete picked me up for the game in his royal-blue Ram 1500.

I climbed in and pointed to the window cling that supported our local mascot. "Go, Cougars," I rooted.

The four of us sat in the same spots in the bleachers as we had for the previous game. Creatures of habit, just about everyone sat in the same seat, which, I noticed, happened in church as well.

By the end of the first quarter, the Cougars scored twenty points to the Lions' three. I smiled so much my cheeks hurt until one of the players had to be escorted off the field on a stretcher during the second quarter. Sean

O'Hara carried the back end of the stretcher. He stopped abruptly. Anger stormed his face. My heart banged against my chest, and I looked away.

Jane caught his glare and grabbed my hand. "What's going on?" she asked.

"Sean asked me out," I whispered.

"Sean is it, now?"

"I told him I had plans for an early evening and I was driving to the exhibit tomorrow, but I didn't think to tell him I'd be at the game."

"What's his problem?" Drew asked, nodding his head at Sean.

Pete shook his head.

"He probably has a lot on his mind with the injured player and all," I offered.

All three sets of eyes glared at me.

"What all?" Drew asked, wiggling his bushy eyebrows and twiddling the end of his Cougar tie.

"He asked Katie on a date," Jane said. "You said no, right?"

I waffled. I'd said no, but I should have said never.

Sean's heated look derailed the evening's enjoyment. "Don't worry," I said. "It'll be fine. Look, he's no longer on the field."

Seconds later, Pete's pager beeped, and he glanced at the display.

"We're ready to leave anyway," said Jane. "We'll get her home."

Pete's hand landed lightly on my shoulder and big questions ignited his eyes. "Don't let O'Hara bother you. Call me when you return from the exhibit tomorrow."

CHAPTER TWENTY-FOUR

I dreamed I was running from cannons mounted on bicycle wheels and woke exhausted to a damp, dreary day, but ideal for an indoor field trip. Carrying his leash in his mouth, Maverick circled in front of the door. I put on my purple Wellingtons and my orange hooded rain jacket, and we sloshed through two miles of the neighborhood.

"Mrs. C said she'd take you out later today, so no pouting." Then I grabbed the SUV keys. "Be a good boy."

Jane spun into the school parking lot seconds behind me. We opened the doors of the metallic gold Chevy Suburban with ISD #340 stenciled on the front bumper and checked it for the detritus of previous use. It was in pretty good shape: no candy wrappers, no snack crumbs, or, heaven forbid, plastic bottles. The gas gauge read full.

The students arrived on time, eager to be on their way. Ashley, Brenna, and Allie wore business casual, looking older than their teenage years. Brock, on the other hand, wore rumpled jeans and a baggy blue sweatshirt with "Cougar Power" silk-screened on the front. His baseball cap perched backward on his head, and his mop of dark brown hair hung rakishly over one eye. He stretched and, with the first huge yawn of the day, mumbled, "Mornin'." Irwin gripped a thin black folder, most likely containing his experiment parameters.

"Climb in," Jane drawled.

"Buckle up. It's the law," came a voice from the back, two octaves lower than it should have been. The girls giggled.

"Well, navigator," I whispered, "do you have any idea where we're going?"

"Nope. But he does." Jane held up her phone, the map on display, and a sexy male voice dictated a right turn out of the parking lot.

Minutes after we left Columbia, the students snoozed. They weren't going to miss out on a Saturday sleep-in for any reason. Soon, Jane followed suit, her head rolling toward the window. Little traffic provided no distractions on a drive with no turns to make until we reached History Center Drive. In the quiet of the car, to the drone of the engine, I wondered, if Ida was right and Elaine was innocent, what I could do.

The late Arthur Condive had relished the power he wielded. He cheated Damon Hastings out of a lot of money. Hastings was a nasty piece of work and remained at the top of my list. Samantha argued with Condive, was known to have had a difficult past, and had disappeared. David Condive had borne the brunt of his father's cruel joke. Ida didn't have many nice things to say about him. And who was Kelly? I had my work cut out for me.

Jane roused when the GPS voice intoned, "Bear right."

"Where?" she asked groggily.

"Where what?"

Stretching her neck to get a better view, she said, "Where's the bear?"

"Very funny—not."

At 9:52, the syrupy voice from her phone crooned, "You have arrived at your destination." My passengers woke simultaneously, refreshed and raring to go, stretching out of their contorted poses.

As we rounded the corner into the parking lot, a majestic apparition coalesced. A gigantic ship's hull emerged from the trees. They had plopped a magnificent ocean liner right down on a pond in Minnesota.

Jane stood straighter as she consulted her phone. "Part of the Midwest Minnesota History Center, it was originally built as a sound stage for a movie production and houses objects of the director's obsession."

Raindrops formed rippling circles on the flat surface of the water surrounding the monolith. Water beaded on the tall windows, reflecting the steel gray of the sky, the streaks looking like claw marks as they trailed down the wall of glass.

With tickets in hand, we splashed across a gangplank to the passage beneath a cantilevered observation deck and came face-to-face with an educational and emotional reality. In exchange for our tickets, we received replicated boarding passes of actual *Titanic* passengers.

History was Jane's bailiwick, so she led the way through a corridor lined with photos that annotated the chronology of the luxury liner from its inception and life on board to its ultimate demise. Jane's passionate voice compelled our group. "This exhibit was made to show humanity in the face of tragedy, stories of heroism and loss, and how people reacted in the face of certain doom."

"Why are they flying a flag of Switzerland?" Brock asked. He didn't look remotely sincere, but Jane took the bait anyway.

"Brock," she said, "where are we?" He shrugged and looked around. The teacher in Jane continued in a most didactic voice, "I'll give you credit for knowing that the flag of Switzerland is red and white, but this is the flag of the White Star Line, famous for the largest and most luxurious ships in the world at the time. The *Titanic* was one of those ships. The company was founded in 1845." Just as the eyes of her students began to glaze over, she teased, "And it went belly up in 1934."

We wandered through the 52,000-square foot exhibit and Jane supplemented the information with trivia she knew by heart. "Thomas Andrews was thirty-nine years old and headed the drafting department of the shipbuilding company of Harland and Wolff in Belfast, Ireland. The construction of the *Titanic* took more than two years."

We followed placards of information detailing Andrews's creation of a floating palace, complete with a gymnasium, swimming pool, Turkish bath, squash and racket ball courts—all for first-class passengers. "Food was plentiful and accommodations were better on the *Titanic* than on any other ship for all passengers—first, second, and third-class," Jane said.

Snippets of old black-and-white films flashed on wide screens. Enlarged snapshots of the ship being built and sent on its way evoked a keen sense of its immensity. Photos taken by amateur photographer Father Frank Browne recorded the first leg of the *Titanic*'s maiden voyage.

"Father Browne was one lucky guy. He requested permission to continue on to New York using a ticket he was offered by a wealthy American. Lucky for him." Jane had us mesmerized. "His boss told him to get off the boat."

We pored over artifacts recovered from the wreck. Many pieces were on loan to the exhibit, but some were Bruckner's personal property. We walked through rusty sections of the ship, past chipped dishes, delicate pieces of jewelry, mottled papers, glass bottles, worn luggage, and tarnished silverware, objects that had borne witness to the souls who perished. To me, the most heart wrenching item was a pair of child's laced shoes, a testament to the senseless loss.

I took a photo of our group standing on the full-scale re-creation of the grand staircase, which led to an artful reproduction of the Honour and Glory: Crowning Time clock. We shuffled through the third-class dining saloon. From there we walked a darkened promenade deck cooled to near freezing, channeling us through a hall where we viewed an extravagant first-class parlor suite, a second-class stateroom, and a spartan third-class berth. The first-class dining saloon tables were set, and my breath quickened at the uncanny likeness. I could almost see Samantha wending her way through similarly set tables at the convention center.

At each juncture, we checked our passes against the lists of passengers to see if ours would have entered this area of the ship. The students read captivating news reports about the sinking, records of the investigation into the tragedy, and facsimiles of newspapers, yellowed to look aged, listing the men, women, and children who had lost their lives. Filmed commentary described parts of the ship in underwater photos of what currently remained of the *Titanic*.

"After discovering the wreck, engineers and architects thought they should try to understand what caused the ship to sink."

"That's what happened, the gashes?" Irwin asked.

Jane nodded.

Irwin read answers to a list of frequently asked questions. "'Up to eighty-seven percent of an iceberg can lie below the water line.' Some survivors reported an iceberg two hundred to four hundred feet high. That left an awful lot of berg below the surface." Rapidly calculating, he added, "Close to three thousand feet."

My students whispered with reverence as we wandered through the amazing exhibit of the ill-fated leviathan. A memorial kiosk at the conclusion of the exhibit would reveal what had befallen the passengers whose boarding passes each of us held in hand. We were overwhelmed by the prospect that the passenger whose role we had assumed for the duration of our tour had ultimately perished.

Brock had pulled the boarding pass of Mr. Edward Beane, thirty-two. "Hey, look at me. 'Mr. Beane moved to New York, but returned to England to be married some days before the *Titanic* set sail. The newlyweds survived the sinking, two of the few honeymooners who weren't parted by the rule 'women and children first' and were rescued aboard lifeboat thirteen.' I'm frugalled!"

"What?" Jane asked.

The girls moaned. Irwin explained, "Frugal means to save." Jane moaned too.

"Doña Fermina Oliva y Ocana." Brenna carefully pronounced the unusual name. "'The thirty-nine-year-old personal maid boarded the *Titanic* at Cherbourg and was rescued in lifeboat number eight.' Me too! I'm frugalled."

Allie read her boarding pass for a third-class passenger. "'Miss Bridget Elizabeth Muhvihill was rescued in lifeboat number fifteen and went on to marry her fiancé and have five children.' Holy cow!"

"I already know what happened to mine," Ashley announced proudly. "'Forty-four-year-old Mrs. Margaret Brown, better known as the Unsinkable Molly Brown, survived the shipwreck, rescued from lifeboat number six. She used her *Titanic* celebrity to advocate for labor rights, women's rights, education, literacy for children, and historic preservation.'" I shared Ashley's smile; she was a survivor as well.

More soberly, Irwin read the fate of his assumed identity, Jacques Heath Futrelle, an American journalist and mystery writer. "'Monsieur Futrelle was thirty-seven years old, returning from Europe as a first-class passenger. He secured a seat in a lifeboat for his wife but refused to board. The last time she saw him, he was smoking a cigarette with millionaire John Jacob Astor IV. His body was never recovered.'"

Jane read her short biography. "'Third-class passenger Miss Bridget Mary O'Sullivan from County Limerick was twenty years of age. Her body, if recovered, was never identified.'" She sighed. "I wish it said more."

I read my boarding pass. "'Patrick Callahan boarded the *Titanic* in Southampton and began his successful journey to America.'"

Color videos recorded recovery attempts and forays into the deep to salvage more of the wreckage, and included lists of excursions, crews, and equipment used on those expeditions. Life-size photos of present-day celebrations stood against the wall. The commemorations took place all around the globe with dinner re-creations in fancy rooms, and openings of similar exhibits in other cities.

"Do you think we could host a *Titanic* tea party?" asked Brenna.

"Maybe," I said.

Candid photos taken at the experimental ice exhibit covered a wall, and revealed the laughter and grimaces on the faces of the guests who braved the cold. In one photo, a tall, intense-looking man balanced atop a ladder with his hands pressed against the large chunk of ice. He wore an old-fashioned trench coat with a fur collar and a felt hat with a dark band. His face scrunched, as if he held his hands against the torturous cold as long as he could. The poster identified the man as Director Robert Bruckner and advertised the showing of his film *Titanic: One Story*. At the base of the ladder in the full-sized black-and-white photo stood Jane in stunning attire, looking up in admiration.

She tittered. "He could only hold out for twenty-two seconds."

"Could we go see the film now?" Allie whispered.

The next showing was in twenty minutes. "We'll finish here and go to the theater to discuss our options."

We paraded through the final exhibit, a series of eight glass cases that housed yellowed pages of personal letters chronicling the life of a man beginning when he boarded the ship in Southampton. He wrote in his letters that he'd always been superstitious and had been spooked at the *Titanic*'s ominous near miss with the *New York* at the Southampton dockyard. He wrote, "It was the worst of omens for the maiden voyage of a ship to come within feet of crashing into another liner, a crash which would have certainly cut short the voyage but saved over fifteen hundred lives."

In another letter, he wrote, "When word of the black face seen above the funnel reached me, I knew it surely predicted doom." Next to the letter sat a tarnished silver frame displaying a copy of one of Father Browne's now-renowned photos of a stoker's sooty face rising above the fourth smokestack. Filled with dread, the letter writer detailed practicing caution throughout his journey, and when the ship struck the iceberg, he grabbed the opportunity to escape the sinking ship.

The letters written after the disaster told of his overriding sense of survival guilt, the obstacles in his path to fulfilling his American dream, his failures and his successes. The faded ink ran in places—the text, at times, nearly illegible—but next to each letter lay a recently deciphered and neatly typed transcription. Patrick Callahan signed each letter, "Always." The name and the circumstances sent a quiver up my spine.

Jane touched my arm to get my attention and pointed to the engraved plate in the last case. "Letters donated by the Flanagan family," and immediately below it, "Authentication initiated by intern Samantha McCoy." I seethed; I would not allow her to ruin our day.

"Hey, all," I said. "We need to decide about the movie, so let's get a move on." I herded my entourage past the disturbing case and toward the theater.

CHAPTER TWENTY-FIVE

We dashed to the theater through the extremes of opulent beauty and staggering grief. The movie likely would intensify those emotions, but the girls had parts in the film so we had to see it.

"Do we still want to try a few experiments after the movie?" I asked.

When they all spoke at once, Jane said in a firm voice, "Take turns. Allie?"

"I vote that we see the movie and stay until we finish everything we set out to do."

"I don't have anything going on, so I'm all for staying," Brock said.

Irwin hung back, which wasn't unusual.

Jane asked, "What's up, Irwin?"

He pushed his glasses up the bridge of his nose. "I'm

supposed to work at five thirty." Sighs were audible to anyone within fifty feet. "Let me make a call," he said. He stepped away from our group to the large block of windows for better reception and pulled out his cell phone. After a short conversation, he gave us the thumbs-up. "I'm covered," he said. Then he grinned widely, and blue and gold bands, Cougar colors, tempered the shining silver of his braces.

We settled into our seats as the room went dark. I gaped at the bold letters crossing the screen; the movie was based on the life of one of Bruckner's ancestors. In the opening scene, ocean waves crashed into the enormous vessel, and our seats reverberated in the surround sound. Again, the majestic ship was captivating on film.

Over strains of popular early-1900s music like "Alexander's Ragtime Band," actors in gorgeous period costumes recited lines repeated for more than a hundred years in other films or on tape and printed in books, and reports. The story followed a semi-fictional second-class family of six and their butler on their journey to the new world. Scenes of memorable importance from the *Titanic* voyage had been re-created with a unique filming technique. Close ups of two characters filled the screen: the mole on the cheek of the stepmother, a lady of leisure, as she sipped her tea with her ringed pinky elevated; her painted bright-red lips as she pouted in the stateroom; the raised eyebrow of the butler in a stateroom as he filched a glittering earring from the dressing table and slipped it into his pocket. Because of the extreme close-ups, I wouldn't be able to identify the butler or the stepmother. They could be anyone.

Our girls had fleeting roles in a ballroom scene. The rich dark hues of their lovely beaded gowns complemented their coloring. They giggled with handsome young men in black ties and tails. I glanced down the row as they gazed at the screen. Movie light cast an eerie flickering glow on their eager faces. They were stars, however briefly.

Jane squeezed my arm, and I glanced back at the screen. The camera closed in on the flaming red curls of an enthusiastic dancer, bouncing amid a lively crowd of third-class passengers, clapping. The girls jostled one another and pointed at the screen too. Mrs. C?

We followed the family through their adventures and mishaps. When the oldest son, a handsome sixteen-year-old, discovered the family butler stealing from a neighboring cabin, he turned him into the authorities; however, the ship's officer released him into the custody of the boy's stepmother.

Just before the sinking, a close-up of the rough red hand of a working-class mother, gently soothing the forehead of her tow-headed daughter, panned out, rotating, spinning, allowing us to view the mother and daughter coming to grips with their destiny as the dark blue-green water swirled at their feet.

I never saw the butler's face, but I recognized the voice. "So you're the little bastard who turned me over to be grilled by the constabulary. You'll get yours," were the last words spoken by the character Damon Hastings played before the sixteen-year-old shackled him to his lascivious stepmother, the butler's lover. The son made certain the conniving coconspirators went down with the ship, to the uproarious applause of the audience. As the ship sank, the boy stood triumphantly on the tilting deck, saluting his father in a final gesture of farewell. The desolate man cuddled his three tear-streaked children as they completed their journey to the New World and gazed at the Statue of Liberty raising her torch against an impossibly wondrous skyline.

The final scene depicted the butler's white-gloved hand clawing at a gaudy turquoise ring on the manicured fingers of the wicked stepmother as they slowly sank from view. We cheered and sighed. We swooned and cried.

As we exited the theater, the mood of our group was surprisingly animated given the gravity of the ship's demise. Then again, some of the good guys made it. Our charges talked nonstop about the ballroom scene. Finally viewing the film in its entirety, I found it enchanting, colorful and poignant. I might have even seen my hands grating chocolate. And I better understood what Hastings had to lose.

"Was it fun making the movie?" Brock asked.

"The dresses were heavy," said Allie. "But the boys were cute," she added with a giggle.

"How did you get a part in the film?"

Ashley drew a deep breath and said, "My grandmother is a friend of the director. We were just extras."

Irwin led us to the science wing. "This is the simulation room. I'd like to try a minor change in the composition of the rivets to see if it would've saved the ship."

"And?" I asked.

"Then we can freeze our,"—his eyes glinted—"hands off."

We watched Irwin enter his experimental parameters into the computer program. Accurate information simulated the ship's actual sinking, and then the application applied the new data. We watched in dismay as the ship sank—again! Irwin's mood sank as well.

We strolled into a dark room that replicated a night sky and housed a massive ice chunk. The line of visitors zigzagged within the confines of velvet cords on metal stands, but moved quickly. After touching the cold wall of ice, patrons promptly stepped toward warmer environs.

Still moping, Irwin frowned and recited, "Salt water freezes at -2° C. This is colder than ice water."

A brisk, raw chill surrounded us. We trooped behind a phalanx of patrons as they pressed their hands into depressions sunk into the ice at various heights and held them there to feel the moment of the utter helplessness and pain the *Titanic* victims must have endured.

The girls and I put our hands into the indentations at shoulder level. Cold immediately leached all heat. We stepped away, rubbing our hands together.

Jane admired the huge wall. "I'd like to try that." She pointed to a copy of the enlarged photo taken of Bruckner. He'd reached his elevated handholds by way of a stepladder. Shock registered on my face, and Jane laughed. "Guys, some help here?"

Brock and Irwin interlaced their fingers for her to step into. Stretching with all her might, she barely reached the indentations but held her hands there. "Time me." She offered a toothy grin as she looked down at us and held out much longer than anyone else. I snapped a quick photo.

The girls' eyes were glued to Ashley's phone screen. "Thirty-eight, thirty-nine, forty," they recited in a crescendo of excitement.

Finally, Jane grimaced and pulled her hands away. The boys gently lowered her. She groaned and she stuck her hands under her arms.

We exited through the gift shop and came away with an

armload of knickknacks and doodads, pens and puzzles, a book describing taking tea on the ship, key rings, and postcards, each of us bringing a bit of the *Titanic* home with us. I purchased a piece of coal brought up from the floor of the Atlantic Ocean at the site of the sinking, complete with a certificate of authenticity. Even the merchandise bag was a souvenir, a stiff reusable frosty white bag with "*Bruckner's New Titanic Exhibit*" inked on the side next to a blue four-funneled ship. Lorelei would be proud.

Jane had a funny look on her face as we climbed into the car. "What?" I asked.

"I enjoyed the film much better this time around," she said. "Robert has quite an eye for the unusual and profound, a great director." She sighed. "But he's still a self-centered cad."

Incessant chatter bounced off the walls as each of us recalled our favorite part of the day. Said chatter ceased when we pulled into the 1950s-style drive-in and contemplated our fast-food choices.

The waitstaff attended to us through a radio then rolled over on skates and hooked our order tray on the driver's window.

Jane popped another antacid from her bottle. She whispered, "Better safe than sorry."

I took a photo of the two-fisted eaters for our archives before the food vanished. As we dined, Jane furiously jotted something on a piece of paper she had pulled from her bag. She passed it to the rear and the students, in turn, passed it among themselves, one hand never loosening its grip on supper.

"I don't get it," said Brock. "Is this supposed to mean something?" Jane nodded.

"Me, neither," Brenna and Allie said simultaneously, looking befuddled.

Irwin scrunched his forehead in concentration, attempting to demystify the riddle.

"I think I get it," Ashley said quietly.

Irwin's features relaxed and he sighed. "Me too." He added, "Ladies first."

She was pleasantly surprised by the token Jane gave her for correctly solving the riddle. Interlocking wooden puzzle pieces fit together to form a replica of the *Titanic*, Jane's purchase from the gift shop. Curious about the piece of paper, I asked, "May I see it?" It read:

"What expression is represented here?

It It It ...

Brock=himselfhimselfhimselfhimself

Ashley=herselfherself

Irwin=himselfhimselfhimselfhimself

Allie=herself

Andrew=himselfhimselfhimselfhimself

Brenna=herselfherselfherself"

I chuckled at the appropriate brainteaser for the day, and caught Irwin's scowl in the rear-view mirror. "Irwin," I said, "next time you get to go first."

CHAPTER TWENTY-SIX

We returned to Columbia early enough for my students to get into a bit of weekend mischief. They had transportation waiting in the parking lot, so after brief thank-yous and spirited goodbyes, they bolted. Jane called Drew, and excited to get home, she also tore out of the lot.

Daylight waned, and as I maneuvered my tired body into the driver's seat of my car, I noticed another vehicle in the L-shaped parking lot, around the corner of the building and partially blocked from view. I could've sworn someone sat in the driver's seat. I peered across the parking lot and thought I saw the door on the far side of the car open and a figure emerge, but the overhead light in the car didn't blink on. I locked my doors and bobbled my keys to the floor; I reached down and searched for them, and when I popped back up, the vehicle had vanished.

I called Pete. I waited—one ring, two rings, three rings. He was never around when I needed him. "Strike three," I lamented.

"Katie? Strike three?"

I hadn't realized the phone had stopped ringing. "Sorry. Just babbling. Would you still like to have that pizza or something? I'm just leaving the school parking lot."

I started the car and kept an eye out for movement, but my overstimulated imagination must have played a trick on me. I had to ask him to repeat what he'd said—twice.

"I thought we'd have it delivered to my place. What kind of pizza do you like?"

"I'll eat anything but ghost peppers." I threw my car into gear and I squealed out of the lot.

"No need to rush. I'm sure it'll take Pizza Party at least thirty minutes. Why don't you bring Maverick? We can take him for a walk."

"I'll do that. Thanks," I spluttered.

Disappointed in myself, I hadn't even asked if I could bring anything, but wine surely would be welcome. I grabbed Maverick and a bottle of Zinfandel.

Maverick thumped his tail and jumped into the rear seat, panting and wriggling, craving human interaction. He tried so hard to please.

I considered Pete's directions and continued to peek at my rear-view mirror. I parked my car on the street outside his house, took one more look around, and carried the bottle of wine in one hand, Maverick's leash in the other.

The bell chimed on the white two-story home. Rich gold chrysanthemums sat primly in the window boxes. Terra cotta pots filled with all kinds of flora festooned a manicured lawn. My nerves jangled as I rang the bell again.

"Coming," I heard. The door opened, and there he stood—black t-shirt, black jeans, bare feet, and the widest smile I'd seen in a long time. "Come on in."

"This is for you." I handed him the bottle of wine.

"Thanks." Pete read the label, nodded approvingly, and ushered me in. I glanced back to make sure I wasn't followed. After letting Maverick sniff his hand, Pete scratched under his collar and won, again, Maverick's undying affection. He unclipped the leash. Maverick wagged his tail as he followed at Pete's heels.

"You need a dog," I said, fishing again.

"I'm not home enough to care for a dog, although maybe someday." He paused and said, "I ordered meat lovers. I hope that's okay."

"Sounds great," I said. I dropped my keys into my bag and set it on the entry table. Then we headed into the living room.

"How was your field trip?"

At the mention of our excursion, tension eased from my shoulders, and I lowered myself to the floor. Pete opened the bottle of wine and set it on the coffee table. He pulled one wineglass from a built-in corner cupboard. "I'm on backup call." He opened the bottle of wine and set in on the coffee table to breathe. As we sat on the plush rug in his sparsely furnished living room, Maverick circled three times, plopped down, and curled up between us, and I recapped the day's events.

Fascinated by the detailed re-creations of the *Titanic* rooms, Pete asked in-depth questions. "Would you go again?" I nodded. "How was Ashley?"

"She seems to be coping well. Her grandmother donated our tickets. But ..." I paused. "Jane and I found letters that Samantha McCoy helped authenticate, and we were afraid seeing Samantha's name might upset Ashley, so we led the students away from the showcase before viewing the movie. I read an article about the sale of a violin owned by one of the *Titanic* musicians. It sold at auction for six figures. I'll bet those letters are worth a bundle too.

"You should have seen the excitement on the kids' faces when the girls appeared on screen. Their dresses were gorgeous. And speaking of clothes, can you recommend a good dry cleaner?" I asked, changing the subject too many times to count.

"I don't wear clothes to work," he said.

I exaggerated a gasp and watched as he turned the words over in his mind and heard the same thing I'd heard.

"I mean, I take my clothes off when I get to work." I snickered and raised an eyebrow. He turned scarlet. He was adorable when flustered. "I mostly wear scrubs." His dimple deepened.

He solved Jane's brainteaser. "Very appropriate. 'It's every man for himself.'"

"Any news on Mr. Condive?"

"His death has been ruled a homicide." That I already knew and I almost rolled my eyes.

"Do you think Hastings had anything to do with the death?"

Pete cocked his head.

"He had words with Condive about an estate sale." I paused. "Or Elaine Cartwright?"

Pete furrowed his brow and said, "I've known Elaine forever and I don't think she has it in her."

"But he fired her?" I paused again. "And Samantha had a heated discussion with him about an old sea trunk." Pete made no comment. "I heard that Condive played a cruel joke on his son, David."

"David? David lives in Wyoming and came home for the funeral. How do you know these things? Why do you know them?" Pete shook his head.

"If I were a member of his family, I'd want to know who killed him. And, well, Maverick found his body and I feel responsible in a way." I knew how horrible the heartbreak of losing a loved one could be. If I could help, I would.

"You were in the wrong place at the wrong time."

"Or the right place at the right time. What if he'd never been found?" I sounded defensive.

"I'm sure they'll catch the guy." Then he surprised me with a question out of left field. "What was strike one?"

Honesty would be best. "You weren't there to remove my stitches." He started to speak but I muddled through. "I read about your emergency. And I was able to step back and figure out what kind of relationship…" The air in the room stilled. "Friendship we could look forward to."

The gentle smile on his face made me look away. Saved by the doorbell. "Pizza." I breathed a sigh of relief.

He returned, toting a can of soda and the red-and-white checked box to the scarred coffee table along with a roll of paper towels to serve as both plates and napkins. As we nibbled delicious melted cheese wrapped around spicy sausage and pepperoni, I thought I'd somehow avoided explaining the strikes. No such luck.

"Let me tell you what I think strike two was." Wheels spun behind those liquid chocolate eyes, and he said, "When I blew by you on the bike path?"

I nodded. "But you were only doing what you had to do."

"These are my people," he said. "I'm sorry, though.

I should've at least stopped to tell you I'd been called in. What a dolt!"

He poured me a glass of wine and a glass of soda for himself. I chewed slowly, savoring small bites, enjoying the company until he asked, "And tonight? Strike three?"

"I was sure you were going to blow me off again," I stammered. "You didn't answer the phone, and I figured you'd forgotten or something."

Pete wore a quizzical look. "Katie, I don't think it rang more than three times. I'm usually quite attached to my phone, as you know."

I didn't want him to think I was another one of those high-maintenance females. "After Jane left, I sat alone in the parking lot and thought I saw someone getting out of a car. I was in a hurry to leave, and it just felt like you took forever to answer."

"Did you recognize the car? Do you think you've ever seen it before?"

"I don't know if anyone was even there."

"So, no strike three?"

"Definitely not!"

I chewed thoughtfully. "Do you think the drugs are related to the *Titanic* exhibit?"

"Why would you think that?"

"Elaine brought it up and—"

"She means well but she's a little…eccentric."

We clinked glasses and our knuckles met with a tingle. I drew back.

"Wild Thing" burst from his cell phone. Pete grimaced, unfolded his lanky body, and reached for his phone.

"Excuse me."

The earnestness in his voice and his movement out

of earshot convinced me that our supper was over. As I rethought strike three, Pete looked my way and vigorously shook his head. Sighing at what might have been, I reached to cork the wine, but instead, knocked over the bottle and it crashed into my glass, splattering garnet everywhere. I grabbed paper towels to sop up the liquid before ruining the rug and sofa.

Maverick bowed his head to lap up the juice.

"Leave it, Maverick," I hissed. "Sorry," I added.

He settled back onto the floor, and I continued to soak up the wine. I glanced at Pete with an apologetic look, and although his voice was serious, his eyes were laughing. He held out a bottle of wine remover. I grabbed it, read the directions, and applied it to the rug and the sofa. It worked pretty well. Then I began to clean up the remains of our meal. I stopped, holding the pizza box in midair, and waited.

Pete ended the call and grabbed the box. "I've got a broken femur to attend to. I'm so sorry. No strike three?"

I furrowed my brow, pretending to think intensely, and heaved a great sigh. "Of course not."

* * *

With my plans awry, I took a drive through the quiet streets of Columbia. Beautiful homes surrounded Lake Monongalia, and I aimed my car toward the intersection of Ivy and Lake. As I rounded the corner, my headlights reflected off the grille of the Bailey's Electric. I parked across the street. "I can do this. I'll just knock on the door and ask the owner if I can bring the kids to see the car." I sucked in a big breath of air, and Maverick barked. I scratched behind his ears and said, "I'll be right back."

I walked through the stone pillars that adorned the drive of an imposing home situated on about an acre of prime real estate. Streetlamps spotlighted the lush green lawn. With all the windows alight, the home looked like a Vegas hotel. I approached with a spring in my step, willing the owner to be friendly and welcoming.

Loud music reverberated around me. I pressed the doorbell but couldn't hear it ring over the jazz. I pressed it again and waited, admiring the arch above the carved wooden door. Then I knocked. The weight of the door drew it open a fraction of an inch. "Hello," I sang.

Maverick's frantic barking between musical tracks yanked me down the steps and back to my car. "Maverick," I reprimanded. He pawed the window. I opened the driver's door, but before I could sit, Maverick barreled over me, up the drive, and into the house. I chased him, calling his name.

The door stood ajar, and I called out, "Anyone home?" I couldn't hear an answer.

I shimmied through the narrow opening and stepped in. "Maverick," I hissed. "Come."

Locard's principle states that it's impossible for a criminal to act, especially considering the intensity of a crime, without leaving traces of his/her presence. I wanted to leave as little trace as possible.

Bright lights illuminated everything in the entry—the ceramic tile floor, the tan walls, a wilting Ficus in the corner, and shelves housing a stash of headgear: ball caps, tams, stocking caps, a cowboy hat, and a felt hat with a dark band. I crept up the stairs of the split level, avoiding the wrought iron banister—I didn't want to leave fingerprints. "Maverick," I whispered.

The masculine space was assembled with exquisite taste in deep dark reds set against jet black and shades of gray. Comfy furniture arrangements in the great room allowed an easy flow for guests. Heat blazed from the massive stone fireplace. Modern art pieces brought vibrant colors to the walls. The artistic flourish fascinated me, but what did a math teacher know? Stepping closer, I scrutinized the signature: *I. Clemashevski*. Is there nothing she didn't do?

I turned my attention to a familiar movie poster. The creative genius behind *Titanic: One Story*, Robert Bruckner had forced a smile as he stood atop a ladder with his hands firmly entrenched in the bone-chilling iceberg facsimile.

I appraised the beautifully furnished room with renewed interest. Bruckner's name was prominently displayed on movie posters, and I stepped closer to the framed photographs of Bruckner, his arm draped possessively over his many conquests.

"Oh," I whispered to myself. Among the scads of photos, my eyes were drawn to one in particular. A pewter frame outlined a striking blonde sheathed in a baby-blue wrap dress, sitting demurely next to Robert, his fingers tangled in her hair as he spoke into her ear—Jane K. Mackey.

I studied the room and my eyes lit upon a plastic bag scrunched on the counter near the garbage can. On the outside, the bag boasted "*Bruckner's New Titanic Exhibit,*" and I was dying to check inside. The clutter around the garbage can sullied an otherwise perfectly appointed room. I peered inside the exhibit bag. I didn't think I could cause trouble by just looking. The bag held a sheaf of aged paper, a Montblanc fountain pen, and a bottle of black ink.

An empty prescription bottle peeked out from under

some vintage-looking papers and I knelt to read what was written on the pages. The same name appeared over and over. The signature wasn't familiar, but the name Patrick Callahan certainly was.

I stood and called, "Maverick."

At the far end of the gold-flecked black marble kitchen island stood three tall mahogany barstools. Maroon liquid spilled onto the floor from a wineglass tipped over on the counter. I followed a trail of wet paw prints around the island to the fourth stool laying on its side.

My gut clenched. I nabbed Maverick's collar, then pulled my phone from my pocket and thumbed 911. "I think there's been an accident."

CHAPTER TWENTY-SEVEN

Megawatt work lights illuminated the vehicles in the drive—two blue-and-white police cruisers and an ambulance—and held the darkness enveloping the nearby homes at bay. Pete dropped from the cab of his truck wearing his "County Coroner" windbreaker, carrying a black medical bag.

He exchanged a few words with a uniformed photographer. "First on the scene said it looks staged." Susie gave me no more than a passing glance before she joined them. They entered the home, and I suspended the daydream I'd be responsible for ferreting out the cause of Bruckner's death and would become irreplaceable to Pete.

From my perch on an iron patio chair, I caught sight of Sean O'Hara leaning against the ambulance, the silhouette of his partner sitting in the passenger seat. He must have known the victim was dead, yet he oddly ignored the bustling activity around him as he carefully picked at his fingernails, waiting and watching. He wore an inscrutable look.

After a lengthy discussion, one of the officers hiked over to Maverick and me. I looked up at an eager, fresh face atop a short, stocky body.

"Evening, ma'am. I'm in charge of the security log, and I have to ask you to sign in as a visitor to the scene."

"Is this a crime scene?" I asked.

"We're not sure yet, so we're doing everything by the book. If I could just get you to sign on the next line, please?" he asked apologetically. He pointed to a line on the page clamped to a clipboard, then handed me a black pen attached by a worn string to the hole in the top. I noticed only one other name on the security log—Daniel Rodgers.

I reached for the clipboard and signed.

"Will everyone be signing the log, Officer Rodgers?"

"I guess so," he said. I watched him circulate among the other officers, requesting signatures. He handed the clipboard in through the passenger window of the ambulance, and finally confronted O'Hara, who looked up and shook his head.

He complained sharply, "Never had to do that before."

"Procedure," the young officer said with seemingly more fortitude gained by each signature.

O'Hara signed rapidly and slammed the pen onto the clipboard. He thrust it at Officer Rodgers and returned to examining his hands. I secured Maverick's leash around the chair, cued "stay," and stepped out of the shadows, mustering the courage to address O'Hara. He glanced up from his ministrations. The icy look on his face froze the chitchat in my throat.

I felt a soft touch on my shoulder, and looked up to see Pete, his face full of questions.

"You shouldn't be here."

"They won't let me leave. I called it in."

His jaw tightened.

I said, "I've already signed the security log and—I can help." Pete's eyes clouded over, and his already-tanned complexion darkened. I added, "Did you see the shopping bag from the *Titanic* exhibit? There were some old papers, pen and ink. And it looks like someone might have been practicing a signature."

Forcing a smile, Pete said, "You shouldn't have gone inside, in case of contamina—"

I said stiffly, "I followed protocol. The door was open. Maverick entered. I went to fetch him. I merely surveyed the room."

"And what did you see?"

I took a deep breath. "The red liquid dripping from the countertop to the floor appears to have come from the wine glass tipped on its side in front of where Mr. Bruckner fell from a high stool. The sink was empty, the countertops—pristine, appliances—shiny. No fingerprints." I hesitated. "The glass door to the deck is closed and appears locked. The lights are on. The fire is blazing, which could mask the time of death. The victim must have been good at what he did. Quite a number of awards line the mantel and bookcase. From your body language, I surmise there's some question as to whether Mr. Bruckner died from the fall." I paused for effect as he cocked his head, and confessed, "I actually heard you say that."

He squinted. "Anything else?"

"I don't believe Mr. Bruckner could have died from just the fall either. His arms are pinned beneath his body so he didn't attempt to catch himself. Are you really asking for my opinion?" I got a nod. "Anything you can tell me about the body?"

"Blood has dripped from his ears and nose and pooled where Maverick, I assume, stepped. Jim and I believe the liver mortis appears unusual, but there's no evidence of foul play. Maybe the blood and tissue samples will help. If we can find out why he fell, then maybe we can determine how he died."

"There is an empty prescription bottle of blood thinner on the floor near the trash can."

"He had his hip replaced less than a month ago so that makes sense and would account for some of the bleeding if he'd taken too much."

"I did notice one more thing I don't understand."

"And that was?" Susie said as she stepped nearer.

I waited for Pete to give me the go-ahead. "I assume Bruckner was drinking the red wine. There's no sign of anyone else. He didn't finish the glass on the counter." They both nodded. "Where's the bottle?"

"And where do you think it should be?" Susie asked.

"Good red wine needs to breathe. The wine should be in a decanter or in the bottle on the counter. There might have been an aerator lying around, but I didn't see one." Because of Drew, my oenophile research was recent. "If the bottle had been empty, it should be in the garbage. If it wasn't empty, where is it?"

"It could be in one more place," Susie said, gloating. "Some of us *regular* folks like to have our red wine slightly chilled." She walked inside, and returned with a pout. "He had one jar of pickles, one jar of olives, one jar of pearl onions, two limes, and a moldy lemon," she sputtered.

"Someone else could have been here," Pete ventured. He turned to his colleagues and gave brief instructions. Then he picked up his case, and took my elbow.

Pete nodded to O'Hara who shoved off the ambulance, stomped around to the rear, and yanked out a gurney and black plastic zip-up bag. Icy fingers crawled up and down my back, and I shivered.

Pete delivered Maverick and me to my car, where he stood hanging over my door. "What were you doing here?"

I searched the empty street for the electric car and gave the only excuse I could think of. "Research?"

* * *

When we returned home, Maverick and I tried playing fetch for a few minutes; I threw the ball, and I fetched it—one way to burn off excess energy.

The huge house was dark. Mrs. C was out for the evening, and in my haste to get to Pete's home after picking up Maverick earlier, it appeared I'd forgotten to lock my back door. We entered and Maverick nudged me. He wriggled and I tripped. I flipped the light switch, but the room remained black. I pointed the flashlight on my phone around the room.

"Maverick, leave it!" I shrieked.

CHAPTER TWENTY-EIGHT

The beam of light pinpointed multicolored capsules scattered haphazardly about the room, on the floor, over the countertops and the appliances. I yanked Maverick outside and redialed the last number I used on my cell phone—Pete. Since I couldn't quite put together a complete thought, he said he'd be right over.

While we waited, Maverick returned every one of my erratic ball tosses.

"*Now* you retrieve," I said, exasperated.

I met Pete at the service door, quaking. We walked up to the house as I tried to explain what I'd seen. I crept in behind him. He flicked the nonresponsive light switch a few times as if he hadn't done it correctly, and then carefully circled the room, flashlight in hand. "What is all this? Where did it come from?"

"I have no idea," I whispered.

He extracted a purple glove from his back pocket and pulled it over his hand. Then he knelt on one knee and picked up a capsule, sniffed, and put it to his tongue. "No! Pete!"

He looked at me. "Sugar."

"Candy?"

"Some kind of joke. You thought it was drugs, didn't you? I think we should call the police."

"No—I mean, what if it was just a prank? I might have left the door unlocked." It was an immature stunt a student might pull. If it was a student. Then again, it could have been the same person who had slashed my tires, who could have been a student too, I suppose. "If it's just candy, I'll clean it up and hope the gag is done."

Pete flipped the switch again. "I'll turn on some lights and help you."

I resisted.

"Mr. Bruckner's not going anywhere," he said.

* * *

The next morning, intent on saving my eternal soul, Mrs. C dragged me to Mass. On the way she asked if I'd received her gift. "And that would be?" I asked.

"I set the candy bags on your kitchen counter. I thought maybe you could use them as a reward for your students."

Too late now. "Thanks, but where did all that candy come from?"

"Mr. Schultz and I won first prize at a Samba competition," she said, placing her left hand lightly on her abdomen, raising her right above her head, and demonstrating her dancing prowess.

"Congratulations," I said, feeling both relief and confusion. "Mrs. C, do you think we might have mice?"

"What? Why?" she exclaimed, a bit insulted, I think.

"I found your candy lying all over my kitchen last night. I'm sorry, but I threw it all away."

She scrunched her forehead. "I'll put out some traps."

While Mrs. C greeted her friends after the service, Jane said, shyly, "Drew invited me to try a new restaurant in St. Cloud. Okay if I bail on our ride?"

Delighted with her good fortune, I found it easy to hide my minor disappointment. "No problem," I said. "Maybe I'll bike anyway and get me some practice." Better yet, maybe I'd take a break from cycling altogether.

"Why don't you ask Pete to go with you?"

"He had to work late last night, and I don't want to bother him. Besides, he rides like you. Fast and faster. By the way, I want details about your date."

* * *

After putting together the week's plan, Maverick and I jogged our five-mile trek. With biking out of today's plan, the exercise would be good for both of us. Happily, he romped and strained only lightly at the leash.

Enjoying another fabulous late-summer day, we skipped through the neighborhood. I skipped; Maverick loped, his ears flapped, and he brandished his thick tail like a machete. At the end of our walk, we practiced the "pull" cue. His floppy hopping back and forth did nothing to instill confidence in me. At this rate, he'd never be able to open Mrs. C's back door. He did "sit" with ease and I gave him a treat. He would make someone a fine dog. I just had to find that someone soon.

My phone buzzed and flashed "Dr P." I smiled as I connected the call. "Hello," I answered cheerily.

"What are you up to?"

"About five six."

I thought I'd lost the connection until he stifled a groan. "That was bad," he snickered. "Would you like to get supper?"

As if it mattered, I asked, "With whom?"

I heard the smile in his voice. "I'll pick you up at six, and I think we'll go Italian."

I would have to use every one of the next forty-seven minutes to finish my walk with Maverick and clean up enough to look presentable.

"There shouldn't be a long wait on Sunday evening," he added.

This time I took a bit more care with my appearance. Having a fashionista as a friend does that to you. I chose a long-sleeve black turtleneck and black leggings with lavender heels and matching jewelry. I curled my hair. I hoped the magic mascara wand worked. I applied lipstick and stepped through a light haze of *L'air du Temps*. When Maverick saw me, he got up from his after-walk, lazy-resting-spot. He waved his tail and I guessed I passed muster—for him anyway. He almost had me, until he pushed his nose into my side, drooling slime onto my leggings. "Maverick," I said, gently shoving him aside.

I dampened the corner of a towel, wiped the drool away, and sent him to his kennel. "Go take a nap, buddy."

My phone rang.

"I would have been a gentleman and come to your door," Pete said, "but I can't get in." He laughed. "The gate's locked."

"Sorry. I'll be right out." I'd be sure to unlock it next time, if indeed there was a next time. *Unlock the gate*, I thought, *but lock the back door.* He waited with the passenger door open and smiled warmly. Was I lucky or what!

"What did you do today?" I asked, climbing into the cab with a hand-up assist.

"Watched the Vikings. They're supposed to do well this year, but they're supposed to do well every year. I did go for a bike ride. Would you have wanted to go?" Saved from fast and faster cycling, I shook my head. "What did you and Maverick do?"

"I found some interesting exercises to use with my students. And we walked. How did last night go?"

"Disturbing. The post mortem is inconclusive, and the lab results will take a while."

"I suggested the first victim could have been Bruckner. They were dressed alike. Do you think there's a case of mistaken identity?"

"Maybe."

If it was another murder, the cause of death as yet undetermined, the cast of possible suspects revolved in my mind: Hastings still topped my list. He said Bruckner was a dead man. Could Elaine or Samantha have a reason to kill Robert Bruckner? Who else could there be? David Condive was still in town. And who was the elusive Kelly? For a fleeting moment, I wondered what Jane's middle initial stood for.

"Pete, do you think Damon Hastings finally made good on his threat?"

"Nope. He's filming an insurance ad in Los Angeles."

Drat. "Elaine held a grudge but she's locked up."

"She's out on bail."

"Oh. What about——"

"Let's not talk shop tonight," he said opening the door. The aroma was ambrosial.

"Dr. Pete," a stout, curly haired man sang when we entered the eatery.

"Romano," Pete answered. "Meet my friend, Katie."

He shook my hand and led us to a quiet table for two.

We ordered the Sunday special paired with a lush Cabernet Sauvignon with a hint of cocoa and spice. I read that last bit off the label and found it much to my liking.

Pete laughed as I listed the possible experiments I hoped to try this week.

"On Tuesday we're going to make cardboard telegraphs with paper clips, thumbtacks, wire, Christmas lights, a buzzer, aluminum foil, batteries, and—wait for it—duct tape. We'll learn a little Morse code and attempt to send the final messages the *Titanic* sent: 'It's a CQD, old man,' or better yet, 'SOS.'"

"What does 'CQD' mean?"

"'CQ', *sécu*, came from the French word *sécurité* and identified an alert. The 'D' was 'distress,' but SOS had been adopted in 1908. The *Titanic* telegraph operators tried both.

"I also plan to make a small iceberg to put into an aquarium, which I have yet to find, and we'll be able to see how much of the berg could have lurked beneath the surface."

"I think I know where you can get an aquarium. They're renovating the hospital, and the aquariums they're switching out for larger ones are all marked 'free.' I'll label one 'taken' and if you give me a heads-up, I'll help you move it. Sounds like a cool experiment."

"I think so too."

He gave me a peculiar look and repeated, "Cool, huh?" I groaned.

We rode home, sated and warmed by the wine. When he stopped in the driveway this time, he came around to my side and gallantly helped me down. I fumbled for my key and finally opened the gate. Pete offered his arm and walked me to the door. He took my key, and when he opened the door, Maverick raced into the yard. We cautiously entered the kitchen, turned on the light, and found it exactly as I'd left it.

"We haven't been able to track down Bruckner's mother, so we haven't released any information on his death."

"Got it," I said.

Pete turned me toward him, his hands throwing warmth onto my shoulders, and I searched his gorgeous face. His eyes were alight with mischief. He reached down and tipped my face up. My heart beat wildly. The blood in my neck thrummed beneath his thumbs. Was I ready? Bracing myself, I closed my eyes. He tapped my chin with his knuckle and said, "Goodnight, Katie," and walked out into the yard. I heard him yell, "Fetch, Maverick."

I grinned and slumped against the door. *Well that was awkward.*

CHAPTER TWENTY-NINE

Having stated to the sixth class on Monday, "Albert Einstein said, 'Pure mathematics is, in its way, the poetry of logical ideas,'" I was flabbergasted when my class erupted in debate. Every student had an opinion on the wording used and whether a scientist, Albert Einstein, could understand the art of poetry. The bell rang in the middle of the robust argument. Maybe the lively discussion was intentional, a distraction to preempt being given the next day's assignment. Even so, I was delighted by the animated yet civil exchange, an uncommon occurrence in a math class.

My bubble burst when a substitute teacher stormed into the math office at the end of the day ranting, "Never again. His first hour students were impossible and they just got worse. I won't be back." Jerry was attending a national math conference in Nashville and would be away for the week. If their bad behavior continued, someone would have to talk to his students. All eyes turned to me and I *volunteered* to do the honors the following morning.

I penned simple words into my journal.

I'll just appeal to their guiltier side.

* * *

Early in the morning, I practiced my spiel as Maverick and I made a quick trip around the neighborhood. To better look the part, I dressed in business attire, a gray three-piece suit with a pencil skirt, a white button-down shirt, and a loosely knotted royal-blue silk scarf.

My fellow math teachers wished me luck and waved me away as they joked with some students, worked through problems with a few others, and handed out stopwatches, athletic tape, power bars, and sports drinks to their athletes.

Jerry's lesson plans were specific, to the point, and easy to implement. The administration merely needed to find someone who could interpret the mathematical language.

Apparently, the last substitute didn't have a math background. She'd merely attempted to babysit thirty-one teenagers for an hour.

The first bell rang and the cacophony in the adjacent classroom doubled in volume. I told my students I had an announcement to make next door and I'd return shortly. I expected them to be on their best behavior. I projected two problems on the SMART Board. "If you work quietly," emphasizing the *quietly* part, "you may work collaboratively."

A smirk found its way to my lips as I left my room and heard someone mutter, "They're in for it now."

I slipped in at the back of the noisy classroom, and one by one, as the students spotted me, all but two of them fell silent. I stepped in front of the boy and girl who were sitting on their desktops, and asked, pleasantly, "Excuse me?"

Stepping away from the desk, the brawny boy answered in a huff, "What do you want?"

The young lady slid into her chair. "Galen, this is Ms. Wilk, our next year's teacher."

"We'll see." Galen slouched against the wall, his arms crossed over his broad chest. Angry red splotches pockmarked his face, and oily hair hung over one eye. He attempted to mask his wariness with belligerence.

As I analyzed his reaction and intention, a deep voice from the front of the room boomed, "Galen, you've got a real shot at a state title this season. Don't mess it up!" Galen shoved off the wall and dropped into an empty chair.

I took a deep breath and addressed the class. "Good morning. Mr. White is at a workshop to improve his teaching methods *for you*. You help him as well as yourselves by being respectful to your substitute teacher." There were a few murmurings. "Meanwhile, the best thing you can do is help whoever comes through that door and make the best of this situation." I wrote the day's assignment on the board. A few students nodded and some grumbled, but they opened books and notebooks and took out writing utensils. "Your sub will be here soon. If you need help, don't hesitate to call on one of the other math teachers in the office. We're here for you."

I felt my little speech had gone over better than expected until I turned to find the assistant principal standing in the doorway, chuckling. The tips of my ears were roasting and probably glowing red-hot. This substitute had clout, and I wondered how long he'd been standing in the doorway. A moment later, the second bell rang.

My students itched for news of someone's impending doom but I began the day's planned lecture. More than a few faces yawned, eye lids fluttered, and chins rested in palms, so, instead, I related the, hopefully, captivating story of Hypatia—researcher, inventor, puzzle-solver, mathematician, and martyr. With string, compasses, and lead weights, we constructed rudimentary astrolabes—an ancient astronomical computer. Their assignment was to measure the angle of the moon from the horizon at 9:00 p.m., if the sky was clear enough.

* * *

We were so engrossed in our discussion we didn't notice Tom Murphy stick his head around the corner until he growled, "Quiet in here. I'm trying to work. Are you planning to hand out more freebies to litter the school?" His glower subdued my science club students. Then he chuckled. "You should see your faces. I was just kidding. What're you doing?" He stepped into the room.

Stunned, at first no one spoke. Then Brock looked both ways, as if crossing a busy street. "Well, Coach, we're learning about latitude and longitude and measurement." He pulled *The Librarian Who Measured the Earth* off the shelf and thumbed through some of the pages. "We're reading about scientists and mathematicians and talking about geocaching."

Brenna said, "It's like a high-tech scavenger hunt using a GPS—that's Global Positioning…" She looked to her friends for help.

"System," Lorelei said, a frown on her face.

"We're going to hide our own cache if we can find a good location and the right container."

"What type of container are you looking for?" asked Tom.

"At the other geocaches we found a coffee can, an old pill bottle, and Tupperware wrapped with camouflage duct tape," Ashley said.

"I might have a container or two you could have. I'll bring some to school tomorrow."

"Thanks, Coach," said Brock, his anxious demeanor relaxing as Tom left the room.

I arranged the precut components for the day's lesson as we watched an instructional video, and five minutes later Brenna exclaimed, "We're making our own telegraphs? Where did you find the Christmas lights? It's not even Halloween yet."

The students bent over their task of connecting wires, slicing plastic coating, clipping and taping pieces to a cardboard base, and successfully constructing crude but working instruments.

Ashley said, "Morse code looks easy, but I'm struggling to read the online translator. Can we dial the relay speed to very slow?"

They took turns writing and telegraphing simple missives and had minimal success reading the signals. They even tried to key in the *Titanic* message but, much to our chagrin, discovered it was difficult to send even three letters—SOS—with too much speed.

"Man, the telegraph operator's hand must have been lightning quick," said Irwin.

"His fist," said Lorelei.

"What?"

"It's called a fist."

"He had a fast fist," Brock said. He stopped tapping his key, and a wide grin broke across his face. "This is antique texting," he said, and continued tapping.

Irwin read Brock's letters out loud as he translated them. "W-I-L-L-Y-O-U-G-O-O-U-T…"

Lorelei said, tersely, "Brock!"

"That's dah-dit, dah-dah-dah," said Brenna. Lorelei blushed, and Brock continued to tap out his message.

At the end of our meeting, I filled a vinyl balloon with tap water and tied off the end.

Irwin asked, "What are we doing with that?"

"Making an iceberg."

Brenna announced, "Meeting adjourned."

On my way through the math department, Tom called me to his desk. "Is this club supervising going well for you?"

"It's fun. I think the kids like it too." I grabbed at the water-filled balloon before it splattered to the floor.

"What are they learning? They certainly can't get much out of reading elementary books and making water balloons." He smiled indulgently.

I felt a slight reprimand. "My lesson plans have specific objectives." My words came out with more fierceness than I intended. He laughed. I guess he was putting me on too.

"Lighten up. You're way too serious, Katie." He chuckled.

An important thought made its way to the surface, and I asked, "What can we do to keep our students safe? Do you think we should offer a help line or provide a tip line? I sure would like to catch the creep who's organizing those

Skittles parties."

"The few potheads and druggies in school don't take much math." He shoved papers into his briefcase and stood.

"It's scary how easy it is for any student to get involved."

"Don't worry about it. It'll all work out. Good night, Katie." Tom stepped out of the office, and a quilt of silence blanketed me.

As I left the building, I spotted Jane heading toward her car and hurried to intercept her. She looked at me through puffy, red eyes. "What's the matter?" I asked gently.

"Nothing." She sniffed, rubbing her hand across her splotchy cheek.

"Jane?" I almost asked if Bruckner's untimely death had upset her, but I hadn't heard a public announcement yet.

"I had a bad night."

"Jane?"

She looked down and shuffled her feet. She looked up and inhaled deeply. "And as my grandma used to say, honesty is the best policy." I certainly agreed. Jane clambered into her driver's seat. I slipped into the passenger seat and waited. Her drawl seemed more pronounced as she said, "My daddy's coming for a visit."

"That's great, isn't it?" I asked hesitantly because I'd never heard her speak of her father.

"I'm not sure. We had an enormous fight when I decided to come to Minnesota. That's the last time I saw him."

"I'm sorry, Jane. Is he trying to make amends or change your mind and make you go home?"

She shrugged. "I don't know."

"Why are you so upset?"

"I told Drew about my dad not wanting me to 'waste my talents teaching a bunch of Yankees.'" I bristled. She added, "Those were his words, not mine. Anyway, Drew tried to get me to think positively about seeing my dad. Then I told Drew what my dad wanted me to do with my life instead of teaching."

"And that was?"

She hesitated. "He wanted me to join him in the family business—airplanes. And I knew I didn't want to do that."

"Airplanes? Building? Buying? Selling?"

"Flying."

"Then, if you like teaching, you just keep telling your father this is where you need to be. Your kids love you. You're great."

She snuffled and took another deep breath. "My dad owns Sapphire Skyway."

"Whoa!" Sapphire Skyway was one of the premiere private airlines in the Southeast, known best for catering to the jet set.

"Drew said that makes me some kind of heiress. At first, I thought he might be angry, but he looked at me strangely and said he was proud of me for doing as much as I did on my own. Then he praised my honesty and said *he* needed to work on our relationship, and he hadn't been completely honest." I couldn't imagine what he'd been trying to tell her. Maybe he was dying. Maybe he hated kids. Maybe Drew was married. He'd better be dying.

"While we were having what I considered a fabulous time, a brunette bombshell sat down at our table and asked how his assignment was progressing. Drew gave her this withering get-lost/you-blew-it look. She apologized and disappeared." Jane stilled. "He said, 'It's not what you think.' And I said, 'How do you know what I think?' Katie, Drew is an undercover agent working for the Bureau of Criminal Apprehension. He's here at our school to see if he can break up the drug ring. He lied to me." She broke down in a deluge of tears. "Maybe," she said between sobs, "he thought *I* might be dealing drugs. He always teased me about how I could afford all my clothes."

Outrage surged through me. Jane wouldn't have had anything to do with dealing drugs to students. She was the most caring, health-conscious person I knew. And then the fury roiled as it dawned on me—if he possibly thought Jane was dealing drugs, he could have thought the same of me.

"Then he asked about my relationship with Robert," Jane sobbed. "Katie, Robert's dead. The police think he might have been murdered."

"Oh, Jane." I wrapped my arms around her and let her cry until she couldn't cry anymore.

"I really liked him. I thought we might be going somewhere. Now I find out I don't know the first thing about him. And when I told him so, he compared what he did to my not telling him about my dad."

"He knows you wouldn't deal drugs." Or me, I hoped. "Maybe there's some other explanation." She glared at me. "Or maybe not. What else did he tell you?"

"He said something about graduating with a degree in education but always wanting to work in law enforcement, so he went back to school. He'd been consulting with the Columbia Police Department, and they thought they could use him undercover. He was hired as a teacher because he had the certification, or they simply would have tried to get him on the substitute list." A wry smile briefly danced across her lips as she sniffed. "By the way, I'm not supposed to tell anyone any of this. Oops."

"I won't say anything, but you might have to tell him you told me."

"I'm never speaking to him again!" Her brown eyes flared, and if looks could kill, someone wouldn't be breathing.

"We'll see, okay?"

The next minute stretched interminably, and then she answered, "I think I'd better go home now." She smiled wanly. "I've got *The Notebook,* cherry chocolate chunk ice cream, and half a bottle of wine to finish." She rubbed her arms to warm herself.

"Call me if you need anything. It'll be all right, Jane. You'll see." I hopped out of the car, but before closing the door I leaned in and said again, "It will be okay." She nodded as she wiped her nose on a sodden tissue. It came away with a little red stain. "Take care of yourself." I closed the car door and she backed out of her parking space, put the car in gear, and sped away without a backward glance.

I put Drew back on my hit list and wondered what he thought he was doing. I wondered why he hadn't told Jane who he really was, and then I wondered why he had. *Men,* I thought, exasperated.

I carried my briefcase to my own car. I found a folded sheet of paper tucked under the windshield wiper like an advertisement. I pulled it out and laid it flat. Glued onto the page were block letters cut from newsprint titles spelling out the message, "You're next." I bridled. *Next what?*

CHAPTER THIRTY

When I arrived home, I found the stuffing from one of my few decorative pillows scattered like fluffy snow at the rear entry. I cleaned it up before calling Jane. "Do you feel like commandeering an aquarium?"

"I'm sorry. I'll have to pass." She sounded dreadful.

"No problem. Pete should be at the hospital to help."

I heard a little smile creep into her voice as she asked, "*Doctor* Pete?"

My ears tingled, a sure sign of guilt.

Jane sighed. "Knight in shining armor. I guess chivalry *is* alive and well."

"Get well, Jane."

I parked my car and stood near the entry. A hospital sign swayed and creaked in the breeze. It felt like dozens of needles danced across my shoulders. I trembled. If I closed my eyes, I was afraid I would see the overhead lights pulse as I chased a rattling gurney down an endless hallway. *Breathe in, breathe out.*

Calmed slightly, I entered and checked in with the volunteer behind the welcome desk. The smell of fresh paint wafted in the air. I wandered to the waiting room and found Susie bustling at the ER admission desk.

Breathing rhythmically, I waited for her to acknowledge my presence. "Oh, it's you," she said. She turned and marched in a door marked, TRIAGE.

A minute later, Pete lumbered through the door, looking haggard. "I can tell you where the aquarium is, but I can't get away to help you right now. One of our orderlies should've put a cart up there for you. If you need help, I can send Susie."

"No, that's all right," I said in a rush. "Just tell me where it is. The cart should work just fine."

"The aquarium is in the second-floor visitor's lounge, up against the wall with my initials stuck to it. Take the elevator in the atrium up to the second floor and follow the signs."

"Got it. Thanks. Now go save some lives." He didn't laugh. "Sorry. I didn't mean—"

He gave me a tired little smile. "I know."

I followed his instructions, a convoluted route. When I reached the lounge, I found an empty aquarium tucked up against the wall. A hot pink Post-it with "TAKEN — PE" written in purple marker was stuck to the glass side. It looked perfect for the experiment, and I could have moved it to my car with a cart, but there wasn't one in the lounge. Maybe I could find one back in the ER.

I retraced my steps and followed the arrows that led

to the elevators. Rounding a corner, I met a nurse and her elderly pajama-clad charge getting out, so I hopped on and pressed "LL."

This elevator had no advertisements for the gift shop on Level 1, no posters with colorful leafy fall greetings. It was clean and utilitarian; a less user-friendly elevator.

I rode down two floors, hoping to get off close to the ER. When the doors opened, though, I stepped out into a stark hallway. There wasn't a single piece of equipment, no artwork, no gurney, no sound, nothing and no one anywhere around. The elevator doors whooshed closed behind me. I shrugged. "Forward, march," I recited under my breath and stepped across the light-gray linoleum in search of the ER.

The narrow halls funneled me past darkened rooms behind locked doors. I heard rattling in the eerie quiet. It continued, so I followed the noise, thinking I might find someone.

At the end of one hall, a single door stood ajar. Fluorescent lights hummed from inside the room. I ventured as closely and as soundlessly as I could, wondering if I'd invaded a restricted area. The sign on the outside of the door read, PHARMACY. I inched the door open and glanced inside.

A person in a white coat stood between an island workspace and the counter with his back to me. He retrieved an item from the floor and placed it in front of him. He fiddled with it, then tossed a tube into a nearby bin. He turned slightly, and jotted a note on a pad on the counter and repeated the process. I patiently watched him repeat the procedure, not wanting to break his concentration, waiting for the opportune moment to interrupt.

He unlocked the cabinet in front of him and pulled down a number of bottles. As he returned the bottles, his face angled toward the door. I had taken a breath to begin speaking, but was silenced by the creepy plastic film covering the part of his face I could see. I leaned back and gently pulled the door nearly closed. It stopped with the whisper of a creak. As I quietly backtracked the way I'd come, I heard a muffled "Who's there?" My heart banged in my chest. I reached the elevator and pushed the "up" button, once, twice and then double time. Soft, halting steps reverberated behind me.

When the elevator failed to open, I stepped through the single door immediately beyond the elevator and pulled it closed behind me. A tiny buzz announced a lock activation on the push bars, and I found a slide for an ID security access card I didn't have. The door only opened in one direction.

I scurried into another hallway. The knob on the first door wouldn't turn, so I frantically tried the second. The heavy door swung open. I entered, drew it closed behind me, and pressed the round button on the doorknob as I peered through the four-by-eight window set at eye level.

The door at the end of the hall slowly opened, and I caught a glimpse of a figure. I held my finger over the lock button to keep it engaged as I slid down the door, ducking below the window. Faint footsteps made their way down the hall, stopping once and then again in front of my door. I couldn't breathe. I couldn't swallow. Someone jiggled the knob, but the lock held. I had the feeling a face was pressed to the window, scanning the room. I crouched closer to the floor and turned slightly, easing my body as near to the door as possible to stay out of the line of sight. I clamped my eyes closed. If I couldn't see him, he couldn't see me, right? It felt like it took forever for the footfalls to continue down the hall.

When the sound of the steps receded, I pried my eyes open. They slowly adjusted to the dimness. The cool air held a faint disinfectant odor. Surrounded by spotless stainless steel and gleaming white tile, three tapered tables with drains occupied the center of the room. A black-and-silver microphone dangled from the ceiling above the tables. Arranged on the opposite wall were four square, padlocked metal doors with black pull handles. I closed my eyes in prayer for the deceased who had passed through this room.

Anxious to leave, I invented excuses for the masked figure. The covering might have helped hide the face of a burn victim who worked in the bowels of the hospital— the Phantom of the OR? Maybe the man was just trying to pull a prank on a cohort. What if it was exactly what it looked like? What if that person was disguised and stealing drugs from the pharmacy? Chest thudding, I slowly rose and peeked through the little window. I couldn't see anyone in the hallway. Reaching into my pocket, I extracted my cell phone. No service.

I held my breath, listening. Slowly I turned the knob. I cringed at the click the lock made as it disengaged, and then crept out of the room. My powers of observation were better in tune with my surroundings, and I clearly read, MORGUE engraved in the black plastic plaque mounted on the wall. I edged closer to the next door, opened it, and peered in.

Ghostly half lights illuminated hanging plastic tarps that lined the hallway, swaying ominously as the air pressure changed with the opening door. A row of buckets held down the edges of a paint-speckled canvas tarp that covered the entire floor in preparation for work to be done.

I hunted for an exit. As the door closed behind me, I heard the lock click and buzz. Without the ID card, the maze of short hallways and locked rooms provided only one direction for me to travel.

The next door led to a long, empty hallway. I heard the rumble of traffic above, so it must have run parallel to the passageway I'd taken to urgent care to have my stitches removed. In the echo of my footsteps, I hoped I only heard my shadow walking the corridor. Another glaring blood-red phone hung on the wall in the middle of the hall, looking like the Bat phone, a direct line, FOR EMERGENCY USE ONLY. I picked up the receiver.

Was being lost an emergency? I pressed the button labeled "operator." The phone was dead. I pressed another button. Nothing. Not a sound. I returned the receiver and laid my head against the wall. Fear wasn't an emergency.

With nowhere else to go, I plodded forward through the dark-gray double doors. I forgot all about stealth and charged up the stairs two at a time to the first level. The door was locked on my side. I took the next flight of stairs more quietly, the fabric of my pants rustling and whispering with each step. The door was locked on level two, as well. I stretched and contorted to the third level, making as little noise as possible.

The door opened to the hospice wing, well past office hours. I propped the door open with my shoe. I pounded on the plate-glass window but I didn't see anyone. Yellow tape crisscrossed in front of a hand-printed sign taped to the elevator door, TEMPORARILY OUT OF ORDER. I had nowhere to go.

I crept back into the stairwell. Steps continued upward beyond a sign that hung from a chain announcing: THIS IS NOT AN EXIT! *NO ES SALIDA!* I crawled over the metal links and tiptoed up to a small landing. A sign on the locked door read, NO ACCESS TO ROOF. I dropped to the floor, my arms wrapped around my knees, and bowed my head. I would meet my fate here.

Someone opened a door below, and a rush of air filled the vacuum. Footfalls spiraled past me. I tried to slow my breathing so I could hear beyond the hurricane pounding in my ears, certain it was audible to anyone nearby. The footsteps stopped and, after a few more steps, stopped again. Plastic swished through a card reader, and I heard the knock of metal on metal as the stainless-steel touch bars were tested. When the footfalls reached the third level, I heard the person stop, take a deep breath, and push open the door.

CHAPTER THIRTY-ONE

I squeezed my eyes closed, pressed my head to my knees, and prayed with all my heart for strength. As the minutes ticked by, the rush in my ears quieted. A sixth sense made me pry one eye open. Elaine Cartwright stood directly in front of me, dressed all in black, silver studs glinting in her ears and nose, chain epaulets draped over tattooed shoulders. Stunned, I scuttled away from her. Then outraged, I began to rise. Smiling furtively, she put her forefinger to her lips to indicate I should stay quiet. I did. She then turned back down the stairs the way she'd come. She looked over her shoulder and, with a nod, beckoned me to follow.

We crept down three flights and stepped noiselessly into a hospital entry behind the stairs. She opened the last set of doors with an ID tag on a lanyard, and we entered a wide corridor. The hallway divided, and she pointed down the right side, backed up against the opposite wall, and allowed me to pass unmolested. I took a few steps into the hallway. When I turned around to thank her, she'd vanished.

Hurriedly I followed the corridor toward the aroma of cafeteria food and found myself in a familiar area of the hospital, outside the ER. With a huge sigh of relief, I set about finding Pete. I walked up to the desk still manned by Susie, who seemed flustered by my reappearance.

"Please tell Pete I'm here."

"What are you doing back? He's just worked ten straight hours in the ER," she said.

"He's expecting me," I said, anxiety filtering through my strident voice.

"Fine," she said tersely.

A few minutes later, Pete appeared behind Susie, sans scrubs and gloves, rubbing his hands together in anticipation, a fatigued but impish grin on his face. When he looked at me, apprehension replaced his grin. I collapsed into his embrace, tears streaming down my face. Susie marched out of the room.

He put his arms around me and smoothed my hair, whispering, "It's okay. I'm here. It's all right," over and over. His lips brushed my temple, and I felt his heart thrumming beneath my fingers.

When I was cried out, he handed me a white laundered and ironed handkerchief. I hadn't seen a cloth hanky since last I saw my father, and I burst into tears again.

We settled into two adjacent chairs. I told him about my inadvertent trip to the pharmacy by way of the peculiar elevator. He looked at me, disbelieving. "That elevator should only be accessible by swiping a hospital ID card. How did you get in?"

"It looked like any other elevator. I got in as a nurse and her patient were getting off. I was so excited to have found the aquarium I didn't even think there could be a wrong elevator. The aquarium looks perfect, by the way." I tried to smile. "But I think the man in the pharmacy was doing something with the bottles of medication."

"That's what pharmacists do." Pete looked skeptical.

"The mask made me turn tail and run."

"What do you mean, 'mask'?"

"He wore a plastic film over his face. I'd never be able to recognize him."

"Could he recognize you?" Pete sounded a little anxious.

"I don't think he saw me, but..." Taking a deep breath, I continued. "I think he might've heard me."

"Are you sure it wasn't a surgical mask? Let's go take a look." He must have seen the terror on my face. "I'll be with you every step of the way." He grabbed a cart, and we headed to the second-floor lounge. Pete put the aquarium on the cart, and then we retraced my steps.

The elevator I'd ridden had, indeed, locked double doors accessed only by an ID card. "Well, it was open to me," I said, a bit miffed. We descended to the lower level. The pharmacy was locked. The room was dimly lit by under-the-cupboard bulbs. Pete had access. I showed him where I'd stood and walked him over to where the masked man had performed his handiwork. I tried to identify the containers I might have seen, but could only guess.

Pete unlocked the cabinet and scanned the bottles. "These are remnants from hospice patients' prescriptions." He pulled on purple gloves, grabbed a brown bottle, read "Hydroxyzine," and poured the contents into the drug tray.

Then he counted the tablets and read the number of pills that were supposed to be in the bottle from a checklist. "This one's good," he confirmed. He tallied a blister pack. "It's hard to know how many Fentanyl lozenges there should be."

He opened and counted the pills from a bottle of OxyContin. The numbers didn't agree. He glanced at the next shelf. "It might happen on rare occasion that a pill or two is lost or a prescription is miscounted, especially those that will be disposed of."

He glanced around the room. "Something's not right."

Up close I could read the labels on the container where they collected biohazardous material next to another that held sharps. Pete furrowed his brow. "The bins should be empty. They just picked up."

I gave him an I-told-you-so look.

He opened more bottles. Most of them were missing at least two pills. He looked at me and shook his head. "We're also short two bottles of Tylenol with codeine. I have to report this." He called security, and a few minutes later, two uniformed men found their way to the pharmacy. They, in turn, called the police, and while we waited, Pete helped me move the aquarium to my car. We returned to the pharmacy and who should appear but Chief Erickson.

"Good evening." Chief Erickson's powerfully built figure was a calming presence. I nodded in reply. He went through a series of questions and finally asked, "And what were you doing down here?"

I explained how I'd unintentionally taken the first open elevator to the basement while trying to find a cart for an aquarium and stumbled upon the pharmacy and its creepy occupant.

Chief Erickson turned to Pete. "Don't these elevators require access cards?"

"I think her timing must have been a perfect storm—a fluke."

Turning to me, Chief Erickson asked, "Why didn't you say anything to the man in the pharmacy?"

"I didn't want to disturb him at work. And then I saw he was wearing a mask."

"What did it look like?"

"I only caught a glimpse from the side. He wore either a clear or skin-tone plastic mask. I backed out as fast as I could, trying not to draw any attention."

I started to tell him about my encounter with Elaine when a tech interrupted. "Excuse me, Chief. Ms. Wilk, we need your fingerprints."

Chief Erickson stepped toward the forensics team, directing them to do a thorough search of the pharmacy. They took my prints for identification and to rule me out, they said. They took Pete's too, although he had every right to be in the pharmacy.

"Did you touch anything?" I shook my head. "Ms. Wilk," Chief Erickson said patronizingly, "are you sure you saw all this? A morgue can make anyone stressed. I assure you there's nothing sinister about the lower level of this hospital." He smiled knowingly. "How do you get in these situations?"

I didn't say anything. The chief lightly touched my elbow, and we walked off to one side. "Ms. Wilk, Katie, your immediate supervisor in the BCA reported that you were irreplaceable when acting in the capacity of consultant, but when you and I spoke, you told me you'd taken some time off in light of what had happened. Maybe you're still under duress and suffering from PTSD."

Breathing deeply calmed my indignation. I knew how debilitating stress and depression could be. However, in this instance, I wasn't under stress and the more I thought about it, the more certain I became. "I saw someone stealing drugs," I said deliberately.

The chief waved Pete over to join us. "Pete, I think Katie should go home."

Incensed, Pete said, "It doesn't matter whether or not you believe what she's told you, there's a discrepancy in the number of prescription meds from the pharmacy. And the security camera is not working." His voice rose in consternation. "We have to take this theft seriously. We have to account for all the meds, keep them out of the wrong hands. Someone bypassed protocol."

Chief Erickson laid his hand on Pete's arm and said, "I know, son."

Swallowing my annoyance, I understood, overall, the chief meant well.

Pete exhaled. "Thanks, Dad."

I turned my disbelieving head to Pete. "The chief is your dad? Wow! I didn't see that coming."

Pete looked at me sheepishly.

Chief Erickson turned to the other officers. "We're looking for a male—" They stepped out of earshot.

Susie brushed me aside. "Dr. Erickson, there's a trauma patient."

Pete said, "Go home, Katie. I'll call you."

"But—"

"Go on," he said. "Leave it to the professionals. You don't have to play detective anymore," He turned and trudged wearily toward triage.

Smirking, Susie followed him.

"Well, somebody has to," I grumbled into thin air. I couldn't determine if I was angrier with Pete or myself. My help wasn't needed unless it suited him.

My journal entry that night would be short.

How condescending! Give me a little credit. Three strikes, Dr. Erickson!

CHAPTER THIRTY-TWO

I escaped from the hospital with an admonition from Chief Erickson to keep myself available. I tramped to the parking lot, unlocked my car door, slid in behind the steering wheel, and steamed all the way home. Men! It's no wonder Jane was feeling shitty.

I resolved to walk Maverick, get to school early, and find a cart to bring the aquarium to my room without any help. I didn't need anyone.

Then I remembered Elaine. She'd helped me and I hadn't mentioned it to anyone. Moonlight frosted the hood of my car and streamed through the window. It was late. My information would have to wait.

Maverick met me at the door. Sensing my gloominess, he wagged his backside and slathered me with kisses, eager to please. Surprisingly, he made everything better. He was never judgmental and his kisses came unconditionally. He was totally trustworthy.

* * *

Early the next morning, I stomped away some of my frustration on a walk with Maverick.

I arrived at school and located my favorite custodian. "Mr. Walsh, may I please borrow a bucket?"

"Thinking of taking my job?" he chortled.

I smiled because he knew, as well as I did, no one could take his place. "No, just filling an aquarium."

"I didn't take you for a fisherwoman."

"Nope. An iceberg."

"Not that either." Mr. Walsh smiled. I must have missed his joke, though, since he shook his head. When I started to explain our experiment to him, his smile turned into a frown. "You may want to check your iceberg. I found a deflated balloon in the sink of the teachers' lounge and tossed it. If it was yours, you might still have time to refreeze the water."

"I guess I should have put a note on it, but really, who would've thought someone would clean out the freezer?" Bucket in hand, he accompanied me to the lounge. "That would've been my balloon," I said.

He filled the first of many buckets and carried it to my classroom. "You really don't have to help me. I can do it," I assured him.

"Actually, I want to check for leaks. I'd hate to have to clean up all this water if the aquarium is not shipshape. I'll fill it and check it at the same time."

I began to protest, then noticed the sparkle behind Mr. Walsh's spectacles. "Okay by me, and thank you."

I filled a second balloon, and before I closed the freezer

door, I attached a note labeling it an experiment. I made my way past the social studies department, but didn't see Jane.

In the math office, students swarmed around Tom's desk. A little jealous, I retreated to my classroom to prepare for the day. Water lapped at the lip of the aquarium. I added the sea-salt solution and activated the SMART Board.

Scanning the calendar to inspect the wording and graphics, I found all the messages appropriate for the day. During my remaining free time, I tried to understand how Elaine had fit into the fabric of school life. Although my opinion of her had changed, it could have been a woman I'd seen in the pharmacy. She could have chucked the mask and white coat and still helped me find my way out of the hospital.

My phone vibrated. "Dr P" registered on the display. I turned off my phone.

Many students volunteered their solutions to our night-sky astrolabe question, prompting another energetic class discussion. This time I assigned homework first. Near the end of my second-period class, Drew poked his head in. It would have been impolite to give him the cold shoulder, so I stepped to the doorway. Dark-gray bags hung under his eyes.

"Jane's not in school today," he said, and looked down at the floor. "She told you, didn't she?" He waited. My silence was answer enough. "Thought so. What do I do?" he asked.

I smiled sweetly. "What did you expect?" *Secrets have a way of sneaking up on you.*

"I know. I'm sorry. She has to believe I never suspected her."

"Were you checking on me?"

He waffled. "I was watching out for the kids to see if we could find out what was happening. That's our number one priority, isn't it?"

I had to agree with him. I didn't feel threatened; I had nothing to hide. The murmurs in my classroom became a rumble.

"She's probably screening her calls and won't pick up for me. Will you try her?"

"I'll call her during lunch." The rumble became a growl. "I have to get back."

"Let me know, please?" he said with some urgency.

"I will if it's all right with Jane."

"Katie, why are you mad at Pete?" They had talked too.

I shrugged and returned to my classroom.

* * *

When I turned on my phone at lunch, I promptly deleted the record of several more messages from Pete. Jane's phone rang and rang and went to voicemail. If she wasn't feeling well, sleep could help. Before I returned to my classroom, I checked the status of our iceberg/water balloon and found Drew sitting in the lounge. I shook my head in answer to his unasked question. He looked tortured. Good!

Punching in the number for Chief Erickson, I planned to tell him about the help I'd received in the hospital from Elaine, to find out what they'd learned about the missing drugs, and ask about the murdered men. He took too long to pick up and the bell for the next class rang. I disconnected the call.

Despite my familiarity with its user interface, I had barely scratched the surface of the SMART Board technology. My students could effortlessly interact with the data, making a math game from assignments, allowing plenty of practice manipulating problems. I maintained a school calendar and was reminded of the comp day Friday—time we would make up at midterm conferences.

Between classes, I downloaded a simulation of the *Titanic* breaking in half before it sank and added it to our science club PowerPoint presentation, along with a few of our geocaching and field-trip photos. I recalled a slide I'd created earlier of the *Titanic* surrounded by icebergs with a question I expected might generate some dialogue typed in the text box below the picture: "How could such a little chunk of ice have had such a damaging effect on the mother ship?" Instead of damaging, however, it now read "damning." I could have unintentionally typed damning—spell check wouldn't have caught a correctly spelled word—but I didn't think so. I edited the text and planned to monitor the display in case someone had access to my work—another prank maybe?

Mrs. McEntee informed me that Jane had called in sick. On my way back to my classroom, I took a detour and headed up to Drew's department to give him a piece of my mind. Fortunately, as I had little time to spare, I couldn't find him. I had no idea what I would've said anyway. What should he have done? Revealed his undercover assignment the first day he met Jane, hoping something might happen between them?

Galen stood in the hall outside my classroom, looking a little surprised and a lot guilty. Although there wasn't much warmth in his greeting, he tipped his head my way, which I read as a small concession. Unsure, I nodded back, but gave him a wide berth.

"James Sylvester," he mumbled. My eyes blinked rapidly and followed him as he passed out of the math area. I rounded the corner to my room. Printed on the board in a neat hand below the jumble of letters YAMOQMTAUCK PE TAL YULPO OY XPAJTX was "Mathematics is the music of reason." Smart kid. He had solved Lewis Carroll's alphabet cipher.

While my last-period debaters put finishing touches on their tests, I researched the name "Padraig Ceallacháin." I found a site listing the *Titanic* passengers and crew. If anything was known about a name on the roster, it was linked to a more detailed description, including point of origin, intended destination, and final disposition.

Third-class passenger Ceallacháin was a toolmaker and had boarded the *Titanic* in Southampton in the company of two friends—Johanna and Thomas Blonigan. Underlined azure text provided hyperlinks to grainy black-and-white photos of the threesome, their eager faces reflecting the excitement of a voyage to the unknown, unaware of the catastrophe that lay in store for them. With the directive of "women and children first," Johanna survived. As the last lifeboat pulled away, she claimed Ceallacháin heard a call for sailors and, having had six years' experience as a crewmember aboard a summer fishing boat, volunteered to serve, saving his life and the lives of those aboard his lifeboat. She witnessed him kiss his ring—"For luck," he'd said. My fingers often found the ring around my neck for the same reason. She thought she saw him aboard the *Carpathia* for an instant, but her maddening search turned up neither Ceallacháin nor Thomas. She never saw either one after she landed in New York.

I was curious about the author of the Callahan letters

as well. A series of links continued to tell the story. After disembarking in New York, a man identified as Patrick Callahan was questioned about a sailor who might have been aboard the rescue ship *Carpathia*—Liam McMahon, a man wanted for two Southampton murders. They'd both hailed from the Dingle Peninsula in County Kerry. The brim of a cap shadowed the fugitive's face in his photo, but the intense set of the jaw gave it a malevolent quality. He was a seriously scary man.

Callahan worked on the docks and, shortly afterward, bought the first of many container ships. He married and had two children. He was a tenacious, some said ruthless, businessman, succeeding on the docks where many others had failed. I examined a family photo included in one of the articles. His face seemed vaguely familiar.

I clicked on a surname link at the bottom of the page, annotating the Anglicization of immigrants' names as they entered the United States. Names were changed erratically. When too many Christiansons were herded through Ellis Island, a random few became Sommers. Other names were translated into the English equivalent, and unfamiliar surnames were modified to look less foreign. The site gave examples of names rewritten phonetically: O'Brien for Ó Briain, Light for Licht, Callahan for Ceallacháin. First names also were altered: Gottfried to Godfrey, Padraig to Patrick. Perhaps Samantha McCoy had followed the same trail while researching Patrick Callahan, or Mrs. C's ancestor Padraig Ceallacháin. They most certainly could be one and the same, which raised other questions.

I slumped in my chair and then realized I still hadn't called Chief Erickson about Elaine.

CHAPTER THIRTY-THREE

Maverick waited by the door, prancing and pacing, standing amid the remnants of a red sock. I grabbed his leash, and we hiked through our neighborhood. Nearly two thirds of the way home, I noticed a golden retriever and a German shepherd roughhousing in the back yard of a small house that bordered the wildlife refuge area. Afraid they might draw Maverick in, I moved to the other side of the street.

The growl of a vehicle behind us made me glance back to make sure we weren't in its path. Simultaneously, from the corner of the house, the German shepherd zoomed in our direction. The black monster truck rumbled between us, and I heard a thump. The truck didn't stop. It didn't even slow down. The dog hit the pavement. Just as quickly, it righted itself and raced to the back of the house. I crossed the street with Maverick in tow and called out, "Hello, anybody there?" That beautiful dog could be hurt.

I reached the front door and rang the bell. Missing the patient gene, I rang the bell again. A short, round man opened the door. Steel-gray eyes, magnified by crooked brown-rimmed glasses, drilled into me. His face was seamed with age, crinkled and craggy. From behind the screen door, he asked brusquely, "What?"

"Your dog's been hit! He ran across the street and a big truck hit him."

"Not my dog."

"I heard the thump and saw him go down. The truck didn't stop."

"Not. My. Dog," the man repeated.

"Maybe he belongs to a neighbor. It was a beautiful German shepherd," I insisted.

The old man squinted then closed the door in my face. I knelt, rubbed Maverick's ears, and buried my face in his fur. "Oh, Maverick, I can't do this."

We followed the sidewalk to the end of the lot and peeked into an empty back yard. I didn't see or hear anything, so we continued our walk home. Maybe the truck just bumped the dog, but I hoped the man would watch for an injured canine.

Mrs. C sat on her porch when we returned. "What's wrong, Katie?" she asked.

I took a deep breath and explained my distress over the German shepherd and the man who didn't seem to care.

"I can stay home with you if you'd like." It took a beat for her message to register.

I forced a smile. "If *you* don't show up at dance, they'll send out a search party and I'll be in so much trouble." We both knew it was true.

I forced myself to write a journal entry.

I pray Jane will recover soon.

* * *

It was unusual for the *Sentinel* to be in the newspaper box in the morning. Mrs. C usually rose early, read the paper with her coffee, then shared her copy with me. Feeling a bit uncomfortable reading it first, I knocked. Maverick pawed the door. I knocked again. No answer. I borrowed the paper anyway.

"Come, Maverick," I said.

Over a cup of steaming green tea, I recognized the German shepherd in the horrifying photo that covered the top half of the front page of the paper. The headline shouted, "Mad Dog Put Down." Two uniformed police officers each held a catch pole with an adjustable strap at the far end encircling the dog's neck. They were a dozen feet away from the snapping jaws of what appeared to be a crazed animal.

I choked down bile as I read the article.

Last night the Columbia Police Department put down a dog assumed to be rabid. The dog was reported running through the Lake Monongalia Park neighborhood with no owner nearby. It wasn't wearing a collar nor did it have a microchip. One of the officers attempting to placate the animal was bitten, and the dog had to be dispatched.

Rabies is a highly fatal viral disease spread by the bite of an infected animal. The virus attacks the central nervous system and spreads to other organs. It can take from thirty to fifty days for symptoms to surface. Death usually occurs within days of becoming symptomatic.

To determine whether the dog was rabid, tests will be performed and results will be published as soon as they are available. Meanwhile, the officer, who might not have been its first victim, will receive treatment as if the animal had rabies until the determination has been made. At press time, authorities warn that the community at large might be at risk. If an animal has bitten you or someone you know, please seek medical attention immediately. The need for vigilance is imperative, as rabies can spread rapidly through the animal population.

I reached for Maverick's silky ears and continued to read the article, heart thumping, trying to silence the thud of the dog being hit by the truck.

I finished my tea and attempted to steady myself for the start of a new day. I'd walk Maverick later. The article could have been about us, and he seemed to understand I couldn't bring myself to venture out just yet. I carefully folded and replaced Mrs. C's paper.

* * *

Allie peeled the ice chunk away from the balloon and placed it in the aquarium. While it settled in the water, I turned on the PowerPoint. We all laughed at our short photo chronicle.

After the video simulation of the *Titanic* sinking, additional footage I hadn't included started rolling. A bathroom with a claw-footed tub filled the screen, and as the camera panned the room it included an open-mouthed fish commode. The videographer zoomed in on a disembodied hand as it reached up to a tall bookcase and stuffed a folded sheet of paper between two thick tomes. I quickly turned off the presentation.

The students began talking all at once.

"Cool."

"Where do you think that house is?"

"That is so dated."

"Did you see that weird fish toilet?"

"Are we going there?"

"Was that house around in 1912?"

"Time to get to work," I chided.

Our experiment proved that most of an iceberg did indeed lie beneath the surface of the water. We adjourned with a promise of more experiments the following week.

"Ms. Wilk, you're awfully quiet," Brenna said.

"Just hoping Ms. Mackey rejoins us soon." No need to worry anyone else, but that was my apartment in the video, my bathroom, and my bookcase. When the students left, I viewed the additional video footage all the way to the end. A selfie filmed a body wriggling through the doggy door with Maverick's electronic remote collar gripped in her hand. I vowed to find out why an amused Elaine Cartwright presumed she could waltz into my apartment. At the hospital, her assistance had been invaluable. She had helped me out of a terrifying predicament. Now she had violated my personal space.

CHAPTER THIRTY-FOUR

When I opened my door, Maverick rushed by me and scratched at Mrs. C's door. The newspaper remained in the box. Taking my cue from him, I tapped lightly at the door and turned the knob. The door opened. As my eyes adjusted to the dim light in the empty kitchen, my stomach rumbled, and I realized, with contrition, how much I'd come to rely on Mrs. C's gastronomical delicacies. As I stepped in and called to her, Maverick sped past me.

"Maverick," I admonished, but he didn't return to my side.

"Mrs. C?" I called. I passed through the kitchen into the adjoining room. Pages of music lay scattered on the piano bench and the floor next to it. Pieces of what may have been a glass figurine crunched beneath my feet. The room was dark, the blinds drawn. I flipped the light switch. Bathed in the golden glow, Maverick's black coat looked bronze. He sat still, his head lying heavily on the couch. Dwarfed by the enormous quilted cushions, Mrs. C, still in her dancing clothes, nestled into the sofa, one hand scratching behind Maverick's ear, the other clasping a pencil drawing.

"Bobby's gone," she said, zapped of feeling.

"Bobby?"

"Robert." She lifted the drawing. The *Titanic* rose.

"I'm so sorry, Mrs. C." I knelt next to her. Robert Bruckner, Bobby, had been Mrs. Clemashevski's art student, whose drawing she cherished.

"After retiring, I began painting again," she said, "and I finally finished a piece to give him in return for all he'd done for me." She closed her puffy red eyes.

"What can I do?" She shook her head. "Can I fix you something to eat?" She shrugged. I cued Maverick to come, but he stayed by her side and nuzzled her hand for more caresses, guarding her heart.

I slid one of my peanut butter, banana, and honey sandwiches into a Ziploc bag and set it on the shelf of her refrigerator next to a carton of yogurt for whenever she was ready to eat. Then I closed the door on the two of them.

In my own apartment, I scoured the bookcase filmed in the video and discovered a pink sheet of unlined notepaper folded in half. I opened it and read an unintelligible jumble of letters: ZAWBWYC FEZABFEZ W1. It was a message I had every intention of decoding. I called Drew.

He answered tersely on the first ring. "What?"

My hackles went on alert. "Hello to you too."

Immediately penitent, he said, "I'm sorry."

"Did you see Jane?" When he didn't answer, I asked, "Are you in the middle of something?"

Drew's voice was rough. "Jane's in surgery. She's bleeding internally, and they can't seem to get it to stop. Can you come to the hospital?"

"What?" I asked, but he'd already hung up.

I stared at the phone in my hand, willing Drew to recant his words. I shoved Elaine's note into my pocket and flew out the door.

When I arrived at the hospital, I slammed the gearshift into park and raced to the information desk, smothering my fear of hospitals by necessity. Winded, I asked, "Can you please direct me to the surgical waiting room?"

The white-haired woman smiled sweetly. "Left, around the corner to the end of the hall, dear."

I found Drew pacing.

His tall frame flopped into an ugly orange vinyl chair and he dropped his head into his hands. Looking up at me with swollen eyes, he replied, "She didn't answer my calls. I went over to apologize and pounded on the door. I acted crazy. I went around and looked in the windows. I thought maybe she left, and then I saw her lying on the floor. So I broke in."

He took a moment to collect his thoughts. "I called 911, but I couldn't wait so I brought her here. I told them she'd been ill, and they put in an IV. Dehydration maybe, or anemia, they said. At first, they didn't want to do much else, just let her rest. I called Pete and he came right away." A slight smile reached one corner of his mouth. "Without him, they might not have detected the bleeding ulcer as quickly. He gave all kinds of orders, and they're trying to get everything fixed now." His head sagged back into his hands. I sat next to him and prayed for my friend.

After what seemed like forever, Pete made his way to the waiting room. I couldn't read the grave look on his face, but I knew Jane couldn't be in better hands. He grasped Drew's shoulder and said, "She'll make it."

"What happened?" Drew asked.

Looking at me, Pete asked, "Did you know she had an ulcer?"

"She said she was taking an antacid once in a while for discomfort. I should have known. She was so health conscious."

"She *is*!" countered Drew.

Pete sank into the chair across from us. "I'm not certain what's going on, but her ulcer started bleeding and finally got the better of her. Hey, man, you saved her life!" He punched Drew's arm. "The blockers didn't work, and the weird thing is, when they made the first incision, she bled far too easily. There is no mention of any anticoagulant in the scant medical records we were able to obtain. The surgical team started an IV with vitamin K."

"She already takes vitamin K," I said. I tilted my head, not understanding.

"How do you know that?"

"She told me all about the supplements she takes because she wanted me to take some myself."

"What do you remember?"

"Just a minute. I can pull up her text."

I handed him my phone, and he slid the list up and down as he disappeared into the surgical suites.

Drew's head fell back, his legs stretched out, and he closed his eyes. "I really, really like her, Katie."

"She knows."

When Pete returned, he asked, "Do you have any of her family's contact information?"

"No, but she said her dad's coming to town this weekend."

"With the supplements she was taking, she absolutely shouldn't have had trouble with coagulation. I think she somehow got an overdose of a blood thinner."

At the mention of an overdose, Drew's BCA agent instincts made him sit up.

"And there have been at least two other recent deaths related to excessive bleeding, although preliminary results have been inconclusive."

"Are you talking about Condive and Bruckner?" I asked.

Pete looked at me uneasily.

"Come on, Pete. Give me some credit." I bristled. "I was there." Drew's head turned sharply in my direction, and I felt his glare. "If there was a blood-thinning drug in their systems too, it could mean…" I trailed off.

"It could mean nothing at all," Drew said angrily. "What connection would they all have? How could Jane possibly fit in? I doubt she even knew them."

"She knew Robert." The photo of Jane and Robert came to mind again. It didn't seem possible she could have had anything to do with his death, but now she was a link in a much shorter chain.

Drew sputtered, ignoring my comment. "What of it? Why would anyone hurt Jane?"

Pete tried to placate Drew. "It could be a random poisoning. I'm going to compare blood samples from each of them." I think he was trying to convince us as well as himself that the three incidents were unrelated, but he wasn't succeeding. The glaring hospital lights glinted off his dark hair. Intense energy blazed from his dark eyes. He stood up and marched through the double doors.

Drew turned to me. "What's going on? What's he thinking?"

"I don't know." We sat quietly for a moment, and then I asked, "Would you like a cup of coffee?"

"Sure."

I stuffed my hands in my pockets, looking for spare change and instead found the folded piece of paper from Elaine. I glanced at it, then at Drew. I jammed the paper back in my pocket and located some cash in my purse. I headed toward the vending machines, debating whether this was an appropriate time to share the note with Drew. I thought not. As soon as Pete returned with information about Jane, I would call the chief.

Jane stabilized, and although she couldn't see visitors, Drew chose to stay.

"Call me with any news, okay?" I said. Drew nodded.

While sitting in my car in the parking lot, I fished Chief Erickson's card out of my purse and punched in the number. He answered on the first ring. "Erickson."

"Hello, Chief," I said. I could feel his unease. "Sorry to bother you."

"Hello, Katie. What can I do for you?" he said a bit frostily.

"With so much going on, I forgot to tell you Elaine Cartwright helped me find my way out of—"

"Ms. Wilk," the chief interrupted. I heard his chair creak, coming to attention. "Elaine is dead."

CHAPTER THIRTY-FIVE

I couldn't breathe.

"Are you there, Ms. Wilk?" the chief asked. A whimper took the place of words. "I'm sorry. Two walkers found her body in Monongalia County Park. She might have been attacked by that rabid dog." I didn't respond. "Katie?"

"Chief, Elaine was at the hospital the night we found the drugs missing. She helped me find my way out. I meant to tell you that night, but everything got kinda nuts." I took a deep breath. "It seems she also found her way into my apartment and left a message for me."

"What kind of message?"

"It's encoded, and I haven't had time to work it out."

I heard the aggravation in his voice. "I'll get someone to stop by and pick it up immediately."

"I'm on my way home," I said, but the connection was already broken. I didn't want to lose the opportunity to crack Elaine's message, so I copied the jumbled letters into a small notebook; I'd decrypt them later. When I arrived home, a twitchy officer greeted me with an outstretched hand into which I placed the coded message.

With my limited culinary skills, I concocted another mean peanut butter sandwich for Mrs. C, along with a cup of chicken noodle soup—from a can. She padded aimlessly about the kitchen until I made her sit while I served her meal.

"I'm fine," she repeated. Her eyes fixed on something in the distance.

I insisted she have a cup of chamomile tea before I bundled her off to bed. I hoped everything would look better in the morning. Maverick settled in with her.

"Good job, Maverick," I said.

I wanted to write about my new concerns, but I'd misplaced my journal, and my eyes begged for sleep. Hunting for it took too much effort.

* * *

I'd finally worked up the courage to decode Elaine's message when Lorelei barreled into my classroom. Discontent rolled off her in waves as she tossed a sheet of paper on my desk. Written on it was an arrangement of letters similar to those of the jumbled cipher from Elaine.

"Where did you get this?" I asked.

She said through gritted teeth, "What do you know about it?"

"Nothing," I said. I could tell she didn't believe me. "I found a note just like it, and I've just begun decoding it."

Her eyes narrowed. "What's the matter?"

"I thought you wrote it," she hissed.

"Me? Why?"

"We all know your little secret—a cryptologist. You're so big into puzzles. You've got to know what it means." Her voice took on a shrill edge. She threw up her hands. "I don't know how to do these puzzles."

"Yes, you do, Lorelei. Look at the repeating letters, just like the message you decoded in class. Just like on *Wheel of Fortune,* try RSTLNE. Then it's trial and error, hit or miss."

"I already did that," she groused.

"First period starts in fifteen minutes. Come back when school lets out, and we'll see if we've come up with anything, okay?"

She couldn't or didn't want to trust me and I could read the conflict in her eyes. "This isn't from you?"

I copied her message. It read: WVYQXZT QRWVUZYX 1Z. "Chief Erickson has a copy of mine. I'm going to give him yours too."

She forced a smile. "I'll be back."

"I'm planning on it."

Chief Erickson's phone went straight to voicemail. "This is Katie Wilk. One of my students found another message." I recited the characters and spaces.

This puzzle wasn't just a game. It held an important key, and even though it brought painful memories of Charles to the forefront, he'd want me to find the solution. Between classes, I decoded possible words for the first grouping: "country," "searing," and "stormed" but then the second set of letters was garbled. I tried Lorelei's code and came up with "himself" and "produce" from the first set of letters. "Impudent" and "somewhat" fit the second part, but nothing made any sense.

When Lorelei arrived after school, she looked as frustrated as I felt. We compared notes. She had worked out "subject" for the first letter grouping, but we couldn't make any more sense of the second grouping. She shook her head.

"What?" I asked.

"I think it's supposed to tell us where something is happening, but I don't know how to read the code." She threw me a desperate glance. "I've seen some kids with these notes before. I think it's a place for one of those parties."

"A Skittles party?"

She shrugged. "Maybe. I'm sorry I've been such a bi— such a jerk. I figured you had to have something to do with the puzzles."

"We'll figure it out. Trust me?"

Her wary eyes were lost in a sea of confusion. She wanted to believe me, but at the same time, she needed to find someone to blame, someone behind the invitations that were hurting her friends. With a gentle smile, I sent her home.

If the code gave a location, I wanted to talk it through with someone, but Jane was in no condition and I knew Drew would stay with her. Unless it was absolutely necessary, I didn't want Pete to catch me still sleuthing without first having a solution in hand. That left Mrs. C and Maverick. I headed home.

Mrs. C was nowhere in sight, but exercise usually cleared my mind, so Maverick and I did a quick two miles. I was out of practice and my decoding skills were rusty, but while I breathed clean fresh air, an idea came to me: what if the letters were encoded in place of numbers?

I pulled the notes from my pocket and counted the number of distinct letters in my message from Elaine. Nine. Lorelei's message contained only nine letters too. There were ten digits possible, and millions of combinations existed. But a code needed some kind of key. If the code was an invitation to a party, maybe I could finagle a solution. Maverick and I rushed to finish our walk.

I assumed both messages indicated a location near Columbia at the forty-fifth parallel and sorted the letters. I mapped the number one to the "W" and wrote a four beneath the "Z." If one, two, and three came prior to "Z," then "A" was 5 and the numbers fell into line.

Using the same process with the jumbled letters Lorelei had given me, I mapped "Z" with one. I knew what the answer had to be, but the coordinates didn't make sense until I reversed the order. If the number in the code came before the letter, the answer resolved by mapping the numbers in reverse order. Translating the second set of coordinates gave me another nearby location.

I plugged the first set of coordinates into my GPS. The display pinpointed a site four miles from the trailhead near the bike path, halfway to the coffee shop. The second set of coordinates looked like they'd put me in a field. I pocketed the completed paper copy.

I changed into my biking shorts and shirt and loaded my bike and gear into my car. I was determined to unravel the mysterious messages and would investigate wherever the coordinates would take me. If anything came of it, I would notify Chief Erickson. If not, no one needed to be the wiser.

"Be good, Maverick. I'll be back soon." He tried to

herd me back into the living room. "Maverick," I scolded. He barked and stood between me and the door. "Kennel, puppy," I said. When he laid in his crate, I gave him a treat and latched the door.

I had a fair idea where I was headed and arrived at the first set of coordinates within minutes. Gravel crunched beneath my tires as I rolled to a stop. I found a shack overgrown with weeds, leaning into a dilapidated barn, isolated and abandoned. Tacked to a tree was a black-and-white sign that read, NO TRESPASSERS—TRESPASSERS WILL BE PROSECUTED TO THE FULL EXTENT OF THE LAW. As I sat wondering why an invitation would take someone here, a small red car rumbled past on the washboard road, kicking up dust, jostling me from my reverie. I continued toward the trailhead.

A little on edge, I checked and rechecked my rearview mirror and found it clear. The parking lot was empty. I unloaded my gear and took off. The breeze cooling my face fought with the warmth generated by my nervous energy. I cycled faster now than when Jane and I had begun our biking regimen. My tires swallowed the asphalt, and the landscape blurred as I considered what I might find.

After three and a half miles of racing myself on the deserted trail, I slowed, closing in on the coordinates. At a tenth of a mile from the location, where the thicket hugged the path, I propped my bike against a tree, hung my helmet from the handlebars, and followed the compass on the GPS. I swiped at the sweat dribbling into my eyes.

The process felt like geocaching. I didn't know what I was looking for, but hoped I'd know when I found it. Searching for a beacon, something unusual in the terrain, I discovered a footpath. I slid behind the bushes and found a circle of stones around cold ashes, hidden by tall trees and a slight incline. I found a plastic bag at the base of a cottonwood tree. Using a twig, I opened the bag and peeked in at the contents. It contained a bowl holding about a dozen rainbow-colored capsules. One of the Skittles parties could have been held here.

I took out my phone. No signal. I took a photo to document what I'd found. I replaced my helmet and hopped on my bike, ready to break records in order to relay the information to the authorities as soon as I could get a signal or get to the landline at the coffee shop. Grayish-purple clouds churned in the distance, urging haste. I careened around and down a rolling hill and noticed, too late, some metal glinting on the path. I tried to slow but ran over the glistening silver tacks strewn across the asphalt. My hands squeezed hard and the brakes held fast, hurtling my backside over the handlebars. My legs tangled, and I had to carefully extricate myself, gingerly testing all pertinent parts for damage and hoping no one was nearby to witness my graceless tumble. I was okay, but my front tire was flat. What was it with flat tires and me?

Bruised, but in much better shape than my bike, I set to work. The wheel rubbed lightly against the dented fender. The seat had rotated in my fall. I set it straight and tightened it into place. It had been a while, but I knew how to repair bicycle tires. The pack under the gel seat held everything I needed to do the job. I started the stopwatch on my phone, arranged my tools, and set to work.

It took me two hundred seventeen seconds—thirty seconds slower than my fastest tire change. I swept the tacks off the pavement with my gloved hands and the tips of my shoes. Then I mounted my bike and beat a path toward the coffee shop.

Yellow caution tape stretched across the trail at the next intersection. I slowed at the sight of flashing hazard lights mounted on sawhorses at the junction and blinked back my amazement.

"Hey, Sean." I jumped off my bike. "How did you find out about the bike path? Has anyone else been hurt?" I turned to look down the path. "About a mile back I ran over a bunch of tacks." Just as I registered the little red car in my mind, everything went black.

CHAPTER THIRTY-SIX

Pain wracked my body. My legs ached. My thick, dry tongue made it difficult to swallow. Every inch of me hurt. I'd fallen harder than I thought. Without opening my eyes, I inventoried my bruised body and listened. Where was I? I felt someone nearby and wondered whether I should open my eyes. I concentrated. Cords bound my hands behind me and bit into my wrists. I sat restrained on a stiff chair. I heard the crackling of a fire and smelled acrid smoke. The stifling heat thickened the air, and I labored to breathe.

I must have tilted my head just enough because an electronically modulated voice intoned, "You're all right."

I dragged my lids open and found myself seated in front of a blistering fire in a sparsely furnished rustic cabin. I coughed. My line of sight took in a large picture window.

Rain poured down the glass and blurred the sagging shapes of trees and shrubs. It was stormy dark outside. Raindrops pummeled the metal roof, and thunder drummed.

I surveyed shelves filled with boating paraphernalia: navigation tools, a brass sextant aged with a reddish patina, yellowed maps, rusty anchors, and a polished wooden boat wheel. My eyes became more accustomed to the dim light, and upon closer inspection of an enlarged black-and-white photo, the familiar four-funneled ship came to the forefront. This place was a shrine to the *Titanic*.

I searched the shadowy recesses of the cabin. Dancing firelight reflected off the shiny features of a masked figure seated in the only other chair in the room. I couldn't stop my sharp intake of breath. My eyes stayed riveted to the creepy fixed smile staring out from under a gray hoodie.

I couldn't move, but I wasn't gagged. I asked, "Why are you doing this?"

"I can protect you here." The eerie robotic sound penetrated the room.

Fear gripped my chest. I wanted to be anywhere else. "From what?"

"Everything."

My head sagged back into the chair. Alarm bells rang in my head. "Maverick?" I gasped. "So help me, if you've hurt him I'll—"

"Maverick's fine."

"I would like to leave," I said, trying to compose myself. "Could you please remove the binding on my hands? It's cutting off circulation."

Memories returned in bits and pieces. I'd been biking, following a lead. I'd fallen, but I'd fixed my tire and needed to get to the coffee shop. How did I get here? Where was here?

I closed my eyes, trying to clear the cobwebs clouding my brain.

When I opened my eyes, the masked face was inches in front of me, tilted parallel to mine. Hideous eyes were set deep in the black holes of the plastic face painted with raised brows, a fake red smile, and hot pink circles for cheeks. I recoiled at the sour breath. My captor stood up and laughed, then again brought the mask down to mirror my face and just stared. My breathing came fast and furious. My heart thumped wildly and I backed as far away as my bindings would allow.

"You don't need to be afraid. I'll keep you safe. No one will ever know. This is a secret place," the mechanical voice droned.

What was happening? What could I do? Maybe, if I could build some kind of rapport with my crazy captor, I could figure this out.

I gazed around the room. "Who's that?" I asked, nodding toward a life-sized portrait above the fireplace. A striking woman with flaming red hair, green eyes, and a rich burgundy brocade dress sat in a high-backed chair, hands crossed primly in her lap.

The mask followed my nod, and with a long sigh the voice muttered, "Mother."

"She's beautiful."

"Yes."

The answer was terse, devoid of emotion. Perhaps the painting brought back painful memories. I tried a different tack. "I'm thirsty. May I please have some water?"

"May I please have some water?" the robot voice mimicked, but a gloved hand held out a bottle of water equipped with a straw. I drank, too fast, and sputtered. The bottle moved away. I stopped sputtering and slowly resumed sucking. The water had a peculiar taste, and then the room faded away.

When I slid back into consciousness sometime later, I decided I'd much rather die of dehydration than allow myself to be put to sleep again and be defenseless. I would figure this out or ... or what?

I resisted the urge to move because I didn't want my captor to know I'd awakened. I listened intently. The fire snapped lightly, and it felt a bit cooler, as if the blaze had died down. I peeled open one eye. The hideous face was inches from mine.

"Sleep well?"

I hadn't intended to be startled again, but I was. My captor snickered. I breathed slowly. I had come so far. I was finally in charge of my own destiny. I wanted out of this predicament. I was ready to live again. Maybe provocation was the way to go. "You think the only way to keep me is to drug me? Coward!" I sounded braver than I was.

"This is the only way," the voice intoned matter-of-factly.

"There are lots of other ways. Untie me. I'll stay," I argued.

The head looked down then slowly shook back and forth. "I don't think so."

I amended my plan of attack. "It looks like you appreciate the sea. You have lots of..." I blanked, trying to find an adequate word to describe the collection around me, and finally settled on the most tormenting word I could think of. "...flotsam."

The figure moved to the table and picked up a solid chunk of black. "This coal was rescued from the bottom of the Atlantic at the site of the *Titanic* remains." It looked similar to the piece I'd bought at the gift shop. "It took seventy-five years to find the wreck. My mother was a member of the crew that made the discovery." The strange voice took on a harsher edge. "But a Flanagan was never given any credit anywhere. Ballard took all the credit."

"It took only seventy-three years, but who's counting," I taunted with a correction. I'd read the list of crewmembers aboard the *Knoor*. I didn't recall Flanagan among the names.

After a deep breath, the masked face looked up at the picture. "The ring my mother is wearing was passed down from my great-great-grandfather." He reached up and affectionately stroked the right hand in the picture—a hand that boasted a wide turquoise ring. I wouldn't be caught dead wearing that ring. At this rate I probably wouldn't be caught alive either.

As the masked figure caressed the frame around the picture, the voice became more spirited. "Her stories made me feel as if I knew everything there was to know, as if I'd been there."

I took another glance around the room. In one corner stood a table littered with paper, labels, inkwells, and a large bag labeled "Ye Olde Auld." There were a number of tan pill bottles and odd-sized boxes on a shelf near the sink, and I tried to make sense of it all. My eyes wandered back to the ring in the picture; it looked oddly familiar.

The voice disguise made it difficult to be absolutely certain, but I thought my captor was male. "The sea has always been a part of our lives. We were born into it. My great-great-grandfather was a passenger on the *Titanic*." The voice droned on and on about the tragic end to the ship of dreams, speaking well-rehearsed facts I already knew, then added, "He was an augur. He told anyone who would listen about his premonition of doom. Of the more than two thousand passengers and crew, only some seven hundred survived the sinking. He was one of them. He survived and thrived."

He picked up a folio, a scrapbook of sorts, and closed the gap between us. Standing next to me, he quickly scanned the gruesome headlines of yellowed news clippings, flipping fragile pages until he found what he was looking for, and spun the pages in front of me to reveal a photo of a man with ice-cold eyes. "His life began when the *Titanic* set sail." Handwritten beneath the photo was the name Patrick Callahan—Padraig Caellacháin. There just couldn't be two of them.

My mind played Tetris with the pieces of information I knew, and then anger swirled. "Truly, he began his new life when the *Titanic* set sail. But that's not Patrick Callahan. Or Padraig Ceallacháin. Maybe his biography began with the sinking of the *Titanic,* but that photo is of Liam McMahon and he was a murderer."

My captor began pacing.

"According to witness accounts, Padraig survived the sinking and made it aboard the *Carpathia*. The real Ceallacháin was supposed to meet his wife in New York but never made it. McMahon took his place and how do you suppose he did that?"

The pacing stopped.

"McMahon didn't know Ceallacháin was married, didn't know his wife had been expecting him. Ceallacháin's wife suspected the list of survivors was incorrect, but McMahon already had assumed his new identity. He killed Padraig, isn't that right?"

My captor slowly shook his head, as if to release the

weight of a gargantuan lie.

"What else is in there?" I asked. "Tokens of the wrongs he committed in his life before becoming Padraig Ceallacháin? When he stole his identity? After the *Titanic,* he invented a new life. Did you make all this stuff up? It's likely your mother was never among Ballard's crew."

His creepy gaze flew back to my face. "Yes. She. Was. Maura Flanagan!" His rage erupted. If I could get him off balance, if I could make him angry enough, he might make a misstep, and maybe I'd be able to figure out a way to escape. Or I'd die trying. Either way, this would end.

An image struck me. The last thing I remembered before waking up here was talking to Sean O'Hara on the bike path.

"You say your mother worked with Dr. Ballard. What did she do, Sean? Magic tricks? Did she sell her female favors? Were you embarrassed? Is that why you changed your name?"

He snatched the hideous mask and threw it to the floor. Wrath etched deep lines in his face.

Angered and beyond terrified, I fought to keep Sean rattled and off his game and began a tirade of arguments. "There's something exposing Liam McMahon, isn't there? Samantha found a sea chest while doing her research. She hinted at an interesting find. She must have found this scrapbook. Liam made references to his illustrious past and maybe Padraig's murder. I saw a photo of the real Ceallacháin. His wife, Sinead, wore a locket that matched that ring. She waited for him at the dock. But she couldn't find him, could she? He was already dead, wasn't he?" I strained against my bindings. "McMahon must have stolen the ring when he stole the real Padraig's identity. And"—

stray thoughts were weaving together—"coming from a family of thieves and murderers, the letters at the *Titanic* exhibit must be forgeries. That's why you have all the old paper and ink. You forged the documents. For what? Fame? Money?"

Sean glanced at the papers and ink. His bravado collapsed and I persisted. "The real Ceallacháin could help operate a lifeboat," I said. "He made it to the *Carpathia*." He looked at me, eyes begging me to stop, to be allowed to continue his lie. "McMahon knew he'd be arrested for the murders he'd committed in Southampton as soon as he landed in New York, so he assumed an impeccable identity and left the real Ceallacháin somewhere in the Atlantic.

"Samantha figured it out because she saw a photo of the real Padraig and Sinead. What did you do to her?"

Sparks flew when the scrapbook hit the coals in the fireplace. The flames burst and consumed the brittle paper. Resignation emanated from Sean as he turned and pulled a syringe from his pocket.

I inhaled sharply. "What's that for?"

"It'll make you be still," he said, then closed the gap between us.

I heard the quaver in my voice. "You framed Samantha McCoy. Did you kill Arthur Condive too?" I raced to complete my arguments before I became another statistic. "And Robert Bruckner?"

He shook his head. Holding the needle erect, he tapped out the air and stepped toward me.

I struggled against my bindings.

Shadows danced on the windowpanes. I felt, rather than saw, a dark shape outside. The silhouette moved quickly. Sean must have felt it too. Even though his back was to the window, he spun around. He set the syringe on the table and a gun appeared in his hand. My heart leapt. Someone had to be there. "Help!" I screamed.

Maverick exploded through the front window, shards of splintered glass flying everywhere. He landed hard, teeth bared, ears back, muscles rippling, sinewy under his shiny black coat. His hackles were raised, and an alien growl emanated from deep within his throat. He took one stalking step forward. Sean snorted and raised the gun in Maverick's direction.

Without a second thought, still firmly secured to the chair, I lowered my head and used my legs to propel me toward the gun hand. A huge and terrifying "No!" escaped my lips. We connected. The gun blasted and dropped from Sean's grip. Tumbling forward, I screamed again. "Maverick!"

CHAPTER THIRTY-SEVEN

Still bound to the chair, I strained to locate Sean in the room as Maverick relished the freedom to lap up my tears. "Maverick, stop." Maverick sat with a grin, panting, and turned toward the door.

A disheveled figure appeared, steel glinting in an outstretched hand. "No!" I cried again, squirming to get free as the figure neared. A knife swiftly sliced the cords holding me. As I rolled away, strong hands gently grasped my wrists and cut through the tape securing them. I backed away then recognized my bedraggled second rescuer. An incandescent smile cracked through the muddied face, illuminating brilliant teeth.

I flung myself into his arms and felt them move uncertainly to my shoulders. Knife still in hand, he held me at arm's length and took stock. He then pulled me into a monster embrace. "You're all right." His voice was ragged.

"Pete," I rasped too. All the emotions I'd held in check were expelled in one pronouncement.

Maverick, beating his tail back and forth, wriggled his nose between us and panted joyfully. His delight turned to a snarl as a moan escaped from the crumpled figure lying on the floor next to the fireplace. Pete pushed me behind him and reached for the gun under the chair, where it had fallen. He then stepped toward Sean. The healer in him took over as he laid the gun on the floor and reached over to take vital signs. He listened to the man's ragged breathing and examined his wound. His shoulders shielded me from Sean. All I could see were the fingers twitching at his side.

I shuddered. "Pete?" I wanted him to secure the gun. I wanted him to back away. I wanted him safe. I wanted Pete.

He looked up at me and gravely shook his head.

"Is he …?" My question trailed off as Pete finally picked up the gun and stood, revealing my jailer. A trickle of bright red blood burbled from the corner of his mouth and down his chin.

Exasperated, I moved toward Sean. Pete tried to hold me back. I shrugged him off and knelt. My anger quickly receded when I saw the amount of blood pooling beneath his head where he had struck the stone hearth.

"Sean," I said. "Why?"

His eyes were an exceptional shade of green. He tried to smile, but the effect was a frightening grimace. He mouthed some words I couldn't understand. I leaned closer and heard, "You've got a watcher…"

"Who?" I whispered. His lips formed the slightest smile, and his bright green eyes faded. Then his head lolled to one side. I scrambled back. Pete knelt in my place and took Sean's pulse.

"He's gone."

Hot, pent-up tears coursed down my cheeks. Questions streamed from my lips. "What was he thinking? What's this all about? Oh, God, I killed him!"

Pete stood and took me in his arms again. "It'll be all right." As he caressed my shoulder, my fear flowed out of me.

We couldn't find any means of calling for help. Pete's cell phone wouldn't turn on after its immersion in whatever hellhole he'd found himself. He was most assuredly disconnected from his ER world. My cell had been taken from me. Nothing surfaced in our futile efforts to scour the building, and it didn't look as if the cabin ever had a landline.

"Let's get out of here," said Pete. We found my car parked outside, sitting low on four flat tires. I sighed. More flat tires. My bike had been tossed into the rear seat and looked as though it had been trampled. The doors were locked too, and the keys were nowhere to be found. Next to my car, under a protective tarp, stood a 1912 Bailey's Electric car, an empty casing where the battery should have been and a big dent in the front fender.

I touched Pete's arm and swallowed hard. "Remember this car? It was parked near Lake Monongalia the morning of the meth explosion. I have a photo of it on my phone."

"That's what I was afraid of."

"It was also parked outside Bruckner's home the night I found his body," I said.

I stepped cautiously on legs still shaky from sitting strapped in so long. I was hungry and thirsty and tired, and I had no idea where we were.

We began our return trek. "How'd you find me?" Pete shook his head and tightly gripped my hand in his, wincing. "You're limping. Here, let me help." I wrapped his arm over my shoulder and let him ease his weight against me.

We walked along a seldom-used maintenance road purified by the light rain. The lambent green leaves, shiny from the lightly pattering drizzle, rippled gently. The air filled with abundant smells of the earth, redolent after a soaking rain. Pete said, "Maverick has a sixth sense. Trust me on this, but if he veers from the path, follow him." I eyed him curiously. "I stumbled into a booby trap—someone dug a pit and camouflaged it with branches and leaves. There might be more."

I stopped walking, looking him up and down. "How did you get out?"

"I had help." Pete propelled me along the path.

"From whom?" I said, searching his face.

"Maverick." His look told me I should have known. He chose his words carefully. "Though you weren't too happy with me, Ida and I both knew you wouldn't have left your kids or him."

"But—"

"You've put on a good show, but you love that dog. After we read your note—"

"What note?"

"Ida found a typewritten note asking her to take good care of Maverick," Pete said. "Ida said you still wouldn't leave him until you found him a good home, and then she laughed and said he already had the best one he could have."

I knelt and cupped my hand under Maverick's jaw and scratched behind his ears. It seemed Mrs. C and Pete knew part of me better than I did myself. "Thank you, Maverick." I buried my face in his soggy fur. My heart heaved.

"Susie said she saw your car heading toward the trailhead yesterday." He tilted his head, remembering something. "I hope they found someone to cover me because I left the ER in a hurry." He snorted, and glanced at my dog. "When I said I needed to find Katie, Maverick went ballistic, circling the yard, barking, bounding toward the gate. It gave me an idea. At the trailhead, I told him to "Find Katie." He shot out of the lot and probably could have gone a lot faster, but he was tethered to me. When I fell in that hole, we were still leashed together. I couldn't get myself out, so I told him to pull and guess what?"

Slime oozed around my knees and wet grass tickled my shins. I dragged my drenched, smelly dog to me, his tail creating a ruckus behind him. I let him wash my face with his kisses as I held his head in my hands. "Good boy, Maverick."

I stood up in front of Pete, looked into the warmest brown eyes I'd ever seen, put my arms around his neck, and gently pulled his face close to mine. His arms went around my back, clutching me. His deep, hard kiss unleashed an unbearable longing. Then he kissed away the silent tears trickling onto my cheeks.

The drizzle was thankfully cooling.

Maverick wriggled between us and we parted shyly. Pete draped his arm over my shoulder. "What was Sean thinking?" Hysteria crept into my voice.

Pete changed the subject. "We completed the comparison on the blood samples from Arthur Condive and Robert Bruckner, and they both had extremely high doses of an anticoagulant, as did Jane." When I started to ask about her, he put his free hand up defensively. "She's going to be fine. But," he added carefully, "Arthur and Robert also had succinylcholine in their systems. It's a neuromuscular blocker. They wouldn't have been able to move, yet both sustained serious injuries."

"And?" The wait was excruciating.

"Definitely homicide."

"If those overdoses were given on purpose, how could it get to Jane?"

"Maybe it truly was accidental."

After a few more steps, I said, "Sean O'Hara is such an Irish name, do you think Sean's nickname was Kelly?"

"Kelly who?"

After a millisecond of indecision, I said, "Fiona Condive told me that her father's friend Kelly might know something about his death. Kelly disappeared at about the same time Arthur died. And there were a few bags from his antique shop, Ye Olde Auld, at Sean's cabin. Maybe Sean killed Arthur."

Contemplating, Pete said, "Maybe."

It took a while to hike out of the trees on the rain-soaked path. The only sounds I heard were faint tappings as raindrops sprinkled the leaves above us. There were no animal sounds, no birds moving. The ground was soft, and I couldn't even hear our footsteps.

"I think I discovered a Skittles party site," I said, breaking the silence again.

Pete stopped and gently took my elbow. "What?"

"Elaine …"

"Katie," he said carefully. "Elaine is dead."

"I know. Your dad told me." Although Elaine's life was cut short, I was thankful Maverick and Pete had immeasurably lengthened mine.

"They believe she was mauled by the German shepherd. Rabies antibodies weren't present in the dog, but it had been shot full of methamphetamines and set loose."

"Poor thing. I think the dog might have come after Maverick and me except for its confrontation with a big black truck." We both imagined what the outcome could have been, and then I continued. "I'll show you the video Elaine made and uploaded to my computer. That's why I was out biking. I translated the message into local coordinates, and I followed them to a clearing where I found an old plastic bag with a bowl of pills in it. I ... I tried to call," I hesitated. I felt the back pocket of my biking jersey and extracted Elaine's decoded messages. The damp paper threatened to fall apart, but the numbers were still legible. As we continued to walk, it dawned on me. "Elaine was my guardian angel, Pete, my watcher. Maybe that was what Sean meant."

"I don't know, but it looks like Drew was right. Someone issued a coded invitation for every party and each one was held at the new location."

"One of my students, Lorelei Calder, also found one of these messages. Your dad has both codes and the coordinates are in my GPS's log history, wherever that is."

The arduous path crossed over some seldom-used gravel roads and through part of a drying cornfield. We entered the parking lot from the trees, and Pete found his bike, still standing where he'd hastily propped it while trying to keep up with Maverick. I didn't know how Maverick and Pete had completed the trek for a second time.

The rain stopped. Precipitation dribbled from the few cars lingering in the parking lot. Pete knocked on one of the foggy car windows. It slid down and the driver smiled. It seemed every time I turned around, I found Susie.

"I thought I'd find you here." She simply glowed, neat as a pin and dry as a bone. Looking over his shoulder, she saw me and muttered, "Katie. You look like a drowned rat."

"Hey Susie, can I use your phone?" Pete asked.

"You're all wet and dirty," she protested. Then she recognized the seriousness in his face. "I suppose, but be careful."

"Thank you." He took her phone and stepped away.

Susie asked, "Well Miss Teach, what've you been up to? You had us worried sick, and now you're both a mess."

Not waiting for an answer, she tossed her perfect locks, and the window slid up. Susie seemed to be everywhere. Maybe Susie was my watcher?

Pete finished the call and said, "My dad was already on his way to look for you. Ida got on his case. I need to take him out to the cabin. He's arranging transportation to the hospital for you."

"No way. I'm going with you."

"You need to be checked out," Pete said. "You're exhausted. You look like death warmed over, and"—he lightly pinched the skin on the back of my hand—"you're dehydrated."

"I'm going with you."

Pete tapped on Susie's window, and it slid down again. As he returned her phone, she gave him a flirtatious smile. "What are you doing tonight, Pete?"

"Looks like we're going to be working tonight, Kelton."

She looked my way and pouted. After giving him a peevish wave of her hand, she rolled up her window and sped out of the lot. Kelton? Susie Kelton? Could she be Kelly?

When Chief Erickson pulled in, Pete climbed into the front seat, and I settled into the back of his cruiser, leaning against Maverick. My heavy eyelids closed, and I drifted off.

Pete's voice breached my dream state as we neared the cabin. His explanation about the booby trap he had tumbled into, the gaping black hole meant to maim or possibly kill him, gave me chills again.

The clouds had diminished, and sunbeams streamed through dark purple and gray clouds. There was promise of a rainbow. When the cabin came into view, it didn't look as ominous, just mournful.

The door was slightly ajar, and we found Sean where we'd left him. Papers were strewn about the floor; the fire had gone out; more than just the temperature had grown bitterly cold.

Remorse racked my soul.

CHAPTER THIRTY-EIGHT

What do you remember?"

My eyes circled the room and I shuddered as I recounted my ordeal beginning with the invitation decryption. Pete finished with the rescue.

One of the officers identified the multicolored capsules as an assortment of drugs and secured them as evidence. He found my GPS, phone, and car keys stuffed behind a fake log in the wall, along with a photo of a much-younger Maura Flanagan, flanked by two identically dressed red-haired children. I swiped through the photos on my phone and came up with the corner of Lake and Ivy. In the next photo, the Bailey's Electric Car grille grinned at us above staring headlights.

"May I?" Pete asked, reaching for my phone.

He and his father examined the photo and conferred.

Pete returned my phone. "O'Hara must have been one busy guy."

"Chief, do you think that paper and ink might have come from Arthur Condive? He collected old business supplies, didn't he?" I said and pointed to the bags from Ye Olde Auld. The deaths remained extremely personal, and I wanted to make sure the killer was identified. "There were stationery supplies at Bruckner's too."

The chief tilted his head and read from a page. "This letter has the signature of Patrick Callahan. Bag it," he said. "Maybe we'll finally get a break."

"There are more of Callahan's letters on display at the *Titanic* exhibit," I said. "Samantha McCoy authenticated them." *Or maybe she hadn't.*

"O'Hara could have made a pile of money from the sale of those fake letters, but how do the drugs fit in?" I asked.

I couldn't verify any of O'Hara's story. Nothing remained of the scrapbook but ashes.

A tech held up a bag with hypodermic needles and unidentified vials. Pete frowned. "They could contain succinylcholine or Warfarin. It won't be difficult to identify because we know what we're looking for. As an EMT, O'Hara would have had access to all kinds of drugs."

Maverick and I returned to the police cruiser. Surrendering to exhaustion, I forgot to ask Pete if anyone ever referred to Susie as "Kelly."

* * *

The Columbia Police Department and the sheriff's department pooled their resources rather than competing for jurisdiction. It seemed the whole town attended the evening briefing in the city auditorium when Chief

Erickson provided a statement regarding the death of Sean O'Hara and his possible involvement in the recent homicides. Our local radio station had reported my rescue by local heroes Dr. Pete Erickson and my own beloved Maverick who'd fallen sound asleep the moment we'd arrived home. Columbia felt vindicated; its *Titanic* story could move forward.

Well-wishers surrounded Pete, congratulating him. He stood across the room, casting tender glances my way, and I warmed. He looked fine in his customary black jeans, black T-shirt, and black leather jacket.

Drew drifted near me. "Just wanted you to know we found the bag at the fire ring, but at the remains of the outbuilding on the rundown farm site, we broke into a waterproof chest that contained a wide assortment of drugs. It looks like the messages you and Lorelei intercepted designated locations in latitude and longitude. Now we have more to go on to stop them." He smiled through his pain, running his fingers up a yellow tie with lime-green polka dots.

I placed my hand on his arm. "How's Jane?"

"Better. Her dad flew in today."

Drew smiled and walked back to Pete.

Muted comments and murmurings about O'Hara circulated dizzyingly in the crowded room.

"He was always around. And so helpful."

"—always around, but so creepy."

"I wouldn't want to be associated with a kidnapper."

"He wasn't originally from here, you know. Can't trust outsiders."

"Probably got his hands on all those drugs at work."

"What kind of security they got where anyone can just walk in and take stuff?"

"Bruckner left quite a legacy."

I listened more intently and also heard an accusatory, "She killed him." Countless other words from my past swirled around me. I felt my cheeks redden. Guilt-ridden and assailed by dark memories triggered by death, I stumbled. As watchful as a guard dog, Mrs. C reached me first and led me down a short hallway to an anteroom. Pete and Drew fell in behind her.

"Katie, what happened?" Pete's voice was tender and concerned.

"I just need a moment."

"I've got this," Mrs. C said. She handed me a packet of tissues and bulldozed the men out of the room. She placed the back of her hand against my cheek. "I'll find some water and be right back. Stay," she said, mimicking my Maverick cue. The heavy door fell into place.

Trying to ward off the lightheadedness, I dropped my head between my knees and closed my eyes, willing Charles's caring face to the forefront. *I miss you.* The last time I'd spoken to him, he was covered in his own blood, shot by a sniper's bullet, shielding me. The feeling of helplessness came in waves, the same way it had when I'd tried to staunch his bleeding. I never had a chance to tell him he was going to be a father. Four weeks later I miscarried. The blush of new life never arrived, a constant reminder of my husband's absolute and total absence from my life. For over a year, I struggled to come to grips with the burdens of loss and culpability, and now responsibility for another death threatened to drag me back into the void. The floodgates opened and I wept.

When my tears dried up, I sniffed and blew my nose. I breathed deeply and slowly, as Dr. Trainor had instructed me, and willed my stiff shoulders to relax. My inner strength tried to flex itself, and I conjured images of my cheerful husband and his calming, easy smile, joined almost immediately by Pete's twinkling eyes, Maverick's lapping tongue, Jane's wink, and Drew's banter.

I felt the hum of the crowd outside the door, and surveyed my surroundings. Embedded in the walls of the room were varied stones engraved with the names of all fifty states. A sign on the wall indicated the WPA project had been completed in 1934. Sounds drifted through the open transom above the door, muffled words becoming more distinct.

"Does Kelly know?" a reedy voice asked.

I concentrated, listening for more.

The same voice said, "I'll take care of it. Or we'll have another one locked up for sure."

I raised myself on wobbly legs and made my way to the exit. I turned the knob and slowly pulled the door, trying to spy the speaker. The hallway was empty. Either there really was a Kelly or I was losing my mind.

At the end of the hall, two plump blue-haired women were having an animated conversation. One said, a little condescendingly, "You just moved back here, Gertrude. How do you know he was a nice boy?"

"I can just tell."

"Excuse me, please. Did you see anyone come through here?" I asked.

"Are you new in town too?" one asked.

"Yes, I—"

They looked at each other, sniffed, and waddled toward the exit.

In the moments it took to locate Pete and Drew, the

women had vanished. "I overheard someone talking about Kelly."

"Who?" Drew asked.

Pete filled him in and steered me toward the door, motioning for Mrs. C to join us. "Let's get you home," he said.

"I told you to stay," Mrs. C said, wielding a water bottle.

"Hi, Mrs. Clemashevski," came a voice from behind me.

"Well, hello, Lorelei."

"Ms. Wilk, do you have a minute?"

Mrs. C touched my hand and headed toward the door. "I'll wait for you in the car."

Looking agitated, Lorelei pulled me aside and said quietly, "I'm glad you're okay. You figured out those messages?" As I thought about how to best to answer her, she blurted, "I found another one. And I think the party is tonight. A bunch of us were at the Y this morning, and I saw a guy throw this paper in the trash can. He doesn't go to any of those parties. He doesn't use drugs, and some kids are intent on taking him down to their level. I don't want that to happen." Her eyes glittered with fury.

"Easy, Lorelei. Slow down. Do you know this guy?"

She bowed her head. I could barely hear her. "It's Brock." She looked up. Her eyes widened. "After his shoulder injury, he was on some really strong meds for a while, maybe OxyContin, but he quit taking it," she said in a rush.

"We have to tell someone."

"I can't. You do it!"

"Show me what you found."

She took a piece of paper out of her pocket. "I copied

it for you. I think this looks like the others."

"Lorelei, go home and stay there."

She gave me a quick hug and fled.

I showed Pete and Drew the piece of paper with "QSKSOOA CAQSAOSY M22" penciled on college-ruled paper torn from a spiral notebook.

Drew asked, "Another one?"

"It has to be."

"Can you decipher it?"

"Yes. We have to assume the party is local, but the M22 makes it different from the others."

Phone in hand, Pete copied the text and hit send. "Dad'll have this now."

"I've got to figure this out," I said. "If you're unhappy with me working on this, that's your problem," I said, glaring at Pete.

"*We've* got to figure this out," he said.

Drew said, "I think Jane would want to help. Let's meet in her hospital room." He turned and jogged toward the parking lot.

Mrs. C wasn't pleased, but conceded. As she slid into her car, Mr. Scott loped by on the sidewalk, more graceful than he'd ever been on the dance floor. "Good evening ladies, Doctor."

"Hello, Mr. Scott," I said.

"Hello, Edward," said Mrs. C, blushing. "To what do we owe this pleasure?"

He gawked at me. "I heard about your terrible ordeal."

"I'm doing all right." I called over my shoulder as I followed Pete to his truck. "See you later, Mrs. C."

* * *

Jane's cheeks were a healthy pink. Her father had visited and the reunion had gone better than expected. There were no specific visiting hours, but we had to be reminded to keep our volume low so as not to disturb the other patients.

I re-created the first two encryptions and demonstrated the decoding process. We each took a pen and paper and scribbled letters and possible number combinations. There had to be some easy way to designate the number/letter pairs or the kids wouldn't be able to find the parties. The M22 had to mean something as well.

Jotting number and letter combinations, Drew said, "This reminds me of my starter detective kit and twisting decoder rings."

"That's it!" A vision of concentric circles spun in my head. "Think of a ring. I'm pretty sure 'M' is 2. If we use every second letter, then 'O' represents the number 3. The pattern wraps around past the beginning of the alphabet."

Drew called Chief Erickson and relayed our solution.

I entered the coordinates into my phone GPS and noted the location and the terrain on the satellite map. Drew kissed Jane. She yanked on his tie and happily kissed him back. Pete kissed me, and then Pete and Drew started toward the door.

"Not without me," I said.

"Hurry up then," said Drew.

* * *

Night had settled. Drew drove almost as fast as Jane did while I dictated the directions given by my phone. He didn't use warning lights or a siren; I didn't even know if he had them. Eventually we approached the Ringo-Nest State

Wildlife Management Park, a 640-acre refuge.

We closed in on the coordinates and Drew switched off his headlights. With only a sprinkling of stars overhead, the blanket of darkness made it impossible to see very far. He nearly hit a parked car. As our eyes adjusted to the inky night, we saw several more cars lining both sides of the road. Forbidding woods closed in around us, and the gravel crunched noisily as Drew pulled to a stop.

"This is it," I said.

Drew leaned over and pulled a holstered gun from his glove compartment.

Pete met his eyes. "Do you really think that's necessary?"

Drew checked the firearm and, with a resigned look, opened his door and climbed out. He strapped on the gun. Pete motioned for me to stay, but I had no intention of being left behind. They might get into trouble. Someone might get hurt. And besides, those were my kids!

I still stared at the app on my phone when Pete touched my arm, causing me to look up. Yellow flames darted between the trees and we heard the fire snapping. Stepping quietly, Drew quickly closed the gap.

Pete had no desire to see anyone hurt. He crashed into the clearing ahead of Drew with his hands raised in front of him. Orange and red flickered on the young faces as they turned toward him. No one uttered a word. The crackling fire flashed and popped. Drew came around behind the kids, who were still frozen in place. Then I heard the keening of a solitary voice. The students slowly turned in unison and backed away to reveal two figures on the ground. A female figure was lying still. The other was Irwin Albright. He had his arms wrapped around his knees, rocking and sobbing. "I'm sorry. I am so sorry."

The kids parted and let Pete approach. He went down on one knee and gently picked up the limp form as if she were as light as a feather. He turned and began the trek back to the car.

We heard the sirens before we saw the flashing lights. Drew stood in front of the kids and told them to take a seat around the fire. None of them seemed anxious to move too quickly, and with reinforcements on the way, I followed Pete.

He gently shifted the rag doll into the backseat of the car. "Get in," he told me. "Hold her head up."

I opened the rear door on the opposite side and slid in. Pete draped the girl's still form into my lap.

"Dear God!" I gasped.

CHAPTER THIRTY-NINE

Hurry, Pete." I held Lorelei close, marveling at her brilliance in deciphering the code, but furious for not realizing how smart and focused she could be.

When we arrived at the hospital, Pete turned into a cyclone of efficient activity. He contacted Lorelei's parents, who rushed to the hospital and gave permission for Pete to do everything he thought was necessary. I wish I could have met her parents under better circumstances. We spent the next few hours watching and waiting.

Drew appeared after he'd interviewed and taken statements from the thirteen students they'd taken into custody. "Not one of them will admit having information about who sent the original text but they know how to decipher the directions and they all knew the rules. They knew what was expected if you showed up at the party.

"Lorelei figured out the message and had shown up uninvited. When she arrived, the other partygoers had been suspicious and asked her to add whatever she had brought to the stockpile of drugs. She hadn't brought anything, so she'd been tagged a crasher. To prove she wasn't going to rat on them, she needed to down a couple of capsules. She'd reached into the bowl and tossed back a few, followed by a swig of soda. As the drugs began to take effect, she'd settled on the ground. A little later, one of the partygoers noticed she'd passed out. That's when we appeared on the scene."

"Lorelei never should have been there," I said. "I failed her."

"She made up her own mind. She was intent on breaking up those stupid parties," her mother said around gulps of air, trying not to cry.

"She can be quite single-minded," Mr. Calder added. "Like her mother."

I knew full well how single-minded Lorelei could be.

"Lorelei can be a handful. But we're so proud of her," said Mrs. Calder, before collapsing into a torrent of tears.

After central processing, the kids had been transported to the hospital. All, but one, were underage. Drew called their parents. The kids had been to Skittles parties before, and fortunately, because we discovered this one so early, they hadn't yet had time to take much. A few had taken nothing at all. Some also knew, through trial and error, which drugs were more potent, which less poisonous, and which gave the desired effects. After being held overnight for observation, the young people would be released to their parents, who were told to watch them carefully and call 911 immediately if they noticed any adverse reactions.

One parent unleashed a dragon when he bellowed, "Well, at least they're not doing *illegal* drugs."

Incensed, Pete clenched his teeth, and the white of his jawbone rose to the surface as he replied, "If the prescription is yours, you could be arrested for dealing."

Irwin Albright remained in custody. He was eighteen and wouldn't consent to having his dad notified. He kept apologizing, convinced that what happened to Lorelei was his fault.

"Katie, the scuttlebutt in school is that Albright is supposed to be some sort of Brainiac," Drew said. "This arrest will derail any plans he had to attend college next fall."

"What has he said?"

"He just keeps saying how sorry he is."

"Can I talk to him?"

* * *

Drew and I left the hospital just as the fingers of burnt orange and gold reached out from the east, grabbing another day.

At the police station, Drew, Irwin, and I sat in one of the sterile interrogation rooms. No one spoke. Irwin rested his head on his arms on the table. Every once in a while, a sob escaped. I reached out and put my hand on top of his.

He sat up and wiped his nose and eyes on his sweatshirt sleeve. "I'm so sorry." He clasped his hands on the table.

Drew pulled a card from his pocket. He reread Irwin his Miranda rights, finishing with, "Having these rights in mind, do you wish to talk to us now?"

Irwin looked incredibly young as he nodded.

"Do you want an attorney?"

He shook his head and said, "I needed the money. I wanted to get out of Columbia. I wanted to go places, but there was no way my dad could afford to send me to a good school, and even if I earned scholarship money, it would be tight. How would I get around? How would I dress? I'd be just some country rube."

It wasn't the information we'd been fishing for, and both Drew and I were taken by surprise.

"I thought you'd be too smart to take drugs," Drew said.

Irwin bridled. "I didn't do the drugs." He sniffled.

"What did you do, Irwin?"

He lowered his head. "The cool kids went to the parties. When the parties were raided last summer, no one wanted to risk hosting, so they needed a different way to get together. Everyone has a smartphone. I sent out the coordinates to invite a list of attendees. Each party was held at a new location and we used a code to make it harder to find—like geocaching." He looked at me out of the corner of his eye. Then he looked at Drew. "You're a cop?" Drew nodded.

"Some kids brought a shitload of drugs, sometimes almost an entire prescription bottle. They'd dump some of the stuff into a candy bowl, and it would look great, all different sizes and colors. Then they'd each take a few pills and be happy for the rest of the night. I'd get paid by the capsule for whatever was left over, and sometimes there were a lot." He looked directly at Drew. "Do you know how many hydrocodones are prescribed for pain when they pull wisdom teeth?" He waited. "Ten. And do you know how many I took when I had my teeth pulled?" He waited again for us to guess. "None. It's so easy to get drugs."

Drew shook his head.

"I'm sorry about Lorelei. I really like her. I didn't even know she was there until it was too late. Will she be okay?"

"I hope so," I said.

"What happens now?" he mumbled.

"Who paid you, Irwin?" Drew asked.

Irwin sniffed and looked Drew straight in the eye. "I don't know." He spun the ring on his hand.

"You must have had some protocol, some way to get your money. Who did you give the drugs to?"

"I don't know. I didn't want to know," Irwin said. "I brought the surplus to the post office and put the package in a PO box. Next day I'd get my money." He dug in his pocket. The clang echoed in the room as he set the key on the metal table. "It's box six fourteen."

We sat silently for a long time. Then Irwin said, "Lorelei might know."

Drew leaned forward. "What might Lorelei know?"

"She might know something about who else used the PO box."

"How?"

"She was always following people. She followed Ashley, Brenna, and Allie because she wanted to be part of the in crowd, and they were all really good about letting her. She follows Brock all the time. And I know she followed me. It was kinda, you know, cute. Like I was worthy of being followed. She might've seen something."

"Irwin, how do the invites work?" Drew asked.

"I'd get a text and forward a group message." He stilled for a moment then removed the ring from his finger and handed it to Drew. His eyes dropped hurriedly to his hands in his lap. There were letters on the bottom half and numbers on the top of the ring. "Most of us have one." A decoder ring.

Irwin needed to figure out his next step so Drew sent him to a holding cell, then drove me home.

"On the street, those drugs are sometimes worth double or four times what was paid for them. There's no watchdog. You can get whatever you want," I said.

"And whoever's selling them is getting them for almost nothing. We might have another problem—fraud. I've heard of meds being resold to unscrupulous pharmacies recycling the cheap drugs and recharging Medicare. That could be one hell of a profit margin."

We pulled up in front of my apartment.

"When you see Jane, say hi." He nodded.

I leaned over and gave him a desperate hug, as much for my benefit as for his.

I was tired and out of sorts, but I couldn't sleep, so I put the finishing touches on three general math logic exercises squirreled away in case I needed a substitute lesson plan on short notice. In my mind, I berated the ne'er-do-wells and selfish drug dealers who preyed on unsuspecting kids, luring them with the promise of a good time or money.

After spending too much of the day feeling nervous and impatient, I drove to Arthur Condive's home, hoping Fiona might be there, and rang the doorbell. She answered and embraced me. "Katie!"

"I'm sorry to bother you. You heard about Sean O'Hara?"

"Yes." She rubbed her arms as if she were chilled.

"When the police investigated his cabin, they found bags, paper, and ink that probably came from your dad's shop. Do you think O'Hara might have been your dad's Kelly?"

She stared at me. "No. I'm certain that O'Hara was not my dad's Kelly."

"Are you quite sure? The nickname of a fishing partner or a drinking buddy? Or—"

A wry smile formed on her lips. "Sean wasn't my dad's Kelly. Kelly was my dad's *girlfriend*, Katie." Her eyes flashed.

She gestured me inside. Selecting a photo of her dad I'd seen at the memorial, she said, "Uncle Ray was shot down in Vietnam and spent seven months in a POW camp. He was a battered man when he returned home. But he was my mom's big brother, and we took him in. When Mom died of breast cancer, Dad was a mess. I didn't think he'd ever get over her death. They were soul mates. But my mom had asked him to take special care of Uncle Ray. I think he and my dad lived as good a life as could be expected. When Ray died two years ago, Dad was devastated again. He became mean and cranky, belligerent, and negative, a regular pain in the ass, especially to David. He went looking for love in all the wrong places and found it. But I assure you, Kelly was definitely female. Just ask Samantha. She and Kelly found that trunk."

That would be difficult.

CHAPTER FORTY

After I left Fiona, I called Pete.

"Lorelei has stabilized but she isn't out of the woods. I'm staying here," Pete said. "And I got a hit on the listserv about another victim of a Warfarin overdose. But I haven't been able to find any connection with our victims yet."

Exercise would clear my befuddled brain, so Maverick and I took our five-mile path. In the hour and twenty-seven minutes it took to traverse, I talked and he listened to my conjectures. My suspect pool was dwindling.

When we returned from our walk, the aroma of fresh sourdough bread and chicken wild rice casserole coming from Mrs. C's kitchen made me smile. She always had enough of her wonderful food to feed an army. And she was cooking again—feeling more like her old self, not that her "self" was necessarily that old.

I was grateful for the company and equally grateful for dinner, which helped ease some of the disquiet caused by Irwin's comparison of locating a Skittles party to geocaching. Lost in thought, I rubbed Maverick's velvety ears and welcomed his kisses until the disjointed words floating around me materialized into sentences and I realized Mrs. C had been speaking.

"Katie, are you alright?"

Snapping to attention, I said, "Of course. Sorry. So much has been going on." *Could I ask her if Samantha could kill anyone?*

Walking toward her living room, she said, "I think you need some rest. Why don't you take a nap here?" She patted a cushion on her couch. "It's very comfortable."

I hesitated. "I need to see Jane." I yawned.

"I'll wake you in exactly one hour—I promise. Sixty minutes and you'll feel better."

I nodded and took her advice. Morpheus took me almost before my head hit the armrest. I woke to Mrs. C gently rubbing my back between my aching shoulder blades sixty short minutes later. *Already?*

"Rise and shine," she sang. I noticed a concerned look on her face. "Someone's here to see you."

The man standing in the entryway wore a short brown jacket over crisp blue jeans. "Ms. Wilk," his voice boomed, "I've heard you're not capable of tending to man's best friend. I'm here to reclaim him."

Mrs. C had a guilty look on her face. "When you were undecided about keeping Maverick, I wrote and told Lady Colton it was cruel to have given you a dog that made you so terribly sad."

The sleepy fog lifted. I pointed to the door. "Get out,"

I said through gritted teeth.

"I won't return," the man sputtered.

"He's *my* dog," I yelled.

"Then this is yours as well." He tossed a fat manila envelope at me. Maverick growled. The British vet from Lady Colton's kennel raised an eyebrow and carefully backed away.

The door closed and I heaved a sigh. "I can't deal with this right now," I said. I handed the envelope to Mrs. C.

I left Maverick rooted next to her. Fortified with a power nap, I retired to my own apartment. I splashed cold water on my face and ran a brush through my tangled hair. Rummaging through my hamper, I found a relatively clean shirt and jeans to wear. Then I called Drew.

"Anything new on Lorelei?"

"No. But her parents allowed me to look through her things. I found a journal with times, dates, places she frequented, her parents' schedules, even favorable notes about you and your science club." He stopped to let that sink in. "She also wrote, and I quote, 'I bet he doesn't even know what he's carrying. I hope he's not involved.' No name is mentioned so it could be Albright. And no description of what *it* might be. She scrutinized everything. If only we could talk to her." He sighed. "Jane's wondering if you would bring some things from her apartment. Her dad's there, so he can let you in."

"Sure. What does she need?"

"She doesn't *need* anything." Lightening the mood, he laughed. "She has me. But she'd like her vitamins and supplements. Pete thought whatever she'd been taking kept her from totally bleeding out. She'd already prepared one of those weekly pill containers. It's in the cupboard to the right of the kitchen sink. And her bottle of vitamin K."

"I'll be there soon."

Before leaving, I gave Maverick, my best buddy and my lifesaver, a great big hug and a treat. Mrs. C, looking contrite, clipped on his leash for a walk, and I headed over to meet Jane's father.

* * *

We sized each other up at the door, he in sharp Armani, me in rumpled Levis. Charisma oozed from every pore, but Mr. Mackey was also filled with great sadness. Although he tried to hide it, his eyes were puffy; he'd been crying.

"Mr. Mackey," I put out my hand, and he gripped as if he'd never let go.

"Katie. I'm pleased to meet you. Janie said you'd stop by." When he dropped my hand, he reached into his inside jacket pocket and pulled out the plastic pill dispenser and the bottle of vitamin K. He handed them to me but didn't let go. "I nearly lost her for good, didn't I?" He patted my hand and then released the containers. As I turned to leave, he added, "I love her, you know."

I looked back and replied, "She loves you too."

* * *

The sign in the corridor read, PLEASE TURN OFF YOUR CELL PHONES. I powered down my phone and slipped it into my back pocket. I delivered the pillbox to Jane, who took her ritualistic titanic cocktail. She looked so much better, but not quite fit for release. I hugged my friend fiercely, wished her and Drew a good night, and went downstairs to check on Pete, making sure I used the atrium elevator. The nurse at admissions led me to his office, where I found him snoring softly, propped up against the wall behind a messy desk covered with water bottles, a half-finished salad, a browning apple core, and a slimy banana peel. I kneaded his neck ever so gently. He closed his gaping mouth and turned his head in both directions, making his neck creak beneath my fingers. He moaned. I stopped massaging.

"No. Don't stop! More."

As I continued, his eyes flickered open and recognition twinkled in them, a smile hovered on his lips. Then he sat bolt upright, alert, as if I'd caught him doing something he shouldn't be doing.

Pete's computer was powered up in front of him—he'd been reading about anticoagulant overdosing. He gritted his teeth. "The female fatality from Fergus Falls delivered packages for MinnviroExpress." He stifled a yawn. "Another victim was a fine arts student at Huntington University in Indiana." He dropped his head into his hands, raked the hair back from his face, then rubbed his tired eyes. "I don't see it."

He paged through photos from the scenes. In the photo of a practical kitchen, a bloody knife lay on the floor next to a large dark stain. "The driver was single, home alone. She had PAD—peripheral artery disease and took medication. She severely sliced her hand trying to open a new pack of steak knives with one of her kitchen knives, and might have become lightheaded or might have blacked out from the rapid blood loss. Never called for help. Bled out." The photos showed a dinner being prepared in an orderly kitchen, a table set with china, and a single crystal wineglass with a touch of dark remaining in its bowl. The report included a comment about the unusual circumstances surrounding her accidental death.

The face in the photo of the second victim had been in

a brawl and had lost. "The student was found on the floor of his apartment, looking like he'd been beaten, and is in a coma. The prior evening, he and his roommate had been practicing taekwondo at a dojo, but not roughhousing, not working hard enough to give anyone a black eye, let alone this. His buddy doesn't show any sign of injury. No scrapes, no contusions of any kind. He was brought in for questioning, but released when all the other students vouched for him."

One by one we examined the photos from the apartment as they flashed across the computer screen. Beer cans, a wine bottle, and an empty pizza box littered the apartment. There were even photos of the interior of the young man's truck cab.

"Wait," I said. "Go back."

Pete squinted, rubbed the stubble on his cheeks, and clicked.

On the front seat of the truck sat a familiar frosty plastic bag. It stood stiffly, like the reusable bags Lorelei had inveigled, the same type of bag from the *Titanic* exhibit gift shop we had found at Bruckner's, just like the ones that held our purchases the day of our field trip.

"Can you zoom in on that bag?" I pointed to the screen.

The pixels gradually focused on the icy-blue lettering and the sinking *Titanic* logo.

"Print that."

We'd connected the student to *Bruckner's New Titanic Exhibit*. But how did the driver fit in? Pete sent an email with explicit questions to the Fergus Falls police: Where had she been in the last two months? Any indication she had visited the *Titanic* exhibit?

Pete sent an e-mail asking the same questions about

the Huntington student. While he awaited replies, even a peck on the cheek didn't break his concentration. I headed up to visit Lorelei.

Questions remained about Jane's connection. She had visited the *Titanic* exhibit, but so had I. I had a bad feeling. A question came unbidden. What did the "K" stand for in her middle name?

When the elevator descending from the fourth floor opened, I stepped back to allow the passenger out, a fine-featured redhead wearing a crisp white coat over green scrubs. The overhead lights reflected off the thick lenses in the variegated-frames. A shiny stethoscope draped around his neck, and a photo name tag read "C Flanagan." I stepped in and pressed the button for the fourth floor. Three visitors caught the door and hopped on, laughing. As the doors started to close, I noticed how the turquoise in Flanagan's gauche ring matched the blue-green in his cold eyes.

I called out, "Kelly?" and caught a glimpse of the redhead's enraged face. Not a he, but a she, and as she spun away from me, the elevator doors sealed with a hiss. Kelly bolted, disguised as a man.

Thoughts whirled in my addled brain. I was so tired. I could be wrong. Was I seeing things? Was he a she? Why was she here? Lorelei was on the fourth floor. I pressed the button again, three or four times. The seconds passed like minutes.

When the fourth-floor doors finally slid open, I pushed through the bodies and rushed toward the nurses' station. I pulled out my cell phone and punched in Pete's number. *Pick up. Pick up. Pick up. Please pick up.*

CHAPTER FORTY-ONE

D r. Erickson," he answered gruffly.
In a breathless panic I said, "I just saw Kelly coming from Lorelei's floor."

I pocketed my phone while speaking to the ICU charge nurse. "Lorelei Calder?"

"I'm sorry," she said, "only family members are allowed to visit."

"Did a doctor just visit her?"

"I'm not at liberty to divulge that information."

I charged down the hall, ignoring the repeated protests behind me, scouring the information sheets tacked to the doors.

Lorelei lay alone in her room; nothing seemed amiss. My heart beat with the same rhythmic pulse as the monitor. The nurse stomped up behind me and ordered me out. I fully intended to argue with her. "You have to check her. I think she might be in trouble."

"You're already in trouble, missy. You can't just go running all over the ICU."

"Please. Just check her and I'll leave."

"Check her for what?" She seized my arm to steer me out of the room. I braced myself and tried to yank it out of her grasp.

"Dr. Erickson is coming. He'll check her. Please let me wait for him?"

She was insistent and forceful. "Leave or I'll call security."

"Yes. Call security, by all means."

At that moment, Pete stormed into the room. As he brushed past the nurse, I wrenched my arm free and followed him. He ripped the IV drip from its source and gently dislodged the needle from Lorelei's arm. "Was a staff person in here recently?"

"Yes, Doctor," the nurse said petulantly. "He said he was just checking on his pediatric patients."

"Her blood pressure is extremely low. I need vitamin K and—"

"Doctor, I don't see—"

"No, you don't. Just do as I say. Stat!"

I stood back against the wall out of the way. Susie had expertly gathered everything Pete would need and followed him into the room. She raised a syringe and tapped the contents. "Inform security to watch for a redheaded doctor. And check with Jane Mackey, a patient down on second floor. See how she's doing. She had similar symptoms." The nurse sputtered her displeasure. "Do it!" Susie stood opposite Pete, listened to and sometimes anticipated every instruction—synchronous teamwork.

When I glanced over Pete's shoulder, I saw a trickle of blood near Lorelei's nostril. *No, not her. Not Lorelei,* I prayed.

Pete called for an emergency response team. When they arrived, they transfused Lorelei, monitored her vital signs, and pushed the meds he'd ordered.

The room was bustling when Lorelei's parents reentered, unprepared for the commotion, each holding a cup of coffee. The confused looks on their wary faces broke my heart; they were anticipating Lorelei's recovery. Pete quietly ordered, "Get them out of here."

I gently took Mrs. Calder's elbow. "Come with me."

She pulled free. "What's going on?" she demanded. "What's happening to my daughter?"

"We have to let them do their work." I couldn't tell her someone might have deliberately targeted Lorelei. She knew something.

I coaxed them out of the room and into the lounge. Lorelei's mother burst into tears again. Her husband moved closer and reached his arm around her. Together they collapsed into seats, rocking, waiting. Time stood still. Even the colorful fish in the aquarium barely moved.

When Pete emerged, he sat next to Lorelei's parents, took Mrs. Calder's hand and breathed deeply before he tenderly said, "I think she'll be all right. She has a ways to go, but thanks to Katie, we caught it quickly."

I didn't realize I'd held my breath until I exhaled. Mrs. Calder put her hand out to me, and I joined them. Pete asked what had sent them out of the room.

Mr. Calder responded, "The doctor wanted to check Lorelei and suggested we take a break and get a cup of coffee." He set the Styrofoam cup on the table, the corners of his mouth turned down.

"Do you know the doctor's name?"

"Flanagan. He seemed awfully young but he was so reassuring. Did he miss something?"

"I don't know, Mr. Calder." Pete looked at me forlornly. He couldn't know Lorelei's outcome yet, but he'd trusted me. I hoped we'd moved fast enough. We led Mr. and Mrs. Calder back to Lorelei's room and made sure they were comfortable. The rest of the response team had vacated. Susie brushed a tendril from Lorelei's forehead, then settled into a chair with a book in her hand and a bottle of water on the floor at her feet; she evidently had appointed herself as Lorelei's guardian. She wouldn't let anyone but Pete provide for her. As she nodded my way, it looked as if we'd declared a truce for the time being. I nodded in return. Nurse Kelton was on the job and off the hook. Officer Rodgers sat outside the door, guarding Lorelei's hospital room.

Pete walked me to the elevator. "Dad will meet us downstairs."

Talking with his father wasn't my favorite task, but I would survive. "Then what are we going to do?"

"You're going home. I'm going to take a nap, then relieve Susie."

A tinge of jealousy crept up my spine. "I can stay."

"My dear lady, you look wretched. Sleep has been scant the last few evenings."

I tried to stifle a yawn.

I strained to hear what Pete told Chief Erickson. "Someone masquerading as a doctor might have doped Lorelei with an anticoagulant. Katie ran into the imposter on the elevator. Security has been alerted. It's doubtful, however, that she's still in the hospital."

The chief said something inaudible. Though faint, I overheard Pete say, "Yup. She sure is a magnet for trouble." But as he glanced my way, an enigmatic smile played on his lips.

The chief asked, "Katie, can you tell me anything else?"

"I was getting on the elevator and he was getting off. I thought it was a he, but it was definitely a she. She was clutching a clipboard, and I noticed she wore a turquoise ring, just like the ring O'Hara's mother wore in the picture that hung above the fireplace at—" I faltered, "—at that shack.

"Can you describe her?"

I shook my head. "Not well enough. She was wearing a white lab coat. She had straight, slicked-back red hair and cold, vivid blue-green eyes. And big ugly glasses. The name tag read, 'C FLANAGAN.'"

"I'll get you a ride home," the chief said.

"Thanks, but I have my own car." I yawned, and he beckoned to an officer.

"Mike, could you drive Katie home in her car? Have Grant follow and pick you up."

Pete and his dad immediately put their heads together and forgot about me. As we walked out to my car, I jerked my heavy eyelids open. The feeling of cotton stuffing filled my head. I couldn't concentrate on any one thought. I passed him my keys, and I might even have slept on the way home.

After the officer parked my car in the garage, he insisted on walking me to my back door. I didn't argue. I pointed out the correct key. He opened the door and I fumbled for the light switch. The room was bathed in warm highlights, but no surprises.

"Thank you," I whispered, letting out another yawn as he departed.

I set my bag on the counter near the door and stumbled into the kitchen. I closed my eyes, counting my labored breaths and found it next to impossible to open them again. When I finally pried them apart, I stood in front of the mirror in the short hallway and was greeted by haunted blue eyes outlined in a tired purple. I staggered into the dark living room to lie down on my plump sofa. If I could catch a few winks, I could then retreat upstairs and finish the day, or start a new one, soaking in my oversized tub, inhaling soothing lavender bath salts. It had been a long, hard week. I closed my eyes and relaxed in the denseness accompanying sleep.

A moment later, a whimper roused me. Maverick rattled in his crate. "Hey buddy. What's up?" I asked as I walked toward the kennel to release him. I didn't expect to get an answer.

CHAPTER FORTY-TWO

A powerful trouble light clicked on and blinded me. I raised an arm to shield my eyes. C Flanagan knelt next to Mrs. C, who was sprawled on the floor, not moving. Flanagan brandished a gun in her left hand. "Can't you ever just leave well enough alone? Sit down," she commanded. I sat.

She paced and continued to lament. "You should've kept your nose where it belongs." Looking directly at me, she asked rhetorically, "Do you know what happens to people who get in my way?"

I didn't want to find out. Instead, I asked, "What happened to Mrs. Clemashevski?"

"I waited until she and that dog came back from a walk. I gave her a little nudge and she put the dog into the kennel." She cackled.

"Kelly," I tested the name. "Is she all right?" Kelly removed the glasses. I recognized her as Bruckner's escort from the movie screening, and O'Hara's EMT partner and deranged sibling.

"How would I know?" she said in a singsong voice. "I always just did what I was told." She cackled again. "Sean didn't think I could ever take care of anyone. I could, you know. I took care of Artie. He was so sweet," she whimpered. "I told him I wanted to play a practical joke on Robert, so he brought me ancient linen stationary, a cool fountain pen, and an old bottle of ink." Her voice was wistful. "And then he asked what I was going to do. I told him *Titanic* artifacts paid better than acting and Robert was buying." She sulked. "But Artie said it wasn't right."

"You're talking about Arthur Condive? The Callahan letters." I began to rise, but she waved the gun at me ominously.

"I am the director. Pay attention!" I dropped back down. Maverick growled, and she pointed the gun at the kennel.

"Quiet, Maverick," I begged softly and cued "down."

"Stupid dog. All she had to do was toss in a treat and slam the door." Her hand hovered over a handheld video camera perched on a tripod next to her. She looked through the viewfinder and angled the lens toward me. "Lights. Camera. Action. I've always wanted to say that." She reached up and pressed a button, morphing the red dot into a flashing green light. "Speak."

"What would you like me to say?"

"Your lines. Didn't you rehearse your lines?" She pointed the gun at me again, her madness dripping like honey.

I tried clichéd film jargon. "I didn't receive the updates. Can you set the scene for me? What's my motivation?"

Kelly rubbed the slate-black barrel of the gun along the side of her jaw. Circling the room, waving the gun in one hand, she examined the ceiling. She stilled when she came to a decision. "You're stealing away from a life where nobody loves you. You'll die alone, just like Sean." That wouldn't be difficult to fake. She stopped walking and carelessly aimed the gun at me. "You took him away from me."

I did, and I'd regret it for the rest of my life. "What else do I need to know?"

She furrowed her brow, staring at the camera. "Pretend to search for a way out of here."

That would be a great trick.

"I don't think you have what it takes. Day after day, I was told how great I was—I should've been a star. I gave every ounce of effort and finished each day exhausted. Take, take, take!" she raged. "After the final shoot, at the screening, in front of everyone, I discovered, after all I'd endured, the close-ups were so close no one would ever know it was me." Her frenzied eyes gleamed.

"So you killed him?"

She inspected the ring on her finger. Then her maniacal eyes targeted me.

I rushed behind the couch. "Am I doing this right?" I asked, slipping my hand into my pocket, searching for my phone.

"Put both hands where I can see them," she ordered. Slowly I removed my hand from my pocket. "Yes. That's it. Creep along. I think I'll zoom in on the top of your head. That's Robert's method. He zoomed in on my ring." She held her hand at arm's length again and glanced appreciatively. Then she reached up and pressed the button on top of the camera. I heard the whirr of the telephoto lens and its retraction. As she recorded my trek behind the couch, she commented, "The part in your hair is crooked."

Mrs. C stirred.

"You're so good at this," I said in a rush.

"We're making a movie here." She was indignant. "Crouch behind the sofa as if you're sneaking up on someone, but keep your head high enough so I can see you."

I crept along behind the couch as per instructions.

"Why does your name tag say 'C Flanagan'?"

She batted her eyelashes. "My given name is Colleen. My mom called me Kelly. When Sean and I were little, we looked so much alike we could have been two little boys. I didn't mind. But Sean hated it when someone thought we both looked like girls. When he left home, he changed his last name." She cupped her red bob in the hand that held the gun and patted her snarled locks. "Do you like it?"

"Why are you doing this, Kelly?" Her brush with reality was fleeting. I pulled at every thread I could find, and she just unraveled more.

"Authenticity. Robert used the clothes Samantha found in an old steamer trunk. She was very resourceful. She studied the faces from old photographs to get a feel for who those people were. She had Robert use real silk stockings. I'd never worn anything so luxurious." Tears slid down her smooth cheeks. "They studied portraits and said no aristocrat had red hair, so I dyed mine black but I hated it, and then they said no aristocrat had straight hair. They curled my hair with an awful metal rod that burned my scalp. I was supposed to be a star.

"I even let Robert drive my grandfather's car. He returned it dented and told me it was a poor reproduction." She held her head a little higher and recited, much the same way O'Hara did, "We Flanagans never needed a phony anything. Our ancestral line links us all the way back to the *Titanic*. I was the only real deal in Bruckner's entire production."

I wasn't ready to burst that bubble yet. "What are you doing *here*?"

"This," she said waving the gun, "makes an excellent truth serum. I knew there had to be more of the movie, film showing my face. Robert lied, though, when he said he'd given it to his *artistic mentor* for safe keeping. He was just trying to save himself." Her voice oozed resentment. "After she put that lunatic in the dog box, she told me she didn't have any idea what I was talking about. Did you know I was there for *every take*? And he never filmed my face. Look at this." She yanked a brochure from her pocket and tossed it to me. "This is the only picture of me!" Among the miniature color photos was one of Kelly, striking, in full costume, the camera catching her haughty features in the perfect light.

She straightened her shoulders. "I wanted Robert to pay. He was willing to cough up a big chunk of money for keepsakes for his stupid exhibit. And I was going to provide some great ones. But Samantha wasn't ever going to let the exhibit buy the letters. She told me about a fascinating journal belonging to *my* great-great-grandfather that she'd found in that trunk. She was going to report that the Callahan letters were fake."

"But they *are* fake!"

"They could've been real."

"Where is Samantha?" I said.

"Stop," she ordered. I froze. She peered through the viewfinder. "How did it end up here?" she said to herself with a smirk. Training the camera on the kitchen, she pressed "zoom." "It's a small world after all," she sang.

I heard Mrs. C's shaggy breaths. She needed help.

My mind was swimming. "Kelly, the Callahan story is fiction. Sean figured it out. He must have had the same conversation with Samantha that you had."

She shook her head then looked lovingly at the gaudy bauble on her hand.

"After the survivors disembarked," I said, "no one ever saw the real Patrick Callahan again. Your ancestor, Liam McMahon, murdered him, stole the ring, and took his place. Isn't that what the journal said?"

Her eyes narrowed, and she screeched, "Lies! All lies!"

"It's true. Your ring opens like a locket, and the photo inside is of the real Patrick Callahan. Let me show you." I hoped it was true.

A voice boomed from the kitchen. "Ida? Katie? Where are you? Helloooo?" Dapper Edward Scott entered, his face full of smiles.

"Mr. Scott, look out!" I cried.

"Hi, Grandpa," Kelly crooned.

CHAPTER FORTY-THREE

Poor Ida looks worn out. Did the old bat do too much dancing?" Scott snickered. The awful laugh echoed Kelly's. "I think we have a murder-suicide on our hands, don't you agree, Colleen?" He walked over and gave her a kiss on the top of her head before sliding the gun from her grasp.

"Yes, Grandpa. But which is which?"

"I think Katie will go off the deep end, worrying about her future alone." He took a cleansing breath. "A pity about Titan. An attack dog on meth isn't a pretty sight. We experimented with a rat terrier, but a German shepherd can do much more damage. Instead of you, though, he got hold of that little twit, Elaine. That's what she gets for getting in our way. Colleen dear, Katie was once considered a fair amateur sleuth, but she has been out of circulation since the death of her husband."

I glared at him as he continued menacingly. "Interesting read. So sad, Katie," he said with all the sincerity of a rock. Scott fanned the pages of my journal in front of me, just out of reach, tormenting me. "You choose life?"

Hot tears pricked the corners of my eyes. Dizzying scenes from the bike trail made my head swim. Dad had yelled a warning but was hit first—a shot to his head—and was downed feet from me. Dark blood stained the blacktop. Charles had charged me, crashing us both to the ground. I heard the air forced from his lungs when the bullet struck him. I gently rolled him off me, lifeblood pouring out. I held his head in my lap and agreed to everything he asked as long as he vowed to stay with me. But when I closed my eyes, I saw the blood pooling in the corners of his mouth. I felt him struggle to take his last breath.

"What happened in that care facility, Katie?" he taunted. "You were there an awfully long time."

My dad had defied his death sentence. He battled his demons daily, but learned how to walk again, how to talk again, how to hold a knife and cup, and press a button. During the early months, I stayed with him, encouraging, cajoling, pressing him until his physician told me I'd inadvertently hampered his recovery and he needed to do the rest on his own. I knew he'd come out on top, but I had no reason to share the pride I had for him with Edward Scott.

Kelly pulled a hypodermic needle from a black bag and said, "It's ready."

After a heartbeat, Edward's eyes glinted pure evil. "We could set it up so that Maverick gets some meth." He tented his long fingers in front of his goatee, inclined his head, and those green eyes bored into me. "Is something bothering you, Katie?"

"Kelly's disturbed. What's your excuse?" She was most assuredly an abused soul. I almost felt sorry for her. Almost.

"Ah, my poor dear, looking for love in all the wrong places. But please don't call her that. She's *my* Colleen!" Scott continued, dripping venom, "When Sean went off to school, I promised I'd watch out for her. She's been so helpful." His lascivious eyes raked over her. She blushed and bowed her head coyly. My skin crawled.

"By the time Sean returned, Colleen had landed a role in *Titanic: One Story*. She's a brilliant actress."

Colleen put her hand out, her face pleading. Scott reached into his vest pocket and pulled out a prescription bottle. He opened it and shook some tablets into her palm, and she tossed them back before he secured the bottle top.

"You orchestrated the entire operation. You're Irwin's connection."

He shrugged and said, "Is that his name?"

"What did you do with all the drugs you collected?"

"As bookkeeper for a modest firm of pharmaceutical salesmen, I maintain a vast system of business connections. Selling and reselling drugs back to those connections is lucrative, with an infinite clientele. Reduce, reuse, recycle!" he said cavalierly.

"Refuse," I added in a whisper. "You're nothing but a low-life drug dealer," I spat.

He snorted.

"Did Sean kill Mr. Condive?"

"Sean didn't have it in him to kill, yet, but he was getting there and would have done almost anything to protect his sister."

O'Hara had said, "Watch her," not "watcher." I had to keep my eyes on her. I had to watch Colleen—the one he'd had kept his eyes on and tried to watch out for. In with the good air, out with the bad. Now I had to keep it together.

"You killed Condive?"

"When Colleen identifies the impediments to our success, I remove them. I thought driving his car into the pond would keep him hidden. It worked for a while." Scott sighed. "I'll tell you a secret—twins run in our family."

"So does murder. You're just like Liam McMahon," I said.

"Ah, you know." Scott raised his eyebrows.

"You won't get away with this."

He sniggered. "We already have." He peered over his frames. "There is no way I'll ever go to prison." He snorted. "Except for you and Ida, Colleen and I are perfectly safe."

I had one card left to play. "Chief Erickson knows all about Colleen or Kelly or whatever you want to call her." Colleen stiffened. Her eyes grew large and she gasped. "I reported seeing her come out of the elevator at the hospital. Her description is everywhere, and they're looking for her. The security cameras recorded her last visit. Someone will recognize her. You'll never get away with this." I turned to Colleen. "Why did you need to hurt Lorelei?"

"She would've ruined everything," Colleen whined. "She saw you at the post office, Grandpa." She turned her empty eyes to me. "This"—she held up the syringe triumphantly— "is an extremely concentrated dose."

I couldn't have survived this long only to fail here; I prepared to fight.

Scott walked over to Colleen. "Don't worry, my dear. Jail isn't an option. I won't let anyone harm you." He put his arm around her shoulder and pulled her close, removing the hypodermic from her hand. He pressed his lips to her forehead and said, "I love you." Then he jammed the needle into her neck and pushed the plunger. She dropped to the ground, clutching at the syringe, looking utterly confused. As she shuddered, he arranged her legs and smoothed her hair, one final act of kindness, maybe his only act of kindness. Then he turned, pulled out the gun, and leveled it at me. "Colleen always did want to be famous. New story line in order, I think." His right hand held the pistol, the left hand came around to form a two-handed grip, his lips curled in a wicked sneer and his eyes circled the hammer, purposefully sighting down the barrel.

I inhaled sharply.

CHAPTER FORTY-FOUR

That's for Elaine." My favorite dancer of all time tripped the light fantastic. A formidable Mrs. C planted her spiky heel in Scott's right knee, and he toppled with a scream. The gun fired wildly. I raced to assist, but she was already straddling the writhing man. I pulled out my phone and punched in 911. Then I picked up the gun and let Maverick out of his crate. My magnificent dog stood watch, ready to tear Scott apart at the slightest provocation, but Scott had become deathly still, a look of disbelief frozen on his face.

Scott had turned his head toward Colleen, inspecting the syringe which protruded from his limp hand. She had managed to wrest it from her neck, and he had fallen close enough for her to jam it into one of his hands.

Colleen's head fell back. I checked her pulse and

watched the turquoise stone in that grotesque ring slowly dull as the light went out of her eyes. Colleen—Kelly—was gone.

I rushed to my landlady, who was scratching behind Maverick's ears. "Thank you, Mrs. C."

She rose and hugged me so enthusiastically my own arms were pinned to my sides. A tsunami of relief washed over me. She looked up with an impish grin and said, "Call me Ida."

Maverick nudged between Ida and me, and we gathered him in our hug.

We reported to Chief Erickson, who listened patiently to our story. Pete provided additional information. "The Huntington student had been a cinematography intern on the *Titanic: One Story* movie, doing scut work for Bruckner during his spring break. Somehow it all comes back to the *Titanic*." Although no one knew how the deadly dose of Warfarin had been administered, it had been found in the systems of all the victims.

Pete shook his head in dismay. "From what we can determine, the MinnviroExpress delivery woman was collateral damage. We haven't found anything to link her to the *Titanic*. Maybe when we check her credit-card receipts, we'll find something. Wrong place at the wrong time?"

Ida, who had been listening quietly, said, "Pete, MinnviroExpress made a wine delivery to me from Bobby. Maybe he gave the driver a bottle in thanks." We walked into my kitchen, and she slid a bottle of Zinfandel from the wine rack. She read the label and looked up apologetically. She held it out. In the corner of the label was a tiny gold imprint of an Olympic ship. "Bobby liked to share his good fortune. You could check each victim for a bottle of Zinfandel."

"Small world." I repeated what Kelly had said. I followed a straight line from my half-full wine rack to the video camera.

Careful scrutiny revealed a pinprick in the foil through which the Warfarin had been injected into the bottles, ending up in all the wrong places, including my gift to Jane. A look of relief flooded Pete's face. I'd spilled the contents of the bottle I'd brought to share with him the night Robert Bruckner had died.

"I hope there are no more of these bottles floating around out there," he said.

* * *

After a successful convalescence, Lorelei sat in my classroom, late one afternoon, wearing a deep frown, gazing at the aquarium. Populated with a pair of clownfish, a yellow tang, a lawnmower blenny, and a few six-line wrasse, this combination of sea life would help maintain the soothing waters according to Mr. Walsh.

"What's up?" I asked. My words echoed in the cavernous department.

"I finished my research paper on Emmy Noether. She would have been a mathematician when the *Titanic* set sail."

"What did you learn?"

"Albert Einstein said the old guard should take some lessons from her. She knew her stuff. In the judgment of the greatest mathematician of the time, 'Miss Noether was the most significant creative mathematical genius thus far produced since the higher education of women began.' I'd like to be remembered as something like that."

"Me too." I chuckled.

"Ms. Wilk, I saw the *Sentinel* today, and Edward Scott was on the front page with a photo of his grandchildren.

The whole story is so sad. I guess it could have been Mr. Scott I saw collecting the box Irwin dropped off at the post office. He was an awful man." She shuddered. "I just can't remember, and I'm so frustrated."

I placed my hand on her forearm. "It'll come, Lorelei. Don't worry. The doctor said it would take time. Can I read your paper?"

She handed it to me, and I took her essay to my desk.

Keys rattled in the lock of the department door, echoing in the churchlike quiet. I looked up from the paper and watched Lorelei scribbling at her desk. The rattling was followed by a heavy thud.

"Coach," a voice cried out. The response was muffled.

When Lorelei glanced up, I gave her a "don't concern yourself" wave as I made my way to the office area.

"I need a better photo," said a gruff voice.

"I won't do it," someone answered, followed by another crash.

"You are so screwed if you don't."

I stood in the doorway.

"I'm screwed if I do," Galen said. Tom Murphy's forearm pinned Galen to the far wall.

"Tom? What are you doing?"

Tom dropped his arm. Galen slid away. "Working on speeding up his defensive maneuvers. Galen has just about all the right moves to get to state. I want him to be able to anticipate the other guy."

Galen's hands balled into fists. "I won't do it," he hissed.

Afternoon sunlight streamed in through the commons' windows, cloaking the light in my room as it flickered off.

"What's really going on, Galen?"

The daggers in Tom's stare made Galen look away. In a condescending tone, Tom said, "I guess the cat's out of the

Mary Seifert

bag now. Galen showed me the photo, and it wasn't very flattering. In fact, it was downright slanderous. I wanted him to toss it, but I think you ought to see it." He gestured to an eight-by-ten black-and-white photo on the corner of his desk.

My heart thudded against my chest as I spun the blurry photo taken in my classroom. A bottle of something was in the photo. Galen was in the photo. I was in the photo. I looked up at Tom. "This never happened."

"That's not for me to determine. I'm sorry, Katie, but I have to turn it in."

I was tired. I was sad. And I was mad as a hatter. I lifted my head in defiance. "Go ahead. No one will believe it happened a second time. First Elaine and now me?"

"They don't have to believe it. You're out of here."

I thought I heard a door squeak. I prayed Lorelei would stay safe. Galen caught my eye and inclined his head toward the department entry door. "Why? What do you have against me?" I kept talking.

He sniggered. "Self-righteous bitch. I thought slashing your tires might do you in, but you kept asking questions. Just like Cartwright. Even after she quit, and no one would have anything to do with her, she kept at it. Then I thought you'd be ready to leave when your students trashed your kitchen."

"She almost caught you, Coach," Galen said sourly.

Tom glared at me. "That photo is proof you're a bad influence. You're finished teaching." He retrieved a padded manila envelope and tossed it to Galen.

Galen opened the envelope. "Wow!" he said sarcastically.

"What did I tell you?" Tom said, reaching for the phone.

Galen said, with exaggerated skepticism, "You mean these?" In his hand he held a number of eight-by-ten photos. He laid them out one by one for me to view.

The first was a photo of Elaine Cartwright sitting on her desk. A cryptic smile played on her lips. The second photo was Elaine in an identical pose with a student sitting at a desk across from her. It looked like they were sharing a bottle of wine. The student in the photo was Galen.

Tom sputtered. "What are those? Where did they come from?"

Galen fanned out the next photos; a photo of me, happily oblivious, proud of the display in my classroom, probably taken when I was telling Tom about my *Alice in Wonderland* poster. In the next, Galen had been superimposed on the photo, a bottle of Jameson between us. The last was a group photo: Edward Scott, Sean, Colleen, and Tom.

From the bottom of the manila envelope, Galen poured out three prescription bottles, rattling with pills. "Let's see," said Galen. He chose one at random and read, "This one belongs to Carmine Elicone—morphine." And choosing another, he added, "This one belongs to Judd Follet— Dilaudid. He died last month, didn't he? And lookie here." Galen picked up a key card. "Pharmacy, huh?"

"Tonnenson. You put those there!" Tom shouted. His nostrils flared. He took a step toward Galen, his fists clenched.

"Witnesses," Galen said and, as he gestured, Brock and Lorelei stepped into the office. "And I think we'll find the originals of these doctored photos on your computer somewhere."

"No one will believe you either. You're hopped up on steroids. You won't ever wrestle again," Tom roared as he lunged at Galen. Brock grabbed him.

"You should know. It's been the steroids wrestling all along, thanks to you." Galen's voice was soft and sad.

Tom tried to shake free and his glasses fell to the floor.

Lorelei blanched. "It was you," she said, firmly. "The man at the post office was you."

Tom Murphy crumpled.

CHAPTER FORTY-FIVE

I pulled the peace and quiet around me like a well-worn quilt. Lorelei and Jane were recovering well. Jane had taken a leave of absence, and, although Drew was temporarily at a loss, she'd be back better than ever. Lorelei's memory cleared almost immediately. She was indeed a very bright and brave girl. She finally remembered seeing Tom Murphy pick up one of the packages she thought Irwin Albright had delivered to the post office.

Murphy and Scott were fraternal twins. Scott was older by thirteen minutes and had headed the entire family enterprise. With a crackdown on his business in the Twin Cities, he'd moved to Columbia, near his only family, whom he cajoled, baited, charmed, bribed, and seduced into helping him, nudging his demented granddaughter Colleen off her precarious edge of sanity. Scott readily eliminated any real or perceived obstacles—Arthur Condive, who wouldn't play hard ball, Robert Bruckner, who determined the *Titanic* letters were forged, and fearless Elaine Cartwright.

Sean had the impossible job of watching out for his sister, protecting her throughout her troubled life. As EMT partners, Colleen and Sean blended into the fabric of the hospital. She'd been able to raid the pharmacy, stealing a portion of prescriptions remaining after patients left the hospital, swiping just a few tablets from random bottles and blister packs before logging them as destroyed, or administering less than a full syringe of medication, pilfering the residual, and turning it all over to her grandfather. In return, Scott gave her whatever she needed to keep her committed to doing his bidding.

Winning consumed Murphy. Scott had provided steroids to help a few athletes bulk up and increase their muscle mass and pain-killers after injury to help them continue toward the ultimate goal of victory. In exchange for the steroids and pain-killers, Murphy contributed the drugs to which he had access from the hospice office— until that source dried up—and what he falsely agreed to dispose of for grieving hospice patients' families as an eleventh-hour volunteer. He'd anonymously enlisted Irwin, who desperately needed the money, to collect all the unused drugs at the Skittles parties they'd hosted. Murphy insisted the fault rested solely on Scott's shoulders, but a number of students came forward to accuse him of providing them with steroids years before Scott moved to the area. We'd never be certain of Sean's role; I certainly couldn't believe a word from Murphy.

Brock played baseball because he enjoyed it, but he had

neither the need nor the desire to be a great ball player, and after his short bout with pain-killers, he avoided drugs at all costs. Galen, on the other hand, was, at first, most receptive to trading photo ops for the added benefit of performance enhancement drugs but would suffer the consequences.

It turned out Samantha had run away rather than face the legal system again when Scott had blown up the meth lab he'd installed in his attempt to frame her. No one thought her guilty, but she'd still have to answer some questions if and when she reappeared. And she might have more to add to the story.

In her own strange way, Elaine had continued to help her students. She'd also tried to protect me.

I witnessed the return of Ida's century-old family heirloom. "I believe this is yours," Chief Erickson said, as he handed her the turquoise ring.

Pete had a set of fine tools with him, and he reverently slid open the delicate ring casing. The glow on her face when she compared the photos in the jewelry spread to everyone watching her. The ring looked at home on her hand. The green gem began to smile again, the color warming from within.

Bruckner's New Titanic Exhibit, which had closed temporarily, hoped to reopen without the Callahan letters, under a new directorship. In his will, Bruckner had requested Ida Clemashevski take his place as chairwoman on the board of directors for as long as she'd like.

I had yet to open the envelope from England that kept wending its way to the top of my to-do pile. There were ghosts among those pages I would need to confront— someday.

Our science club underwent scrutiny, but the kids

vouched for me. I owed them my life. We had so much out there for us to study, talk about, and try. We even added a few new faces.

Ashley asked, "Could we read and discuss *An Inconvenient Truth* or *Truth to Power*?"

"Absolutely," I said. Lorelei beamed.

"I hear Chief Erickson's new prescription collection center has brought in tons of leftover and unused drugs for disposal," Brock said. "What's happening with Mr. Kidd?"

"He found he actually enjoyed teaching, but he's making his career in the BCA. However, he thinks he might substitute here once in a while when he's between assignments."

"When will Ms. Mackey be back?" he asked.

"She went home to recuperate, but she loves Columbia. And all of you. She'll be back soon, I hope."

"Why did you move here?" Ashley asked.

Charles loved teaching and would've been a great educator. But he lost his life protecting mine. Smiling through the sudden salty tears stinging my eyes, I said, "I'm following in the footsteps of someone I love."

I shared the riddle Ida had given me that morning. "Five girls are in a room. Amy is playing chess. Maria is sleeping. Eve is reading a book. Sandi is watching television. What is Joan doing?"

A disembodied voice crackled from the intercom. "Ms. Wilk?"

"Yes."

"I'm forwarding a call from Mr. Wilk."

The students turned their baffled attention to a shuffle at the doorway. As I stepped to my desk to take the call,

I turned to follow their gazes. Pete's shoulders slumped and the bouquet of yellow roses in his hand dropped to the ground. He turned and walked away. He couldn't have known who was on the line. Pete was going to drive me crazy. I wondered what he thought he'd heard. I smiled to myself as I picked up the phone.

"How're you doing, Dad?"

TITANIC COCKTAIL

¾ oz Gin
¾ oz Crème De Violette
¼ oz Blue Curaçao
3 oz Champagne
¼ C Lemon Ice Meringue
4 lemons
1 ½ C superfine sugar
Water
2 Egg whites
¾ C sugar
3 oz water

To make the Lemon Ice Meringue: Make lemon water ice. Peel the lemons, taking as little of the pith as possible. Add the peels to a bowl and completely cover with the sugar. Let sit 1 hour. Add 1 cup of lemon juice (which 4 large lemons should produce) and stir to dissolve sugar. Strain out peels. Add enough water to make 1 quart of liquid. Freeze in an ice cream maker or pan until partially frozen.

Make Italian Meringue. Beat the 2 egg whites to stiff peaks, and set aside. Combine the ¾ C of sugar and 3 oz water in a saucepan. Bring sugar mixture to a boil over medium-high heat, stirring occasionally to dissolve sugar. Heat to "small ball" candy stage (candy thermometer reads 236-238° F). Remove syrup from heat and, in a very slow trickle, fold into beaten egg whites. Stir until all syrup is added and mixture is smooth.

In an ice cream maker or chilled bowl, add meringue to lemon ice, stirring gently until combined. Just before serving, add to glass.

Stir the gin, Crème De Violette, and Curaçao into a mixing glass. Top with the Champagne. Place the lemon ice in the glass. Garnish with a light dusting of edible silver powder or blue sugar. Enjoy!

~ ~ ~

Thank you for taking the time to read *Maverick, Movies, & Murder*. If you enjoyed it please tell your friends, and I would be so grateful if you would consider posting a review. Word of mouth is an author's best friend, and very much appreciated.

Thank you,

Mary Seifert

~ ~ ~

What's next for Katie and Maverick?

Katie Wilk and her black Labrador retriever, Maverick, are training for Search and Rescue certification, and Katie is well into the school year with her math and science students. But a series of shocking events rock their small town—a teenage beauty queen is found dead in a state park, Katie's neighbor's three-year-old daughter is abducted, and Maverick's SAR certification exercise turns into a real emergency. Doctor Pete Erickson, the man Katie was starting to have feelings for, seems curiously out of touch with her these days, but the new veterinarian in town may turn out to have quite a lot in common with her.

Can Katie put together the pieces and learn if the crimes are connected, or will she and those dear to her be put in even greater danger?

Don't miss *Rescues, Rogues, & Renegade* **coming soon!**

Mary has always loved a good mystery, a brain teaser, or a challenge. As a former mathematics teacher, she ties numbers and logic to the mayhem game. The Katie Wilk mysteries allow her to share those stories, as well as puzzles, riddles, and a few taste-tested recipes.

When she's not writing, she's making wonderful memories with family, walking her dog whose only speed is faster, dabbling in needlecrafts, and pretending to cook. Mary is a member of Mystery Writers of America, Sisters in Crime, American Cryptogram Association, Dog Writers of America, and PEO.

Connect with Mary, get her free newsletter and free recipes when you sign up!

Visit Mary's website: MarySeifertAuthor.com

Facebook: facebook.com/MarySeifertAuthor

Twitter: twitter.com/mary_seifert

Instagram: instagram.com/maryseifert

Follow Mary on BookBub and Goodreads too!

Made in the USA
Monee, IL
03 June 2023